# What's Left Behind

## Angela T. Edgar

– Lancaster Gate Press –

First published in 2022
by Lancaster Gate Press

Copyright Angela T. Edgar 2022

Angela T. Edgar has asserted her moral right
to be identified as the author of this work

ISBN: 978-1-7396822-0-0

Printed by ImprintDigital.com, UK

*For Mum*

# – 1 –

The sight of the police cars and ambulance shocks me as I drive towards Mum's house. Rapid flickers of blue light bombard the edges of the surrounding buildings and cars. Walking through this terrifying electric light show, I glance at the caged police van with excitable sniffer dogs, parked at the kerbside. I have no idea what is going on. I catch sight of my brother, John, on the pavement, one side of his face strobing, blue and white, standing tall and rigid. I had phoned him. 'Mum's had a fall and I'm on my way now,' was all I had said a few minutes earlier. It's what they told me.

The stiff policeman shifts hastily to the side as I walk through the front door, midway through announcing who I am. Didn't really afford him any time to deny my entry. The living room is busy. Mum is lying on the floor. Two paramedics in green and in control are kneeling beside her. There's another awkward policeman and Mum's upstairs neighbour's daughter Anne. John's followed me in briefly, I think, then retreats back outside. The scene doesn't make any sense to me, there are too many people in this small room, and before I know it, I'm light-headed with tangled silk thoughts, grappling to steady myself amidst a dull, humming noise in my ears and head.

'Don't touch anything,' the officer snaps.

Although I hear him, it's like a muted playback as I once again scan the room and feel troubled so many people are in Mum's living room. Why is Anne here? And how did the paramedics get here? Who called them?

'Grace, your mum's in a really bad way,' Anne says calmly and quietly. I look at Anne and no words come out, not that she's expecting me to say anything. Anyway, she's turned away and is gazing down at Mum on the floor.

Joining the kneeling paramedics, I crouch at Mum's back, aware of her sobs and moans weaving through this confusion. I can't make out what she's trying to say.

'We need to try and turn your mum over and get her on a stretcher chair to carry her out to the ambulance.' There's an urgency in the young, fresh-faced paramedic's voice.

'Tell me what to do that will help.'

The words tumble out and I am still trying to work out what's happened, playing catch up. I pull the blanket over Mum, covering up her cold back.

'Try and comfort your mum, talk to her, keep her as calm as possible.'

The paramedic's not looking at me, too occupied with duty and attention to turning Mum over.

'Mum, it's Grace here. You're going to be okay. I'm here now.'

My words are reassured by the police officer's hand on my shivering shoulder. That's when I realise that I'm shaking.

'He hammered me, oh God, he kept hammering me,' Mum cries out. A painful, shrill cry fills the room as the paramedics turn Mum over. Her face. Her battered face. Bloody eyes ballooned up and staring wildly at me. Mum's hand is safely in mine now. There's more blood on her arms. God, where's all this blood coming from? What a mess. Blood is smeared below her ear and neck. Her nose is dirty and bloodied.

'Oh, he gave me a hammering, help me, where is he?'

The scared and desperate words, clear and piercing, follow the path of a thin stare from Mum's eyes, struggling to find a safe face.

'I want my glasses. Give me my glasses.'

'Can I put her glasses on?' I ask the officer after spotting them on the footstool.

'Best not to touch anything, sorry.'

'It's okay, Mum, I'll get them later. It's okay, I'm here.
You're going in the ambulance.'

I'm trying to change the subject quickly. I can see the glasses bent and twisted on the footstool. Not much use anyway.

'I've no pants on. He took them off.'

Mum's crying now. I'm shaking. The enormity of what has happened is dawning on me. More shaking. I look around the living room. What for? Clarification of what was obvious had happened? Mess. Clothes in heaped dirty bundles. Mum's blue tweed skirt strewn awkwardly and not neatly folded over the back of her chair. Where it always is. Where it should be. A vile sick feeling hits me. It smells, there's a smell in the living room. 'I'm going to be sick.' Another wild stare, seeking my face. Frightened. Terrified.

'There's a small bowl in the bathroom?' I offer, waiting for permission to get it from the police officer.

There is a sense that access around the house is now totally restricted. Mum's house with all its familiar photos and ornaments.

'Just don't touch anything when you get it,' says the police officer.

'I'm away to get your bowl, Mum; only be a minute, okay?'
I release Mum's hand to get the bowl, stepping awkwardly
through the living room to the back of the house and the
bathroom. Mess, more mess in the bathroom. Still that smell,
that smell that doesn't belong in Mum's house. 'Has she been
sick?' I ask the paramedic as I return with the bowl and a towel.
Oh, the towel. Did I say I was going to take a towel too along
with the bowl? The police officer doesn't appear to notice the
supplementary item.

With Mum and John safely in the ambulance, I make my way
over to my parked car and begin the 12 miles to the hospital. My
fingers tremble, clenching into fists around the steering wheel,
worried that any loosening of my grip might cause me to lose
control of the wheel. The streets and the houses are familiar to
me; it's a route I've taken on numerous occasions, as bad chest
infections and small transient strokes had taken Mum off to
hospital for treatment. But today is different, and on arrival at
the hospital, I'm greeted by more local constabulary before I get
to the medical team.

The ambulance pulls in with Mum cocooned amidst
blankets on the stretcher trolley. I rush up to meet the trolley
and look around the waiting room, only to find the few people
there are staring at me, questioning my accompanying police
presence. Their whispers uncomfortably resonating with my
raised heartbeat, numbing the sound in the room as I steady
myself on Mum's trolley. I'm taken through and Mum lays
quietly in the cubicle of the accident and emergency room.
The cubicle's curtains offering little private comfort from
the hurried and unbelievable thoughts stabbing at my mind.
Nurses in and out, saying very little but so kindly towards
Mum. Every movement met with sobs and painful moans

from the hospital trolley. Another nurse sweeps in between the curtains. Blood pressure, heart monitor machine. There is a cannula now in Mum's hand. When did they put that in? Mum silent now, steady breathing. And then another nurse.

'We'll take your mum for an X-ray shortly,' says the nurse. 'We need to see the extent of her injuries. She's in a lot of pain when she moves. I've given her something to help in the meantime.' Another swoop of the curtains and she's away. I'm standing, awkward, and for a moment, I feel enormously redundant. Thinking my brother will want to join me and see Mum, I sneak a peek through the cubicle's curtains. Police officers stand out in the corridor. Black uniforms and suits keeping a safe distance. They've been told by the hospital staff to let the nurses tend to Mum. They'll have to wait for their business. I smile at a young, blonde female officer standing opposite. Her police hat is off, sitting on the medical trolley beside her. No sign of my brother close by. I can't leave Mum. I head back behind the curtains. Mum lies peaceful, the medication clearly providing some solace. Where is John? I don't want to be alone anymore with Mum lying here.

'Can I just say,' the curtains part ever so slightly by the female police officer as I turn around, half expecting another nurse to appear, 'when your mum wakes, it's best not to ask too many questions. She may get confused or mixed up by what you say.' The female police officer smiles. I nod and acknowledge the advice being offered.

John appears. 'How's Mum? Has she said anything?'

'They're taking her for X-rays soon. She's not said much. They've given her something to settle her,' I reply.

'Hi, Mum, it's John.' He leans over Mum, who has woken

up. 'Can you remember what happened, Mum?' he asks. I'm mortified.

'Don't ask her any questions. The police said not to, otherwise it will confuse her or get her mixed up.' I try and whisper so Mum doesn't hear me.

'Mum, did you see who did this to you?' comes the next question from John.

'John, don't ask questions! It's what the police have said.' John reaches down for Mum's hand and stands over her, smiling and reassuring her. I'm glad his interrogation appears to have ended, his curiosity adopting an element of patience. Not like him, I thought to myself. 'Can I go out for a moment?' I ask, looking exhausted towards John.

He nods.

The hospital corridor moves with nurses and staff getting on with what they are supposed to do. I meander around them, seemingly unnoticed, very little eye contact. It's busy but quiet and calm. I don't get very far before a grey-suited police officer catches me.

'Grace, I'm DC Mackie. When you can, I want to take a statement from you. There's a family room off the waiting area that we can use. I've spoken with your sister-in-law already. I need to get statements from you and your brother. I know it's never a good time, but the sooner we can do it, the better.' DC Mackie is clear about his duties.

'Yes, of course. Yes. Mum will be going for X-rays shortly. We can do it then. My brother's in with Mum just now. I'll let him know.'

'Great, thanks.' DC Mackie continues to hang about.

I walk out into the cold morning air of the hospital car park. I need to ring my daughter Jenny and let her know. I'm still shaking. It's too cold to stand out in the open, so I head back the short distance to my parked car and get inside, pulling the door shut on this welcome, private domain.

Across the road, the curtains of a neat bungalow are pulled open to welcome in the new day, revealing the inside of an elegant bay-windowed lounge. For a moment, my eye is drawn to the large artworks hanging on the walls. Colourful and abstract, the image of a modern landscape comes into focus, confused lines and shapes forming a typical, remote island cottage below red sunset mountains. The work above the fireplace is too much at an angle for me to determine the style and subject. My artistic eye has come to a timely rescue, pulling me away from the day's horrific events. I'd give anything right now to be sitting in the back workroom of my small Edinburgh gallery, tending to my latest work. 'Labours of love' is the sentence that stays with me from the article a local newspaper had written about my preview show a few months back. The reviewer gave very little away as he pored over each work, making his way around the gallery space, notebook in hand, scribbling away. My mind jolts back, and I suddenly remember why I'm outside now. I should be phoning Jenny and making arrangements for the day. Clearly, I'm not going to be leaving the hospital anytime soon. I'm not going to be able to open the gallery either.

Opening the cover of my mobile phone, I look down at my screensaver photo. It's a picture of Jenny, taken after a concert, and she's smiling. It's taken a while to get her to a place where she is enjoying life. This will come as another blow for her, another blow for us both really. Six years have passed since we lost her dad, and it has taken most of that time to tentatively pick our way back to begin a new life for just the two of us. We were given daily reminders that our family structure was lacking, missing an essential ingredient. But we made 'us' fit and over time the traditional routines kindly adopted our minimalist set-up and it grew to be the norm. So much so that we convinced ourselves of the normality of our existence. It still mattered, but it didn't matter so much now. Just myself and Jenny; a content double act, blending in to each day. Whatever happened to Mum has sent shock waves in our direction, and I'm not convinced there is adequate buffering to protect us. So I protect her for the time being, until I know more. As far as she knows, Mum's had a fall, because everything else is speculation, and as I utter those words, I feel myself choking on the misrepresentation of it all.

Back inside the hospital, Mum's bedside has become busier since I left. My sister-in-law Pamela and niece Rose have joined John and are hovering over Mum, who is awake and talking.

'Has she said anything more?' I ask. Then I wonder if that is wise to ask. It will only invite John to launch into his next round of questions for Mum. Questions he's not meant to ask according to the police. John doesn't answer.

'What did he do to you, Mum? How old was he, same age as Rose, or older?' John is clearly in full swing with the questions. I leave him briefly and off he goes on one. Does he never listen? What confusion is he introducing for poor Mum? Why can't he just wait like me for things to come out when the moment is deemed right?

'Don't, John, no more questions. You know what the police said.' Was this just me, classic me, determined to be in charge? Of course we all want to know what happened. But sometimes the family really are spanners. There can't be mistakes. What nonsense has he introduced now into Mum's mind? Has she not been through enough? And here he is, relentless and hungry for every morsel there is. Jesus Christ!

'Yes, about the same age. He looked like the devil,' mumbles Mum.

It's all coming out. But was he the same age, or did Mum just say that having been offered up the option of an age-related Rose? What if he is older, and now she's got that in her head? More to the point, what did this man do to her? The shaking starts again, and I feel like my head is about to burst.

'The police want to take our statements, John. There's a room out there to do it. Some DC chap is waiting for us. Said we'll give our statements when Mum goes for her X-rays.' I'm trying to adopt a civil tongue, when inside I'm reeling from his inability to do as he's told. My shaking, nerves and inner anger are disturbed by a posse of nurses and a porter, parting the curtains of Mum's cubicle.

'Mrs Fallon, we're going to get you X-rayed. We'll take you there, okay?' says the nurse.

'Mum, they're going to take you for your X-rays now,' John says, leaning over Mum and explaining what is happening. She isn't deaf, well, she is, but he is annoying me now by repeating things. The hospital cubicle is empty. Mum is carefully wheeled out for her X-rays.

'We'd better go give our statements now,' I say to John as I stride out towards the waiting area. John follows.

DC Mackie is left-handed. He writes page after page with an awkward slant of his wrist the way lefties do. It doesn't look comfortable. There are many questions about Mum in general, her background, how she lives, what she does on a day-to-day basis, what she was like in the days prior to the incident. The 'incident'. But of course, how else can he describe the horror?

Then questions about what I was met with when I first arrived at Mum's house. The layout out of the room. The positioning of certain items on chairs and on the floor. I also have to recount what Mum has said to me. DC Mackie is carefully repeating what I'm saying, ensuring there is precision and clarity and agreement as his wrist continues to stumble across each sheet of paper. Every word noted down. Sheet after sheet turned over, comprehensively accounting for everything being said. I look at the bundle of paper as the process of taking my statement concludes. And I'm shaking again; actually, I never stopped. I feel shattered and drained. DC Mackie gathers up the sheets and taps them into a neat bundle, slotting them into a plastic wallet. The plastic popper seal clicks, and he reaches down to place it into his briefcase by his feet.

'She was naked when I got to the house.' Suddenly, it comes out.

'Sorry? Mum was naked, on the floor, naked?'

DC Mackie abandons his briefcase and un-pops the wallet, flicking back through the pages, but I know he won't find it anywhere because I haven't told him. I know what I told him, about the blanket being over her, the clothes on the floor, but not about her being naked, and now it smacks of an apologetic omission. Hiding her nakedness during my stifled account feels like a communicative modesty, but not on a deliberate level. Saying it out loud makes it real for me. DC Mackie writes it on a fresh page, and I sign it, just like the other bundle of pages. 'There will be a family liaison officer joining us soon, Grace,' adds DC Mackie. 'She will guide you through what will be happening next.'

'Is there any news on who did this?' I'm desperate for any update now.

'I can't really say at the moment. What I can tell you is the police with the dogs arrived very quickly. It's early in the morning and any trace or scent will still be there, ideal conditions. It's all very positive,' he reassures me. Well, that's something at least. I go back to Mum's cubicle, allowing DC Mackie to take my brother's statement. There is no sign of Mum having returned from her X-rays. The blonde police officer appears to have been replaced, and the new officer introduces herself. Behind the cubicle's curtains, I sit down, staring around at the empty space where Mum has been. It's as if I have lost her.

'Oh, hello,' says a nurse, parting the cubicle curtains. 'We've done the X-rays and your mum will be moving to a ward shortly. I'm just waiting on a porter. Do you want to come out and stay with Mum?' The nurse smiles.

I stand up and follow the nurse towards where Mum is waiting, just in time to see the porter tap down the brake release on the trolley and start to wheel Mum to the ward. No words are exchanged during this solemn walk down each corridor, slowing on the turns, passing bland pictures periodically plonked on the expanses of pale mint green walls. Wafts of the morning's breakfast meals seep out of industrial-size crates, positioned like sentries at the entrance of wards. Their scrubbed stainless steel walls will be opening soon to the expectant patients, some grateful for the offerings, others perhaps like myself, viewing the contents of plastic plates and bowls with trepidation. Mum has a room on her own within the ward; we arrive at it. The nurse explains it offers privacy, given there will be continuing police activity.

I regroup with John and the family in a family room off the ward and allow the nurses time to settle Mum into her room. It is the first chance we've had to privately share and discuss all the events since those early hours. I feel distant but absorb all that's being said in the room, settling back into a chair in the far corner. John's becoming very vocal on the likelihood of whoever did this being caught. He vents his near excitement of his recollection of the promptness and sense of urgency from the scene he was met with outside Mum's house. This is then followed by his horror at recalling what has happened, from what Mum has told him. It dawns on me; Mum has clearly spoken at some length to John. Must have been when I was outside the hospital phoning Jenny. Then John spouts a barrage of what ifs and hopes, how things will unfold, what needs to happen, then anger. Anger and disbelief. He was meant to be there for breakfast; that's what he'd arranged. John wishes he had stumbled across whoever did this. He'd have fucking killed him. If only he'd got there earlier. I feel his every word being launched towards me. I try to take it all in, but I'm lost for any response. It's draining, my own thoughts darting in and out of John's preaching.

A knock at the door of the family room is followed by a friendly and enquiring face entering. DC Diane Bain comes into the room and introduces herself as the family liaison officer. John promptly shuts up at this stage.

'I'm so sorry to hear about your mum. It's absolutely terrible. We are all so shocked to hear what happened. How are things?' asks DC Bain.

She's up against four of us, all of us silent since she came into the room. I'm drawn towards feeling sorry for her, sorry for her intrusion into this family situation. If I don't respond, then it isn't likely anyone else in the family will say something. So I politely bring her up to date with things, but her expression tells me she already knows, and all I am doing is ending the deathly silence.

# − 2 −

Dressed in a pleasant, beige, checked suit, and carrying one of those large purpose-built handbags, DC Diane Bain doesn't strike a typical constabulary pose. She calmly defines her role as family liaison officer. Acting as a go-between for the family in dealings with the police and the Crown Prosecution, she will offer a veritable deluge of useful updates on what will be happening over the coming days. All of these promises are met with my brother's intense nodding and almost blissful gratitude. For me, it feels like a hostile takeover that I don't want to be part of. John glances over at me as DC Bain finishes her role-defining speech. He's clearly looking to me to respond to DC Bain, with a display of my usual select and proper words. Those words that will represent the family in a dignified and correct manner. All very important to John; just a pity he's not prepared to oblige by volunteering his own verbal dexterity.

John's anticipatory look smacks me out of and away from the less than gracious argument going on in my head. Sitting up and fixing an expression on my face, I smile at DC Bain in acknowledgement of her offer of assistance over the coming days.

'We don't know all that's happened to Mum. I think more has happened than what she is managing to tell us so far,' John adds. This is met with a look from me that says it all. Here it comes, the results of John's own interrogations with Mum earlier as she lay on her hospital trolley. A combination of John absorbing the facts and adding his own interpretation to them. Clearly the absence of definitive responses from Mum earlier have only heightened his appetite to explore the realms of what could have happened, and then share them with the newly appointed family liaison deity who has entered the room. Oh, I think, the sweet bonding of a family in crisis and the constabulary's finest family liaison personnel. I can't comprehend my brother's ease of acceptance into this carefully managed police process. And for a moment, I feel left out in the room.

'Is there any news on an arrest?' I ask, pulling myself out of my dark hole of isolation.

'Nothing as yet, it is still early on, but the police are confident they will find out who did this. They will do everything they can,' DC Bain replies. 'You and your brother have given your statements and it's important that we get a statement from your mum on what happened,' DC Bain adds. 'I know it will be very upsetting for your mum to do this, but it is important we establish the facts that will help us find who did this.' DC Bain can't be faulted on her genuine and tempered words, seeking the necessary next steps to progress the case. There is another glance over from John to me, seeking my response to this latest request.

'Mum said to me she wants to do everything she can to find who did this to her.' I'm recollecting more and more of what Mum shared with me earlier. 'She will want to do this.' John nods in approval. DC Bain explains the method of taking the statement will involve video recording it too. I feel a rush of anxiety as I consider Mum's reaction to not only having to provide a statement but that it will be recorded too. 'I want to be there with Mum when she provides her statement,' I say. 'I need to explain to her what is happening, and if she gets distressed, then I want to ensure someone is there for her. I can't begin to comprehend what she has already gone through, and I have no idea what this might do to her.' I'm clearly defining my own set of rules on how things have to progress carefully and with Mum's best interests. It's up to the police to accommodate this.

'I will be in the room asking Mum questions, alongside DC Mackie. Grace, you can sit in the room too. It's not a problem, that's fine,' replied DC Bain. 'You won't be able to say anything; just be present there for your mum. But I understand.' DC Bain leaves shortly after this and says she will be in touch with a time for taking Mum's statement. It will be tomorrow though at some point. She'll phone me to confirm the arrangements.

John and I head back into the hospital room to see how Mum is doing. She is awake in her hospital bed and spots us coming in. She begins to cry as John leans over to take her hand and reassure her. I notice Mum's face is changing. The earlier puffiness and blood staining is replaced with a cleaner face but with tell-tale signs of the internal bleeding behind each and every cruel blow made around her face and body. Each injury still pale but with an indication of things to come. Mum's voice and words bring a sense of normality. She sounds like my mum always sounds, but the choice of words as she recollects the assault are quite alien. The soft look I cherish from Mum's dark eyes are ruined as she glances towards me and John, straining to see through the gnarled and disfigured area around her eyes, nose and mouth. Her mouth is twisted and sloping, but Mum's attempting to ignore it as she speaks about the assault. I sit slightly away from the bedside and watch my brother's caring and calming words and touches. Mum and John clearly engrossed and engaged in sharing the awful events. I notice I'm still shaking.

The results from the X-rays show the extent of Mum's injuries. She has a broken shoulder socket and humerus which will require surgery. Injuries on her face and other parts of her body are restricted to severe bruising. The psychological injuries I can't help but think will be a different pain for Mum to endure. An injury which, despite its hidden qualities, will no doubt haunt Mum for a long time to come. Just how it will manifest itself and how Mum will deal with it is a huge burden I begin to try and imagine. But how can I even begin to gain a sense of this?

John and I spend the entire day at the hospital. It's getting late and the nurses come in to settle Mum for the night; they encourage us to go home and rest. It has, after all, been a long day and the forthcoming days are likely to be as full and as tiring. I ponder over plans for the coming days too, my need to close the gallery, and my daughter's reaction. I feel I haven't even had time to explain the day's events fully and this is something I need to do. My mind is clearly on my duty to my home life now.

My Mini adopts a mind of its own on my journey back home. Or so it seems. Truth is I can't truly remember getting home, but clearly I am home and rewarded with the familiar sound of crunching gravel on the driveway of my cottage. Key in the front door and the warmth grabs me into the comfort of my dining room and kitchen. Jenny wanders up to meet me.

'Hi, Mum, how is Nanny after her fall?' she asks.

'She's okay. Let me get my shoes off and get sorted first,' I reply. But I get a look from her, one that registers a sense of missing information. Jenny smiles and lets me take my things off; she'll get the full news after this. I unzip my boots and gather them up and head towards my bedroom, keen to get out of the day's claustrophobic clothes. Carefully placing my boots in their usual space in the wardrobe and placing my raincoat on a hanger, I sweep aside a hanging space then slide the coat carefully into its correct slot, smoothing down the silk Union Jack flag lining in the process. I dismiss the rest of my outfit into the wash basket then wrap my bathrobe around me. For a moment, I feel unburdened of the day's events.

Jenny pokes her head around the bedroom door and smiles. Stepping around the bedroom, she heads towards me and looks up at me. With one hand, I sweep aside her mop of hair and kiss her forehead. 'You look tired, Mum. Have you eaten anything today?' She's now examining my face.

'I'll get something just now, just fancy porridge maybe. Not overly hungry.' I smile at Jenny and make my way through to the kitchen. 'I'll put the kettle on and make us a cuppa. Want one?' I ask.

'Aye, I'd love a cup, then think I will head off to bed shortly. Might read a bit. Is Nanny going to be alright, Mum, after her fall?'

'Yes, she will be fine, darling. Nanny's going to be in hospital for quite a while, but we are all looking after her and she will be fine.' I try and reassure Jenny. I want her to sleep minus the day's worries. With a hug, she reaches for her cup of tea and makes her way to her bedroom. I think I've succeeded in achieving a sense of calm.

I sit in the living room, just sit, with the corner light on, casting a glow over the room. There are no streetlights outside and the telly is off. And I just sit, nodding off occasionally then wakening up, again and again. Each time I wake, I'm reminded today did happen. And it's enormous and overwhelming and, if I'm honest, has all the hallmarks of the day the police turned up at my door and told me Jenny's dad had been found dead in his flat. Oh God, tell me it's not going to be like that all over again.

# – 3 –

It hasn't gone midnight when the phone rings again. The nurse is clearly worried about Mum's condition.

'She's getting terribly upset, having flashbacks, Grace. I think it's best for you to come in and see if you can calm her down. We're worried about her becoming increasingly upset and the effect it might have on her. We don't seem to be able to reassure her.'

'I'll head over straight away. Please tell her I'm on my way. Be about 30 minutes,' I reply as I awake from my pathetic excuse for sleep. I'm now totally alert thanks to an instant surge of adrenalin through my body.

It's not so much a drive as a trundle along the dark country road before I'm welcomed into the street lamped townscape, making my way to the hospital. The skin on my face feels tight and cold. I lick the remnants of toothpaste from the side of my mouth, tell-tale signs of a hasty spell moments earlier in the bathroom. I feel like shit and wonder just how shit I actually look. Blessed with a relatively clear complexion, I'm not one to frighten too many folk despite the early hour and negligible spread of makeup. Glancing up at the internal car mirror, I clock the area around my eyes. God, I look old. I examine the top I've chosen. How long have I had this black tee shirt? Does it matter for a visit to the hospital in the middle of the night? I switch the engine off and park up outside the hospital. My thoughts now return to poor Mum, upset and having nightmares after what that bastard did to her. After what that bastard did to us all.

Hospitals in the middle of the night are different. Spooky by the absence of visitors and staff that normally litter the corridors at each and every turn. I glance at my reflection in the dark, endless windows that line each shiny linoleum-floored walkway. *Wards 20 to 26 this way*, the signs indicate. I head towards the ward, passing a seated waiting area where two people are sitting, one noisily eating a bag of crisps. I think about the bacteria seeping through the hospital air. Wouldn't catch me eating in a hospital.

The nurse is expecting me and comes up to meet me at the ward's locked double doors.

'Sorry, Grace, to have to phone you, but your mum is getting anxious. We are worried about her heart and her getting worse with the anxiety. We've tried to settle her, but it's you she wants. Keeps talking about what happened. It's so awful.' I smile at the nurse and walk with her to Mum's room. Mum is sobbing and trying to establish where *he* is and crying about not being safe. She doesn't want to stay here where *he* can get her. I walk over to Mum's bedside, after accepting the offer of a cup of tea from the nurse.

'Mum, it's Grace, I'm here. You don't have to worry. You're safe now.' I try to sound calm and softly spoken. Nothing but nothing should make Mum think she isn't safe in the hospital. '*He* can't get you here, so try and get some rest. I'll be here.'

Mum's face has changed yet again in what seems to be a frequent occurrence now. I don't know what to expect next. Her face is wet from crying and I reach over for a tissue and wipe the discoloured areas of what was once Mum's soft round face. It's ugly and ruined now. The left eye has puffed up big time; the upper and lower eyelids fighting to co-join and escape from every morsel of light on offer from the hospital strip lights. Mum's lips have morphed into cushions of purple fatty blobs on one side. A dark yellowy purple line of bruising follows what was once the natural smooth wrinkle under her eye, sitting proud above a larger than normal cheek area. It's a mess, what a mess to such a precious area. How dare *he*, how fucking dare *he*.

My cup of tea arrives. I decline the offer of a biscuit, given the climate of germs I'm engulfed in. Mum has stopped sobbing and her breathing settles into a natural rhythm. Her eyes are calmly closed. I feel rewarded that she seems to be heading towards some form of slumber now.

An hour goes by with me sitting at Mum's bedside, absorbing the quietness of the room. Reciprocating maternal duties, where once as a child I lay fighting off a fever, Mum's hand never leaving its resting spot on my forehead, her intuitive thermometer patiently waiting on the dip. Her hand holding mine making the full remedial circuit, with a gentle circling of her finger in my half-closed palm. It's a wasted hour of nothingness, dropped memories cementing my bridge to my mum, who has now relented and given in to sleep.

'Another cup of tea, Grace?' whispers one of the nurses on duty.

'No, no, thanks, I'm fine,' I reply, glancing at my still full cup. Clearly, denying myself the prospect of sharing a mouth of tea with hospital air has won in the argument between rational thought versus my irrational cleanliness disorder. Pity, I'm quite thirsty now; though not as thirsty as the crisp-eating folk I passed earlier in the waiting area, I think smugly to myself.

'Looks like your mum will settle now, Grace. You should go home for some rest,' offers the nurse.

'Yes, think I will, but if she does wake, just phone me.' I'm desperate for my own personal sleep but only if Mum is going to be okay.

Back home, I put the key in the front door and step quietly inside. There's no noise or movement. Jenny is still asleep, which is good; no point in us both losing sleep. The wretched old tee shirt and jeans I'm wearing are tossed into the wash basket and I slide slowly into bed. And sleep.

## – 4 –

BEEP BEEP BEEP. The dulcet tones of my alarm beckon me to the new morning. Feels like I managed some sleep, I'm sure of it. I reach over and press off the alarm. I savour the warm soapy water from the shower. The fragrance from French olive oil soap wiping away the remnant smells from the hospital. I've been ordering and using the soap for years, favouring it for keeping my skin moisturised, whereas before it always felt dry. However, this morning's furious scrubbing is heading some way towards negating the nourishing effects of all that olive oil goodness. Once again, I let my mind switch over to mindless cleanliness, in an attempt to steer clear of all the worries and panics I'm having about Mum.

Pulling on my robe, I wander to the kitchen, stopping briefly to pop my head around Jenny's bedroom door. She's sound asleep. It's still early for her, though, to get up and get ready for college. I'll give her another quarter hour. I open the cupboard and catch a glimpse of organic porridge. Not worth the effort making it up. I opt for a small helping of muesli instead. Back in my bedroom, I pull out some jeans and a black polo neck. Smart enough, given there will be continued police activity at the hospital. I fix my face and ensure today's makeup at least masks some of the pale tiredness registering on my face. A surging blast of the hair dryer and I'm ready. Returning to Jenny's room, I poke my head around her open door again.

'Morning, Jenny, you want breakfast?' I ask cheerfully. It takes a while and a bit of turning around amidst the mass of the duvet and bedspread before Jenny replies, with her usual order of toast, peanut butter and jam. Back in the kitchen, for a brief moment, I absorb myself in duty and domesticity preparing Jenny's breakfast. I don't get to do it that often, with me heading to work early on and her later for college. Jenny is never a morning person. A trait she's inherited from her late father. You just never spoke to him until coffee number three. Crabbit as hell he was in the mornings. For once, the agony of the morning rituals makes me feel things are normal despite the hell that's brewing.

And it's within this hell that Jenny will soon be finding herself swimming in as well. Working out a way to tell her the truth that is emerging is not going to be easy, but she needs to know. Over breakfast, I tell her as softly and kindly as I can, her dark eyes penetrating mine, as if looking for the flaw, the crack that will arrive at just the right moment to dispel the awful truth. But my story ends on a raw, bleeding note. Our cups of tea are drained in silence, beating the same tune in unison, lifting, sipping, lifting and sipping. We put both our empty cups in the dishwasher, and we finish getting ready to head out.

We leave the cottage together, filled with a shared sadness, and go our separate ways. Neither of us wanting to over-talk events in case it leads us to the edge of a mutual decline. Jenny looks tiny and exposed as she drives off. I head to the hospital. Mum had woken again during the night, after I left, but the nurse managed to sit with her until she went back to sleep. Things start to get busy again around 11am, when DC Bain comes into Mum's room looking for me. She explains they will set up the camera for recording Mum's statement after lunch. She also updates me on how things are progressing.

'Grace, we brought someone in for questioning yesterday afternoon. We will be continuing to question him today.'

'Has he been arrested? Are you sure he's the one who assaulted Mum? Is he local?' I've been somewhat taken aback by the latest news but ramble on just the same.

'All I can say is we will continue to question him. Yes, he is local. I'll know more soon.' She's trying to ensure her updates are tempered by what is still clearly very early doors. DC Bain also mentions the possibility of doing a computer-based photo ID parade with Mum. That's likely to take place in the next day or so. 'I'll head off now, Grace, but see you after lunch. If I need to get hold of you before, I'll ring you on your mobile?'

'Yes, I've got my mobile on me,' I reply as DC Bain heads off.

The nurses come into the room to freshen up Mum, so I wait it out in the family room. On my way, I see DC Bain speaking to the ward sister at the end of the corridor, no doubt getting her own update on how Mum is doing. In the hospital ward's family room, I sit on my favoured corner chair at the back. I take my mobile out of my bag and check for any missed calls or messages from Jenny after telling her the news earlier this morning. There's nothing though, and I know my worrying will continue. The door opens and John and Pamela come into the family room.

'Did you hear they're questioning someone?' John's eyes are wide with excitement at the latest news. 'Must be a fucking nutter.' I sit quietly as John continues a blatant character assassination of the man they have arrested. 'What's going to be happening with Mum today then? They're taking a statement from her, aren't they?' John asks.

'Yes, video statement after lunch. I'll sit in on it to make sure she doesn't get too distressed. Then in the next day or so, they are doing a photo ID thing on a police computer.' I look over at John, who has a preoccupied, glazed look on his face. Clearly, he is pondering over an impending arrest which is feasting on his over-zealous imagination.

Lunch comes and goes in a shroud of gastronomic disappointment. Vegetable broth in an orange plastic bowl enjoys limited success with Mum's taste buds. With her Italian background, she's more accustomed to glorious, sticky mounds of pasta in all shapes and sizes, with steaming tomato sauce harbouring the secret family ingredient. I remember perching on the kitchen stool when I was young, hanging over the blue Formica-topped table, watching Mum fill the small attic flat with delightful food smells. As Mum added the secret family ingredient from the brown paper bag into the pasta sauce, I would giggle as she raised one finger to her mouth and went 'shush' and I knew I must never disclose the secret ingredient to anyone in the world. It was the law. The brutal irony of it all flings me out of this trip down memory lane. Christ, it was only dried celery leaves, after all.

Like a hasty scene change from an amateur dramatics play, dirty lunch dishes and cutlery are whisked off and trolley tops wiped down as the police camera crew arrive. The limited equipment seems to be at odds with the amount of clattering and racket being made. It isn't a huge hospital room and the policeman setting up the camera is working tirelessly, shifting chairs and curtains out the way, then bringing in more chairs. I'm wondering if another minor deity is arriving.

'Mum, the police will be taking a statement from you, like I told you earlier.' Mum is silent and emotionless. 'You don't have to be afraid of the camera. It's recording your statement so they can play it back later. You can just ignore it; it's nothing to worry about. I'll be here with you all the time.' I scan the room's newly appointed seating arrangements and wonder which chair has been reserved for me. 'Just try and listen carefully to the questions they will ask you and answer them with what you remember from yesterday.' Mum is still showing a worrying lack of emotion but appears resigned to giving her statement now.

DC Bain and DC Mackie both arrive in the room. After briefly chatting to the policeman to check the camera is in position and operating correctly, DC Bain turns to me and says they are ready to begin. I'm suddenly thrust into the horrible events of the previous day. DC Bain picks up on Mum's every word, relentlessly squeezing clarity from each and every phrase and description given in the responses.

'Mrs Fallon, you said he *hammered* you. What do you mean by that; he *hammered* you?' Mum just looks at DC Bain in disbelief, then looks over to me for the answer. 'When you say *hammered*, what is it exactly you mean?' Again DC Bain attempts to rephrase unsuccessfully.

'He took my pants off and wanted to have sex and I said no, I said get away,' comes Mum's response.

'Okay, Mrs Fallon. Before that, you said that he *hammered* you. Can you tell me what you mean by *hammered*?' Excruciating. Utterly and totally excruciating. At one point, I'm sitting like a feckless object, unable to offer reassurance as Mum struggles to hear at times and fully understand the level of detail needed by the police. With a pathetic straight smile and daft nodding, I try to transmit some comfort across the room.

Hopeless, I feel bloody hopeless.

'He looked like the devil, and in a suit he was, like the prime minister.' Mum, uneasy with the lull from the previous question, offers another instalment as if to please, as if to cover up some embarrassing silence.

'Where did he *hammer* you, Mrs Fallon?' DC Bain appears to have conceded and accepted her own definition of what *hammered* means and is now moving on with the statement.

'He had dark hair, like the devil he looked. He wanted to have sex and he started to hammer me, hammer me, and he kept hammering me and I screamed at him.'

There is an immense difficulty in sequencing events and questions. Mum demonstrates, God only knows where from, but an inner strength and enthusiasm to pour out painful fact after painful fact, but she can't follow the order of the agenda DC Bain has in mind. She restates what happened to her, what he did to her. Mum's face is now anxious, exhausted and ready to give up, as if they are not listening to what she is saying. They are ignoring her and instead keep repeating these stupid questions. Another awkward silence. DC Bain regroups her thoughts then pauses, deciding which way to go with this whilst looking towards my mum. I'm powerless to do or say anything and move sideways on my chair, as if manoeuvring my position will relax me. How stupid. How frustrating. How long is this going to go on for? How much more can my brave mum take?

'I can't hear you. You'll need to speak up; I can't hear what you are saying,' sobs Mum, thinking she has missed something being said. I can't contain myself any longer and, despite being told I must keep silent throughout, decide I'm going to have to say something.

'DC Bain, you will need to speak louder, go near Mum, near her side and speak loud in her ear. She is used to us doing this at home.' There, it's out, has to be said or I feel the room is going to somehow implode into itself.

'Mrs Fallon, can I come a bit closer so that you can hear me better? Your daughter says you are used to this, and it will help.' DC Bain repositions herself as Mum watches her, waiting for her to resume, impatient to get more of her statement out. Just wanting this bit to be over with.

For over an hour, the questioning continues with mixed success. Between another debate about how to interpret the expression *hammer*, to how he got in the front door, to what clothes or nightwear she had on, to what he was wearing, any noticeable things about his appearance, did he smell of anything, and did any of the family smoke; it was unrelenting and punishing. Question after question after question.

Towards the end, DC Bain flicks through the notes she has made on her notebook, and all I can think is, stop, that's enough, she's told you the whole shebang, she cannot take any more of this. Then DC Mackie turns to DC Bain and says to her he'll give it a go. Fuck, Fuck, Fuck, I'm reeling, upset, ready to burst. What the hell? All of these emotions and thoughts mincing my brain and insides.

'Mrs Fallon?' DC Mackie pipes up, then remembers he needs to get near Mum's side so that she can hear. He shuffles around the compact space in the room, avoiding knocking over the camera and, in a slow un-balletic way, swaps places with DC Bain to get the best seat in the room, the best seat to be heard. He stands up, then leans over. 'Did he say anything when he hammered you, Mrs Fallon?' DC Mackie finds a new question that he's either thought of himself, or it's on the notes DC Bain has in front of her. But it is yet another question for my tired mum.

'He wanted to have sex, he took my pants off,' repeats Mum.

'And what did he say that made you know he wanted to have sex? Did he say anything specific?' DC Mackie persists. Why the hell would he strip her naked? How many times does this have to be repeated? I am totally tense beyond comprehension now. DC Bain calls it a day with the statement, offering Mum the last chance to say or add anything else to what she has already said. The police leave the room. Equipment is retrieved. It is over. I feel like a bad smell is being evicted. I go over and sit close to Mum, with my hand resting on hers. Mum's eyes are heavy, ready for sleeping. Within minutes, Mum falls asleep. I creep out of the room and go to find John. I don't have to go far; he is talking to DC Mackie along the corridor. He says his goodbye, and as he clocks me, he trudges towards me.

'Well, how did Mum get on? Was she able to tell the police everything?' John's voice lifts at the end of both questions, seeking what he hopes will be a positive reply from me. If only he'd heard what I just sat through. What an evil, vile ordeal Mum suffered at the hands of that beast.

# – 5 –

I wake up and yelp as I discover I've fallen asleep awkwardly on my favourite leatherette chair in the hospital family room. Hauling my head into a near upright position, I pummel away at the corner of my neck that is suffering the greatest from my distorted sleeping pose. 'DOODLEDOODLE DOODLE DOODLEDOODLE DOODLE DOODLEDOO-DLE.' I glance down at my handbag where my lit-up mobile is seeking my attention. Flipping the cover off, I touch the screen.

'Hello?'

'Hello, Grace. DC Bain here. Sorry to disturb you again and so soon.' I look at the hideous plastic retro wall clock on the faraway wall of the room. It's 4.30pm.

'Oh, that's alright,' I lie, since my neck is now jittering away, still not recovering full sensation.

'I'm phoning to ask you for your help, Grace. My colleagues are heading over to your mum's flat, and I wonder if you can meet them there shortly? There are a few things they need to check out with you. Would that be alright?' asks DC Bain.

'Eh, yes, that's fine. Just now or what time?' I ask, still concerned whether I'll be able to walk without looking stupid. I've still to fully straighten my right knee, which has been left in a bend worthy of the Indian rubber lady. I never sleep in that position. These days, I never sleep full stop.

'They are on their way now, so it would be great if you could head over shortly,' DC Bain's optimism was clearly evident in her voice.

There is no sign of the police outside Mum's house as I park up. I gaze at the house from across the road. It's hard to imagine it was such a short time ago, what with all the hospital trips and inevitable waiting around. It feels like weeks have passed. My imagination is harping back to the brutality of what had gone on, and the rawness of it all returns. What time did he get to Mum's house? And was the door locked, or did Mum unlock it to let him in? She was safe in her home as long as her door was locked.

Glancing up at the flat above, I picture the scene as the neighbours rushed down to see what was going on when they heard Mum's screams. And then to find her lying there, all bloodied and bruised. Jesus.

A silver car pulls up and parks immediately outside the house. Three men in grey suits get out. Detectives, I think, all sporting the same short haircut. I get out of my car and head across the road to join them. I recognise one of the three detectives from the hospital yesterday. On approaching them, one of the detectives turns and introduces himself and his colleagues. DCI Gordon spends a few moments outside the front door talking to me. He is in charge of the investigation and is genuinely horrified at what has happened to Mum and is keen for an update on how she is doing. And of course how the family is coping too.

'I'm sorry, Grace, to have to ask you to come back to the flat. It's going to be difficult, I know. The forensics have taken

samples and fingerprints of all relevant areas and we just need
to check a few minor points to be sure. Oh, and I'll warn you
now the flat is a bit of a mess with the black fingerprint dust.
It comes off easy enough with some warm soapy water.' DCI
Gordon speaks with authority as one of the other detectives
opens the front door and we all go inside, with DCI Gordon
ushering me in, in front of him.

I'm suddenly faced with a crime scene. The living room is
covered in fingerprint dust. It is all over the door panels, the
sides of the doors and window ledges. He wasn't kidding when
he said it was a bit of a mess. And then familiar signs and
memories come back. I spot the bowl and towel I had carefully
brought through for Mum when she felt she was going to be
sick. Clothes which were lying on the floor have either been
taken away or are sitting across one of the dining chairs. Her
glasses are no longer sitting on the foot stool; they must have
taken them away too. Mum's plastic water jug sits redundant
on the table beside her maroon floral armchair. A few items of
mail sit beside it, perhaps waiting for me to visit and collect
and deal with like I usually do. Or more typically, junk mail
that needs to be binned. Family photos adorn every shelf and
hang proudly on each wall. Some more photogenic than others,
but snaps Mum loves and wants to keep. Each one hastily yet
lovingly framed and placed in an order, an order that's familiar
to me, as every now and again, I lifted up and dusted under
each one. What had these family images witnessed the previous
day? There's a photo of Mum and Dad standing opposite each
other, jointly holding a newly born Rose in their arms, both
absorbed by Rose's wrinkled face. In the photo, both Mum and
Dad are turned away from the scene of horror that took place
in the home, but Rose's face is painfully puckered and facing

forwards, as if being forced to see the ugly assault. I scan the room, the detectives silent and just watching me mentally take in each and every corner of the room. I'm overwhelmed and feel a surge from my chest rise up to my face, pushing tears closer to the corners of my eyes. I fight to try and contain my mouth turning down, as if preparing to cry. I want to cry at the whole fucked up scene I'm now having to absorb again. 'What am I looking for specifically? Did you want to ask me about things?' I cling on to a moment of focus that has kindly arrived, like a long-awaited bus on a pissing wet day.

'Take your time, Grace,' says DCI Gordon.

'I'm fine. I can't yet see anything obvious that's out of place,' I reply matter-of-factly, still taking in the room and mentally visualising the extent to which the room conforms to its correct state. 'Has the blind been touched by your forensic people?' I blurt out accusingly, staring at the window that overlooks the pavement to the front of the house. The detectives swing round towards the blind, then look at each other to gauge a response or reaction, but nothing is apparent. 'It's been pulled down. It's too low; she never has it that low. Even at night time she doesn't have it that low. It sits precisely a third of the way down the window during the day, and at night, Mum lowers it to about here, just below where the top pane meets the bottom pane of glass. But its right down at the bottom and it's not right. Someone pulled the blind down.' I'm standing making animated gestures in front of the blind, anxiously wanting them to understand it isn't right and being overwhelmed by the audacity of whoever it was who adjusted the blind. 'The toggle on the blind, *look*, no one has fingerprinted the toggle yet.' It's out before I can stop myself. The toggle is devoid of black fingerprint dust. I turn and see one of the detectives scribble in his notebook whilst the other has his mobile phone out and is mumbling to someone. DCI Gordon stands still, and in charge, with that air of authority as the two detectives scurry about as if they have been found lacking. The scribbler detective looks up at me.

'Most folk pull their blinds down at night for privacy. Are you sure your mum wouldn't do that?'

'She doesn't do that!' I hit back in an instant.

'Get it fingerprinted,' orders DCI Gordon calmly.

I move to the kitchen. There, in a small saucepan, sits two broken eggs and some milk and a lump of butter. She was making scrambled eggs for John, just like she had promised him the night before. A bit premature in the preparation, but sure as hell, there it is, my brother's breakfast to be. He never got his scrambled eggs that day; that bastard saw to it she wasn't going to make her son's breakfast. I feel palpitations in my chest become faster and more profound, like someone has clamped my chest and is tightening and tightening it to hinder my breathing. A moment of light-headedness engulfs me, and I place my hands on the kitchen worktop to steady myself and regain my composure.

'Do you want to get some air?' offers DCI Gordon.

'No, I'm fine, just give me a minute. I want to get this over with and get out of this place.'

'You're doing just great, Grace, strong just like your mother.' DCI Gordon smiles.

'It must be the Italian in us then,' I retort with a reciprocating smile.

I complete the review of the house with a look in Mum's bedroom. The detective has taken a cylindrical Pringles crisp tub out of Mum's wardrobe.

'Do you recognise this, Grace?' asks the detective, who is now opening the tub and showing me the inside. It has money inside it, a few notes and some change.

'I didn't know she had that. Where was it?' I ask, disappointed that a small aspect of Mum's life has suddenly revealed itself to me.

'It was hidden away towards the back of one of the shelves in the wardrobe,' says the detective, pointing at the tub's clandestine hiding place.

'She likes Pringles, always buys them. Is there much money in it?' I ask, as if an inconsequential amount of money will go some way towards making it more palatable.

'About £35,' says the detective. I shrug apologetically. 'Would your mum keep a larger amount of cash in the house, Grace?'

'No, I doubt it. I get Mum money from her pension each week. She gets enough to keep her going with food shopping, and if she needs more, she will ask me to get it, you know, for something special, or if her neighbour upstairs buys her some plants for the rockery, that sort of thing. I pay her bills too so that she doesn't have to worry about paying them. I deliberately discourage her from having large sums of money in the house because it isn't safe,' I reply without realising just how lame my last sentence is in the grand scale of things.

'It doesn't appear to look like robbery was his motive,' adds the detective, and I glance up at him with an expression that demonstrates how blatantly obvious it isn't robbery, considering how poor Mum has suffered at the hands of that beast.

We all head back to the front hallway and prepare to leave the house. One of the detectives in front turns and re-enters the house. He mutters something to DCI Gordon as we proceed outside. They lock Mum's house. Across the road, three youths sit on a wooden bench in a small park-like area overlooking the row of houses. DCI Gordon catches their eye as they laugh and joke away.

'Where are you parked, Grace?' asks DCI Gordon.

'Just across the way behind the white building,' I say, pointing to an invisible spot behind a building, behind where the youths are sitting.

'I'll walk you to your car,' he says without hesitation and without offering a reason for doing so. I put it down to the presence of the three youths. Who are they? Are they known to the police? It suddenly strikes me they might be acquaintances of the bastard that assaulted Mum. With pressure building up inside, I take a deep breath and convince myself of the need to calm down and not let my imagination run away with itself. I immediately sense the police know more and are excluding me from proceedings. Yet it doesn't seem the right moment to ask. Back at my car, DCI Gordon thanks me and again says how sorry he is. 'We're doing everything we can, Grace, don't you worry.' And with that, he heads back to his car with the other detectives, and I make my way to the hospital.

In the hospital car park, I quickly check my mobile and note a missed call from DC Bain. First, I ring Jenny to see how things are with her and she tells me of her plans for later, meeting up with friends then staying over at her friend's house. She sounds cheery enough and it will be good for her to be with friends she can talk to. Not sure how much more I can say to her about this whole sorry state. Then I call DC Bain.

'Hello, Grace, thanks for calling me back. How did you get on at your mum's house today?'

'It wasn't nice going back, bit sickening really to think what went on there.' I sound deflated, exhausted.

'Can't have been easy. I can only imagine how awful it must have been. Anyway, Grace, I was calling to let you know the police have charged a local man, Darren Rodden, the man they were questioning in relation to your mum's assault.'

'Are you sure it was him?' I'm at a total loss how to react or say anything else, so it's the first thing that comes into my mind.

'The police still have a lot to do, especially in pulling together all the forensics. We will be continuing to question the accused, but we have enough to go on just now to charge him.' DC Bain then continues. 'There's a lot to take in, Grace. Tomorrow, I have set up a meeting with you and your brother and the procurator fiscal. With the accused being charged to appear in court, it will be up to the Crown Prosecution Service to take proceedings forward. I want you to meet them since they will be key to the ongoing proceedings.' I agree a time with DC Bain and tell her I will contact John to let him know. 'One other thing, Grace, we want to get the computer photo ID set up soon, whilst your mum is still recalling details of the incident.' DC Bain waits on my reaction, no doubt conscious of allowing time for me to take in what's happening and when. Mum, after all, remains desperately poorly in hospital.

My mind goes completely blank. Holding my phone to my ear, I panic trying to forge or salvage some sense from a head full of mangled information overload. It's the photo ID that has thrown me. I'm sure of it, but not sure why it has rendered my thought process to the point of useless. My eyes are heavy, sleepy; I've hit my first wall.

'Grace, are you still there?' comes DC Bain's voice from my mobile.

'Yes, sorry, I'm just thinking, trying to take it all in, things that need to happen. I haven't seen Mum since lunchtime today.' The words just spew out of my mouth as if playing for time, time for me to think straight.

'Will I go ahead, Grace, and organise things and we can speak more tomorrow at the meeting at the fiscal's office? It will give you a chance to talk things over with your brother. I'll speak to you tomorrow,' offers DC Bain. And at that, she hangs up. I feel pushed into a corner, a victim of my own debilitating slowness at processing all these questions and requests. Stupid stupid.

I suddenly remember where I am, in the hospital car park, and want to head in and see how Mum is doing. She will have had her tea by now. The automatic hospital doors hiss as they welcome me in. I make my way along the now familiar, shiny floors towards the ward. The nurses smile as I head into Mum's room. John, Pamela and Rose are there already, chatting loudly for the whole world to hear. Mum is somehow managing to snooze through it all. She looks calm despite increased bruising over her soft face. It isn't as puffy, but colour-wise, it has grown into a palette of blues and purples.

'Best let you know the latest from the police. They charged a 19-year-old guy, same one they were questioning yesterday, Darren Rodden. We have a meeting set up at 10am tomorrow with the Crown Prosecution Service at the procurator fiscal's office; it's just off the end of the motorway. We should write down any questions we might have. DC Bain will be there. And a computer photo ID will take place soon.'

'That's quick, eh, charging someone? And 19 years old, crikey that's young.' John is satisfied with this latest milestone.

'Yes, it's good the police are making progress. Well, if it's okay with everyone here, I'm going to head home and get some rest. I'm just exhausted. Mum seems settled, eh?' I try and contain my yawning just enough to lean over and kiss Mum's forehead.

* * *

Back at the cottage, I settle down on the sofa for what is left of the evening. A large mug of steaming tea sits beside me, and I flick through the TV channels for something to do; I'm restless and unsettled. I wander up to Jenny's room at the far end of the cottage and slowly swing open her door but choose to leave her light off. There's a glow from the moon through her two large windows, allowing me to see the room's familiar set-up. She's not there of course, and through the darkness, I take in her mess on the floor, salvaging companionable thoughts from the clothes that haven't quite made it to the laundry basket. Their outlines, like deflated mannequins with arms and legs in non-conforming skeletal poses, make me smile, heartened by their familiar presence. Her MacBook sits on her desk, a technological hedgehog with random sticky notes jutting out and framing the screen. I've forgotten how untidy her writing is too, but it's too dark to read them, not that I would. And the small silver photo frame holding the final photo I took of her with her dad has relocated from her desk to her bedside table, perhaps for comfort.

The corner of my eye catches a flicker; a slither of a reflection passes Jenny's window at the side of the cottage. Why would someone be here at this time of night? There's been no knock at the door. For a split second, the already darkened room dulls as something briefly shields her room from the light of the moon. I can't move and a panic surges in my chest. I'm hoping it's a trick of my eyesight struggling to adjust from the small hall light to Jenny's dark room. Instinctively I listen; surely a noise must follow. I stare towards the second window. It overlooks the driveway and front garden. I'm rigid, can't move my feet. And there it is, the slow steadfast crunch of gravel. Suddenly I lunge towards the wall at the side of the window, hiding, tracing, timing the crunching before it turns the corner and passes the window. The cold wall is firmly against my back, and I can't bear to look, holding my breath, making my chest pulse even more. The room dulls again. Someone's outside.

Front door's locked, chain is on, but I'm still terrified. The phone is in the kitchen and my mobile is sitting on the sofa in the living room. If I move, I'll be seen. If I was still sitting in the living room, I'd be seen. This is stupid, but I can't seem to do anything except remain pinned to the wall, listening. And then a slow creak, I know what it is, the letterbox. Oh Jesus, they're looking inside, they know I'm in here. I hold my breath, the pressure filling my throat and chest. And then a click, the letterbox closing, then crunching, noisier this time on the gravel as whoever it is runs away from the cottage. I slide down and crawl, crawl into the hall towards the lounge. There's no way around it; if they're still there, I'll have to be seen from the front lounge window to reach for my mobile on the sofa. Crawling near to the front door, I'm already deciding I need to stand up and make a bolt for the lounge. That's when I see it, the bit of folded paper lying on the carpet below the letterbox. God, how stupid; it'll be a flyer for the village hall quiz night or something like that. And for a moment as I grab the bit of paper, I feel relieved and can't understand why I'm so jumpy. Unfolding it, I read the message.

*HE'S DONE IT BEFORE, BUT IT'S GETTING WORSE. YOU NEED TO BE CAREFUL.*

Someone knows him or knows of him. I'm back to being terrified and listening, listening until I can be sure whoever is outside has gone. I grab the phone in the kitchen and pull the wire around the corner, the corner hidden from any outside view. With the phone on my lap, I think, too scared to ring anyone. Panicking, I ring Jenny.

'Hi, Mum, sorry about the noise, it's busy in here though. Wait, I'll go outside, see if I can hear you better.'

'*No!* It's okay, I can hear you, *stay* where you are, *inside.*'

'Mum, you okay? You sound funny.'

I don't know what to say to her and suddenly I'm caught up in a silence following my hasty decision to ring her.

'Didn't think you could hear me. Sorry, did I deafen you?'

'Is everything okay, Mum? You sound out of breath or something.'

'My tea went down the wrong hole.' I just want to end this conversation.

'Is Nanny okay? I should be home. I'll come home, Mum, is it Nanny?'

'No, no, don't be silly. There's no change with Nanny, she's still in hospital. Just checking in, making sure you got to your friends okay.' And I force out a stuttered laugh.

'Right, well, if you are sure, I'll get back to my friends. I'm staying over but will be back lunchtime sometime. Byeeee.'

'Bye, darling, see you tomorrow. Oh… mind how you go now.' And with that, she hangs up, oblivious to what's just gone on here, I hope. I replace the receiver and sit and think.

I decide to ring the police, the non-emergency number. There's silence at the other end of the phone as I explain who I am, what happened to Mum and mention someone is outside the house, but they're gone now. Rather than tell them about the note, I go to great lengths to explain why I'm terrified and start to convince him of the unfairness of whoever did this to Mum being out there somewhere.

'Well, he's not likely to come anywhere near you.' The officer assumes I think the attacker is outside my house and I'm annoyed I've led him to believe this. 'He wouldn't be so stupid,' he adds.

'Well, I'm glad you are reassured about him because all I know is what he did to my mum!' I snap back and now realise the conversation has gone so far off kilter that mentioning the note will have the police rank me as a paranoid time waster. I thank him, not sure what for, and hang up. I put the note in a safe place at the back of the cereal cupboard, behind my box of porridge oats. What's the point of calling the police?

# – 6 –

The tired-looking curtains remain drawn at 16B Haw-
thorn Close, shielding a glow from a low-level table
lamp in the front room. Light strains through gaps
in the poorly hung maroon fabric, illuminating patches of a
neglected flower border in the front garden. Carefully parting
the curtains, Darren Rodden checks for anyone outside. This is
the longest few hours the police have left him alone since firing
questions at him down at their headquarters a few miles away.
Abandoning the mess in his flat, he had gone with them when
they called him in yesterday for questioning.

They were interested in what he was up to that night. 'Just
walking,' he'd told them in a confident tone, which came out
sounding more like a guess. The detectives' knowing glance
at each other panicked him into a fake, helpful mode, so he
mentioned walking past the old woman's house, seeing a light
on, but that was about it; it was very late. Switching to a casual
voice, he told them he went back to his flat after that; it was
freezing outside and he was hungry. They made him wait alone
in the interview room, and he had been dying for a fag but
couldn't find them in his pocket. Leaving the room to ask for
one would trigger an alarm, an alarm he imagined would go off

the moment he even stood up. Maybe there were wires under his chair. He couldn't hide his agitation when the police came back in again with more questions. He told them he needed a fag and his medication. The cocky detective asked him what medicine he took, so he told him he had ADHD. His right leg was twitching by now and he'd forgotten the last time he had taken his meds. Amidst informing the police about his *genuine* ailment felt a good time to come clean and tell them he'd seen the old woman, especially after they'd asked him *how* he knew it was an old lady that lived there. It was getting complicated since the blind in her front window was down and he was meant to be across the road.

They said he was free to go, but it was short-lived. He'd just put the washing machine on in his flat when they rang him, and soon he was back in the same interview room, on the same wired chair, with more questions. They pressured him until he told them how he'd gone into the old woman's flat and saw her lying there, got frightened and ran away. Well, he thought someone would catch him and think he did it. That would have been when he dropped his fags on the carpet, fags the police found later in her house. They'd gone to his flat after that and taken stuff away, clothes and shoes. It all happened so quickly. Getting mixed up with his story, and choosing to stare at the tiny red light on the police video camera, he was frightened, thinking things needed to slow down. After announcing a date and time again, the detective reached over towards the recording switch beside the red glow, stating he'd been charged and told to appear in court the following day.

It was pretty big stuff compared to his previous misdemeanours, when the police were okay about it all. This situation was different, more serious, so he told his mum about it and then his grandad came over. They looked worried as he explained he hadn't done anything wrong but still the police took away his clothes from inside the washing machine. He'd be more careful next time and keep out of trouble, he told his mum. His grandad had shouted at him, said it was becoming a habit now and he worried what he was doing wandering the streets at night. The last time it happened, he stayed with his grandparents and wasn't allowed out late at night. After a couple of days, things were just getting stupid, so he escaped out of a window at the back of their house and headed back to his own flat, where he could do what he liked.

Today is 'court day', and once again he looks through a gap in the curtains and checks outside. It's still early, with no one about. Picking up his mobile phone, he begins clicking through his contact list, anxious to find a distraction.

Meeting up with his mates after court is tempting, but he isn't sure how much had been said the previous night, the same night the nosey police were keen to unravel.

Being blitzed and high from the vodka and cider led to arguments over a lassie from his work. He remembered that okay. Rarely did he talk about girls and sex, but a few vodkas had loosened his tongue, leading to an unexpected outpouring of how he'd fancied her for ages but working next to her made it awkward. It provided his mates with a believable excuse for why he hadn't got round to asking her out. Deep down, it masked his flaccid impotence when it came to dating. The argument erupted when his mate announced he'd asked her out, and now they were an item. Acted like he never knew he'd had his eye on her. Fuck sake, she was all he talked about, so it should have been pretty obvious. Now he'd stolen her, and it would be ages before he would have the courage to ask out another lassie.

He'd ruined it, his mate, and after swearing at him and pushing him over, he had grabbed his vodka and stormed off, left them drinking in the field behind the high school.

Stumbling through the bracken and gorse to get to the footpath, he could still hear them laughing at him. He didn't feel like going back to his empty flat after that. A mild early morning breeze was clearing some of the fuzziness inside his head. Which was good in a way, as he'd been staggering since leaving them drinking in the field. But he knew a lifting of this internal fog would invite the return of his irritation, a mood only cured by his meds. The quietness of the morning was playing tricks on his mind, still imagining his mates laughing at him running off like that. Frustrated and angry, he had taken a last gulp from his bottle of vodka and launched it into someone's front garden. Thankfully it landed in amongst bushes and didn't appear to smash and wake the residents of the house. He'd lost track of time after that and made his way back to the flat where it had all become a blur.

After a somewhat drunken and clumsy arrival at his flat, he fancied chips to soothe his hunger, so he put a box of them in the microwave. The five-minute greasy feast led to some hasty undressing, with him only managing to pull on tracksuit bottoms before passing out with exhaustion. It was the heavy knocking on his front door that caused him to jolt and sit bolt upright. Jagging into the palm of his left hand were the last few microwave chips in the discarded box by his side. Wiping off the sauce from his chips, he noticed the bleeding on his knuckles and it stung like hell. Grabbing a hoodie, he stumbled to the front door. By now the knocking had become angry thumping. He opened the door, and it was the police, and things just went from bad to worse after that.

Today he's alone, waiting for his court appearance, deciding it isn't a good idea to get in touch with his mates. He looks around the flat for something to do before his mum arrives to take him to court. With the help of some milk, his tablets seem to go down a treat. His mum had left them out and warned him about forgetting to take them on time. Jumping at the sound of another knock at the door, he momentarily panics before hearing his mum's key in the lock and the familiar sounds of her letting herself in.

'You not opened your curtains yet, Darren? Open them and open a window whilst you're at it. Stinks in here.' It must still be the chips, he thought.

Desperate to avoid any argument with her today, he tentatively pulls open his curtains, not quite fully but enough to keep her happy. Lifting the latch on the top window, he recoils as a gust of healthy outside air pelts him before blending in with the rancid interior air particles like a failed odour eating laboratory experiment. Turning to his mum, he attempts a smile then recognises the same strained, empty return look. A dead expression that shrouds her hollow eyes, saddened by the darkened rings which have long begged for a decent night's sleep. Fed up, she's fed up with him, and it's plain to see. After tossing aside some of his strewn clothes, she sits down on his sofa in unison with a sigh that sings her utter disgust with him. He'd have been better just booking a taxi to take him to court. She looks around his room for a clock or something to indicate a time, half laughing at the possibility he'll even have an item so sensible amidst all the rubbish and crap that sketches out his existence.

'You'd better hurry up and get ready, Darren. Doubt we'll get parked outside the court, so may have to park and walk up.' His mum dusts down the front of her coat, terrified of an encroaching disease that may be rising from the foam of his sofa.

The one grey suit he owns has appeared and is hanging up on his bedroom door. A pressed, white shirt and random tie sits on his bed. He shudders as the cold cotton lands against the pale veiny skin on his back. The subsequent suit does little to provide warmth, despite the grey cladding making him feel like a trussed-up turkey.

Rummaging in the bottom of his wardrobe, he grabs a pair of black shoes and sits on the corner of his bed to tie his laces. It all just feels a bit unreal to him, as if he is going somewhere he doesn't want to go, like his dental check-ups when he was younger.

'You nearly done?' his mum shouts through the bedroom door. He presents himself to his mum in the living room, but she hardly looks at him, just picks up her bag and car keys and heads for the front door. Feeling like he's been told off, he sheepishly follows her out towards her car.

There's no conversation as they make their way to court, the car simply filling with a suffocating annoyance. She hates him as much as he hates the prospect of this court appearance. By the time they get to the court and make their way in, his grandparents are already there, standing in a quiet corridor. His solicitor is there too, standing at the front of them in an orderly queue, just as some more police arrive and wait with them. A court officer speaks to his solicitor and says he'll be called in shortly and suggests his mum and grandparents may want to go into the public gallery soon.

Darren watches them walk away, abandoning him in favour of a good viewing seat.

The court proceedings are speedy and business-like. If he blinks, he'll miss something, but not the fact he's charged and feels instant disgust by what they are charging him with. He didn't think that's what had been agreed during his last police interview, if indeed he had agreed to anything. But standing here in court today makes him feel scarily important even if his heart is racing a bit. The strange feeling is new to him, something he's never felt before, and he wonders if he will get used to it.

Parking is a nightmare at the procurator fiscal's offices. The meagre selection of visitor parking spaces has been scooped up and the remainder of the car park is riddled with spaces set aside for companies who have offices in the building. It reads like a who's who from the yellow pages. I recognise some company names as I crawl around waving at John and Pamela, who have already arrived and are waving at me from the front of the building. It's like an un-enjoyable fairground ride passing and waving, passing and waving. Eventually I find a space, albeit a distance from the entrance. Picking up my notebook, I make my way to the entrance, noting that a car has just reversed out of one of the precious visitor parking spaces. Just my rotten luck. The foyer is quite grand considering the uninteresting company names I've seen in the car park. Glass and stone are in abundance as we make our way up the stairs to the first floor. There is a dirty mop smell permeating in the air. That or an old apple core that has been overlooked from last night's cleaning. I can't quite place it but just scrunch up my nose and hope the smell will disappear as we arrive at the entrance to the fiscal's office. John pulls at the door handle but fails to open it on two counts. Firstly, it says push, and secondly, there is a sign that says *Buzz to enter*. Pamela presses the buzzer and just looks at John as if he is stupid. I announce our arrival at the reception desk and am relieved the girl nods to confirm we are expected, and she tells us to take a seat in the waiting area. The buzzer goes again and DC Bain walks through, saying a cheerful good morning to us all sitting there. I return a smile and wonder if DC Bain has been the lucky beneficiary of the recently vacated visitor car parking spot.

We don't wait long before an attractive male in a pricey business suit comes out and introduces himself, then gestures us into the conference room. I shake Frank Callaghan's hand and note his impeccable grooming. There is also the hint of a fading suntan, no doubt remnants of a summer holiday. John and Pamela warmly greet him. DC Bain nods at him halfway through a familiar hello; their paths have obviously crossed before.

The conference room is large and airy with wonderful views of the Wallace Monument. Teas and coffees are distributed amongst us as two more staff find their way into the room and sit down around the light oak table. Frank initiates formal introductions before sitting forward and clasping his hands to begin the meeting for real. 'DC Bain will have told you the news about the police questioning a 19-year-old male called Darren Rodden in connection with the incident involving your mother. He's due in court today and we expect him to be formally charged. The court will also determine bail.' Frank Callaghan clearly sets the tone of the meeting. 'Given the fact an arrest has been made, myself and my colleagues here at the Crown Prosecution Service will be taking over proceedings from the police but will continue to work closely with them. We will be your primary contact from now on.' His tone remains consistent. 'I can only say how shocked I am by this terrible incident with your elderly mother and in her own home too. This must be very difficult for you all to come to terms with and I am sure you have questions you want to ask. I must, however, state that whilst the investigation is ongoing, there may be aspects of it that I can't discuss with you; I'm sure you understand.' The procurator fiscal *hath* spoken.

With this, he looks over at me and my permanently knitted eyebrows. I naively thought this meeting would work differently, but I'm not sure why, since we are all venturing into the unknown. I have already virtually thrown back earlier offers of support from the police family liaison and yet here I am somehow wanting to feel embraced and cossetted by this next bunch from the Crown Prosecution Service. Maybe I want them to be warmer towards us, more touchy-feely. It will be down to their diligence and expertise to bring the bastard in and convict him. And what do I know about them? Are they any good? Is Frank the best in his field, and has he a decent track record? I'm suddenly expected to accept these individuals as being of sufficient calibre to own this important and very personal situation. How can I feel more comfortable when all I can imagine right now is having been forced into some bubble of trust and acceptance without being given the benefit of a background check?

And then there's the note I got pushed through my letterbox. I'm intentionally *not* sharing that, but I have no idea why I'm keeping that to myself. I curse my own unfair and unreasonable logic but can't help thinking Frank's pricey business suit looks cheap and shiny now. Cutting through the clinging tension, DC Bain smiles over at me and suggests I may have some questions for the fiscal. I lower my heavy head and examine my list. That bloody note is also etched on my face, I'm sure of it, and I feel my face reddening. John is now wearing, permanently it seems, an expectant face and is eagerly waiting on my first question. He hasn't written anything down.

'Given the severity of the assault, at court today he's not likely to be granted bail, is he?' I ask. It is a question halfway down my list but one which beacons above the others on the list. I feel I somehow know him better than they do, especially given the note says he's done it before.

'It's a decision that will be made by the court, and although on the face of it, you'd expect the accused to be refused bail, it really depends on the individual circumstances, whether he's likely to do a runner, or his past history and how likely he is to reoffend. I don't want to guess which way it will go; best wait to hear what decision the court make.' Once again, a rehearsed reply by Frank. It's like phoning an insurance company and hearing the robotic individual at the other end reading from a script on their screen.

'So he could be released and free to come and go as he pleases?' I feel nervy and exposed at the first realisation the police have caught who done it but are now planning on potentially losing him. And it doesn't add up, not if he's done it before, but the police must know that.

'That can't happen, surely. I mean, you do know what he did to our mum? She told us he tried to rape her, *rape* her, and the courts might just let him go?' John uncharacteristically utters his disbelief. I'm silently with him on this, but Frank offers no other detail and manages to keep up this impartial pretence that none of us can grasp and understand. We are all quite dumfounded. It feels like a waste of time. As the meeting is about to finish, Frank looks over at us as if on a final note.

'Just to make you aware, there's likely to be considerable ongoing press interest in what happened. Crimes of this nature are very unusual of course in this area, but it will be more down to press interest in the accused, Darren Rodden. Darren is one of the children who survived the school massacre.'

We're all silent. I can't feel what direction this lightheaded wave hits my body, but all of a sudden it engulfs me. Sheer utter shock that something more has been added to this catalogue of horror and it's as if it's never going to end.

* * *

If I didn't know any better, I would have said the walls of the fiscal's office leaked like tea bags. Pressing an invisible launch button, the news was out about Darren Rodden, with rumour and speculation seeping out into any newsworthy jet stream. I'm not long home from the meeting with the fiscal when my brother rings my mobile to warn me some journalist from a popular national newspaper has been at his door.

'It's in case he heads up your way, Grace, just to warn you.'

'I hope you sent him packing. Can you imagine the story they'll want in light of who he is? Stirring all that up again. It's irrelevant really. For whatever reason, he is just an evil lowlife who did this to Mum. Don't speak to any of them and tell Pamela and Rose not to either.' I'm starting to sound bossy now.

The whole day is filled with this continuous hell. My phone rings again and it's a lady from the fiscal's office. Her purpose is to inform me of the outcome of the court hearing earlier on in the day, the hearing that would formally charge him and decide on bail. Stumbling over the exact wording, she apologies for what must be the third time amidst the nervous undertone of the words she's been told to say. And then she tells me the news I am dreading. He's been released on bail. My attempts at sabotaging her official stance fail because she isn't able to provide further insight or rationale behind the decision. Of course I want to know where he is; she can't tell me this information. What happens if he tries to go anywhere near Mum? She can't tell me this. I've asked for reassurance they are aware where Mum stays in relation to him; she pauses at this one, no doubt wondering how I know where he stays. But the truth is my brother found this out; I had no idea. I only hope they have measured the distance and taken this into consideration. Not that Mum is expected home anytime soon, if at all. As her pause lengthens, I prepare myself for telling her all she has to do is walk through the town and the chatter-infused air will hit her with a wealth of information on him, including where his flat is. She isn't taking the bait, there's silence, so I enlighten her of the meagre distance between his flat and Mum's flat. She almost admits they hadn't considered this, then quickly withdraws this confession by the offer of the procurator fiscal phoning me back with perhaps more information. Stepping back from the line she's been manoeuvred into crossing, there's this glorious relief in her voice as she ends the call.

It isn't long before Frank, in his shiny suit, rings me back, offering little more than I've already been told. He does confess that instructions have now been given regarding his bail conditions, mainly that there's a time curfew and he isn't allowed to approach Mum or go within an agreed distance of Mum's flat. As if anticipating my next question, he informs me he obviously cannot tell me where Darren Rodden is residing. I bloody well know this thanks to my brother. I want to pressure

Frank into declaring this, but he's clever, I'll give him that, and he manages to maintain a steady controlled tone that isn't giving anything away.

My mind flicks back to the note I got through my letterbox just as the phone call ends and I hang up. Someone out there knows him better than we do. *And* they know me too, and where I stay, where Jenny stays! I'm terrified at how unprotected I feel, vulnerable to whoever it is keeping one step ahead of us, knowing so much more. What else is there that he's done? I should warn Jenny; she's not here and he's out there, somewhere, anywhere! I need to know what we are *not* being told.

I notice my hand is still clutching the phone receiver; I haven't let go of it since I plonked it down. A sick feeling rises in my chest. I pick up the receiver again, dialling my brother's number, with one prevalent thought. How on earth do I tell John that Darren's been granted bail and is in effect out there?

* * *

The press are not allowed to report on his background before the trial takes place. And things are eerily quiet, no more calls, no one knocking at the door for a story. Without that 'hook', I guess it isn't newsworthy. And so we are left alone.

But as the press shuts down to the possibility of the story, the news slowly finds its way in amongst the town gossip. Never exaggerated, just sporadic, simple confessions of the truth of what happened. There is shock, of course there is, what a terrible thing to happen to an old lady. But it's hard to describe the subsequent mute effect that seems to descend. Fourteen years since it all happened, the school shootings, and the town has come a long way in dealing with its legacy. Darren Rodden has opened the hatch, peeled open the Pandora's box, one that has been so carefully closed and shielded, never to be forgotten but with new saplings offering hope over those years, a protective glaze for those who survived. He's tarnished it, caused an upset. But his membership of this sanctified club places him out of bounds, beyond reproach. And in all the heartache in trying to cope with what Mum has gone through, I am losing sight of it being his caustic fault. Instead, I am apportioning the weight of blame firmly in Mum's hands, as if she is in some way responsible for the renewed unwelcome attention. The severity of the assault refuses to curb or dampen its effect. There really is no way of overcoming a sense that I am holding the poisoned chalice.

# – 8 –

Julian Brodie steps into my gallery. I don't know him, and I find myself wondering who he is and where he comes from. An uneventful morning with viewers browsing the latest exhibition has quickly changed and I am curious about this latest admission. He halts in front of *Study II*, allowing me to ponder over his tall, confident pose and balanced proportions. The intelligent, sidelong face isn't overly young, with a protruding distinguished aquiline nose and ears with elongated lobes and fine, groomed hair that looks soft to touch.

I search his clothes for the clues they suggest, an occupation perhaps. Suited trousers fold and curve where a toned calf meets his ankle, then drop over buffed leather business shoes. His briefcase is aged, buckled and with a Rumpolean scholarly oddness to it. I'm drawn to his hands gripping it, mature and long-fingered, slipping out from under the cuffs of his black wool Crombie coat.

I want to know what he is thinking of *Study II*, and I suddenly wish he'd chosen a work of a more noteworthy title. It's not my favourite and shows my laziness. Turning on his right foot, he moves on and around the gallery, his eye contact constant, interested and curious of each work. We stand in the now empty gallery, the pair of us giant ornaments, aware of each other's presence through the space.

'Hello, I saw you in court yesterday and you dropped something.' He stands close. His eyes are boyish and impudent, in a way defying his age, late fifties, 60, I'd guess. That's when he introduces himself and tells me his name.

Two months have passed since the violent assault on Mum. A visit to the court yesterday was by way of preparation for the forthcoming trial. Never in my life have I been in court or experienced its harsh reality. He'd picked up my business card, which I assume must have fallen out of my glasses case, although I don't recall, just as I don't recall seeing him there either. They were new cards I had printed for my forthcoming exhibition in my gallery. An exhibition he's spent the last 20 minutes getting to know.

I'm not sure how to respond, but logically there is a requirement to bring some correlation between my day in court and the first week I have felt able to open the gallery again. I just couldn't face the three-quarter hour commute to Edinburgh.

Neglecting friends with excuse after excuse about hospital visits to Mum and trying to get my head around events leading up to the court case had more or less made the last couple of months reclusively unfulfilling. There isn't anything normal about choosing to do a grocery shop at the 24-hour supermarket from midnight onwards. My latest exhibition has forced me to resume normal service.

'Yes, I was at the court, although I don't make a habit of sitting in on criminal trials.' It was best to rule out any notion he had that I was either a weirdo with an unhealthy liking of the inside of courtrooms, or worse still, I knew the hardened Aberdonian crook in the dock.

'I like your work, by the way. The larger pieces must take ages. Such a talent.' I seem to have appeased him since he is now back on the subject of my work and less on the nasty business of the court case, which I truly don't want to share with him right now. Our exchange lasts several minutes, almost superficial in nature, but it feels important, or different, and I don't know why. And then he leaves. The lack of history or knowledge of each other is at odds with the inappropriate feeling I'm left with, and I let my silly mind wonder if he feels the same.

The International Book Festival and Edinburgh Fringe are in full swing with amorphous crowds flocking to the streets, sashaying into the cycle lanes, soaking up the city's offerings. I'm not complaining since despite being off the main thoroughfare, my gallery visitor numbers remain quite buoyant throughout the day. A German couple are very interested in my largest work, a work with a proper title this time. Hand sewing features heavily, and I'm amazed it holds such appeal when their country exudes precision engineering. But they like it and I've suddenly become party to a discussion over the size of a wall in their morning room back in their Hamburg home. Balancing between the push for a sale and simply listening in on this stimulating Germanic rant, I place a polite hand on the German lady's arm whilst excusing myself to see to another customer who has saved me by walking into the gallery.

This new viewer requires no assistance, purely browsing, so I do a non-evasive float around the gallery. The German couple I can tell are nearing a decision, as their conversation moves to more conclusive, stuttered pauses and much nodding. I put the sale through and take details for the international delivery.

Closing time is at 5.30pm, so I alarm up, twist the keys in

the locks and verify the secureness with a turn and firm pull on the door handle. I glance down the street to the left and right, checking if anyone might be there. I'm still nervous about going out on my own, what with Darren Rodden being out there somewhere. It's a feeling I can't seem to shift. Staring up at the buildings the town has fought hard to prevent being swallowed up by dodgy eateries and short-term sad shops. What's there remains trendy and inviting as I stroll up the lanes of popular historic architecture, accented with just the occasional planning authority disaster. The streetscape cuckoos my own enveloping spasmodic misery. Dormant weeds growing in tarmac and concrete pavement cracks are good practice for the cobbled sections that follow. My footsteps are hopeful, steady over other peoples' footsteps, maybe Julian Brodie's footsteps, since he headed in this direction.

A ghost moon accompanies me on my drive home. The lunar illumination seeps through torn and shredded fractus and settles on my little cottage. There's a damp nip in the air, and the crystalising gravel indicates an emerging frost. Best put the fire on, as I will be reading as usual into the noiseless early hours. Marilynne Robinson's latest is chosen, brand new, and I savour the smell and delicious crack of its spine. Nothing nicer than breaking into a fresh literary treat with my flickering, snapping friend the coal fire.

The first few pages make me warm and gratified.

## 9

Mashed up memories is the only way to describe Mum's continued descent. It's the mix of trauma and loosened memory that are most cruel. She's remembering the assault but forgetting the good memories. All I ask for is a careful measurement, an intricately orchestrated sequence of highs and lows and not this confused cacophony. And when this variegated memory does hit her, there isn't a resplendent vocal complaining, no bitter venting of the absurdity of it all. Instead, her eyes show a distant loss that chills me. I ache when I see it.

I'd often joked with her previously about her forgetfulness and regrettably shown my nasty impatience too. I feel bad now. Before this all happened, we had toyed with the idea she might have the start of dementia, but her happy life trundled along nicely and there never seemed a need to grant it solidity through medical labelling. What difference would it make when she had the love of her family and a workable care package? She was happy in her home and sustaining her independence despite those troublesome aches and pains.

Unknown to us, those neurons in her working memory had been venturing into old age territory before the assault.

Overstocking her cupboards and repeating the same story or complaint to me over and over again had become acceptable behaviour. Diplomatically, I'd rearrange and syphon down food before it wasted, joking about us all coming over for tea on Sunday, since the army weren't available to attack her bulging stock levels. John's hollow legs made the biggest dent, as did Rose and Jenny's target of maintaining a maximum of ten Milky Ways in the left-hand kitchen drawer. We all did it so well with soldierly precision. We were her army.

I've been listening to the psychiatric nurse today, explaining what might be occurring with Mum's mind. Hippocampus is too jolly a name that radiates such positivity it makes me sick. A medical oxymoron hiding behind its equivalent clumsy maritime creature, suitably coroneted to reign high in the brain structure hierarchy. Mum's hippocampus is not her friend right now. Damaged and worsened by the attack, there was a slim hope the broken memory segment would make her forget the recent trauma of the assault. A sort of selective kindness in its damaging rampage. For reasons only known to itself, it's decided to keep that one firmly on its radar and instead erode the cells from happier times. Cruel, cruel bastard.

Leaving the hospital behind, Mum has now moved to her new home, a permanent nursing home. More trickery for her mind to fathom. I have done my best to condense the front room of her flat into her own room at the nursing home. The single bed is the carbuncle in my well-intentioned plans. Her wicker blanket chest bolsters up the foot end and, if I am honest, takes up more space than is desirable. The chest played such a critical part in Mum's plight for the perfect storage solution, its simple clichéd appearance won hands down in the war against a more noble ottoman. It pains me to recall the shopping experience that safely procured the wicker chest. I've picked a selection of framed family photos too, and anchored them strategically, second guessing where she might sit and hence where she might look. The ergonomics of the room are flawed, I can see that, and I am damn sure Mum will see it too. A nervous transition awaits us.

'Let's go for a walk, Mum.' I try and remove Mum from her room before her analysis of the alien room concludes it's not really her room, and she wants to go home.

'Pass me my walking stick and you can help me go to the laundrette. I need to help the girls there since they are busy; it's terrible what they expect them to do.' Oh, Mum's got a 'job' now and it makes me smile that this 76-year-old has defied the futile dole queues and secured employment at the laundry. I find humour therapeutic. 'A bloody mess they made of my cardigan too *and* they've lost my crocheted blanket. If the manager is there, I'll tell her I'm not happy. It's ridiculous.' Surely if she's 'working' there, she'd have been on top of her own laundry and to hell with the other residents.

My mind is slowly losing it.

I pass Mum her Zimmer frame to prepare for her walk to 'work' since it's what the physio says she needs to use now. 'Pile of shite, that. Pass me my stick.' Mum was never one for profanity, but clearly she's awakened something from the depths of her cerebral cortex. It's funny at times but not so funny. She called the auxiliary a bloody pest the other morning. Clearly, she's forgetting she is a stickler for tidiness when the lady comes in to hoover and polish her room amidst Mum bad mouthing her.

Thankfully there's no venom in her tone and the staff seem to take it on the chin.

We walk along the wide corridor to the sounds of Mum dragging and clumping her Zimmer. Her facial expression is borderline argumentative, like she's dragging an old sow to slaughter. Doors with an old photograph display the history and past lives of residents. Room 27, Mrs Rosemary Davidson, looking not a day older than 21 in a black and white picture of a nurse. Room 29, Mr Charlie Beattie, a dapper young man in a suit, shirt and tie. Room 31, Mrs Geraldine McCabe, holding a brush and comb in front of a floral balloon-headed customer, drying her hair in a salon. We pass the day room, and Rosemary, Charlie and Geraldine are eating cake now with arthritic hands. I note Geraldine has clearly had her hair done recently. I shout in a compliment, and she salutes me with her slice of Battenberg cake. Charlie's struggling with his jam scone and *Trash in the Attic* is blaring out from an enormous TV screen.

We've passed the laundry room now with Mum showing little interest and reneging on her laundry duties. Passing the small dining room, I read the menu board and ask Mum what she has chosen for her dinner. As soon as I say it, I know how futile the question is. So instead, I tell her she has rhubarb crumble and custard to look forward to tonight.

Tomorrow is a big day for Mum with a visit to Dad on the cards. Dad's in his own nursing home, has been for a few years. Before it all happened, Mum would visit twice a week, a mixture of organising her own taxi to take her and either myself or John taking her. She's not been able for the visits since the assault and I'm conscious that I have been tentatively fudging her absence with Dad. It was another domestic decision or adjustment that needed to be sorted out. What do we say to Dad? I mean, he is definitely going to notice if she doesn't visit. We struggle to know what the right thing is to do. An honest declaration or conjure up an illness that might believably occupy the weeks for Mum's recovery. 'Mum's had a fall and broken her upper arm, Dad. She's in hospital and will be for a while. Well, the physio itself will take a while.'

And each time we arrive for our visit, Dad slowly twists his head around at the opening door, hoping her recovery has arrived and she'll surprise him with a visit. The bananas and box of Matchmakers chocolates are a consolation prize that never dampens his longing.

After her operation in hospital and finding Mum in one of her more lucid moments, I remember standing staring out the third-storey window of her hospital room. The Royal Infirmary building sits high above the rose beds and stumpy hedging, boxed around precise tarmac parking bays. Hospitals and their association with healing and kindness, special sheltered places, and I am now inappropriately about to shatter it all.

'Mum, what do you want us to say to Dad?' I feel pathetic at the delegation of this decision. She's clearly thought about it before, been dwelling on it, and I have caused an emptying of her expression. Just how much she'd thought about it came as a shock.

'How can I tell him then leave him behind to just keep thinking about it? It will hurt him, and he can't see me until the next visit. He will worry how I am.' Naive and ill-thought-out, that's what struck me about my immediate choice of being honest and telling him. Years of separate living arrangements had somehow managed to find a way to kindle their loving marriage. And it was after this we told Dad about Mum's fall in her living room.

As if to remedy my ill-thought-out plans, I meet with Mum's

care worker at social services to try and establish whether it would be possible for Dad to relocate to the same nursing home as Mum. Given the unusual circumstances, it would create the chance for Mum and Dad to be back together and for Mum to tell Dad what happened but be there with him during her recovery. She was honest, expressing the difficulty with so few spaces available in nursing homes generally, let alone the popular home Mum was now in. But I admit I didn't anticipate what turned out to be the flaw in the plan.

Tomorrow arrives, and with Mum safely seat-belted in, off we head to Dad's nursing home to break the 90-day abstention. I'd bought red carnations at Mum's request, since she often took in a bunch when she visited Dad. A shared memory of the Polish crystal vase that sat in front of their lounge window, a vase Dad had brought back from a visit to his relatives in Poland many years ago. They are all pleased to see Mum, the girls at Dad's nursing home, and cuddles are dished out amidst sad expressions at the horrors Mum has faced. But they never mention the assault.

Dad's in his room and we are promised tea and biscuits shortly. I'm nervous and excited. Excited about facilitating this reunion, nervous about what Mum is here to say. I tingle all over at the delight in Dad's face when he sees Mum. His sunken eyes sparkle with happy tears and he beams, his mouth carefully manoeuvring his loose false teeth. He stretches up to meet Mum's kiss and I settle Mum into a chair next to Dad, facing him. Dad's telling her he missed her and she's crying.

'How is your broken bone in your arm? You need to keep it moving or it will stop working. Look at me, a cripple here in this chair; I can't walk now since my broken hip.'

'She's getting physio, Dad, to try and get it to move about better.'

Dad doesn't look in my direction; he's still contemplating Mum.

'Grace says you can't manage now and have given up the flat?'

'I've moved to the nursing home just down from the big hotel up the road from where we stayed.'

'Are you okay there? It looks nice, nice and new. Are there many men there or all women?'

'Grace made my room nice, and I want to see if we can move you there, you old goat. Social services are going to see what they can do, but it might take time.'

Dad thinks for a bit and it's as if he knows he is going to upset her.

'Your nursing home is better than mine, but the staff here know how to handle me, how to lift me. With my crippled legs and feet, I had better stick to it here. I worry they won't manage me at your place.'

And it's like a youthful courtship, with Mum being turned down. She manages a smile that understands yet hurts her heart. If he only knew the full story, he'd want to be with Mum. I can't say or do anything. I can't disclose the full facts that go against Mum's wishes. With a long silence in the room, I know she won't tell him. She just won't tell him, and I'm devastated to witness all of this. But I say nothing.

Twenty minutes of small talk next. Mum putting on a brave face. I gaze out of Dad's window at the Ochil Hills beyond. Heather mixes of purple and green cloak the lower sides of Dumyat. Splashes of yellow bracken sparkle, giving hope to the day. And then the burnt blackened area dying back, where the farmer torched it. Hills where Dad walked in his youthful days, stretching out towards the Forth estuary and nearby industry. It's not a hopeful landscape; it's one that hides behind a dying autumn, with little new growth to feel an improved future lay ahead.

## 10

Regularly opening the gallery is a huge boost to my routine. After parking my car, the walk from there to the gallery doesn't feel so laboured and depressing. Whether it's the hint of sunshine this morning or simply a happier disposition, stonework and bricks on the front of buildings appear to shine, as if making the effort. Careful of the pavement cracks, which are prevalent in this stretch, I am somewhat lost in thought and haven't picked up on his footsteps approaching.

'Good morning, how's things?' It's Julian Brodie, tall and interestingly handsome, just as I remember him from the day he appeared in my gallery. I haven't forgotten him. I quickly come to a halt and face him. This time there is a chance for me to see a full-frontal face. Dark tortoise-shell-rimmed glasses and those impudent eyes again, wise and wry, hinting at a pounce. I feel slightly overwhelmed, but I'm not rushing to open the gallery just yet.

'Oh, morning. Eh, I'm fine, thanks, just on my way to the gallery. Are you heading to court then?' I ask. During our chat at the gallery, he'd spoken about work he was doing with senior officials at the government. He's a doctor, consulting on medical aspects of cases.

'My office isn't far from here and then yes, in court, same shit just a different day.' And it's then I notice it, an almost lascivious smile, or maybe I imagine it. His words to describe his court days seem out of kilter with what I picture him to be; it ruffles the stuffy aura I imagine his professional world to be like. There is something odd about him and it elicits a warm internal feeling.

We part, quite literally part since I am aware of how close he is standing. The traffic rumble and vibration noise dissolves upwards to the morning's promising sky. As I walk, I imagine his face, thinking that if I persist, his face will manifest itself in front and smile over at me, calling my name. It's as if he is trying to gain some hold on me, drawing me in like he drew me in by placing his body so close when we spoke. I finish my walk, slowly coming to terms with this strange new feeling, my gallery door a timely hiatus, not so much at the end of a rush, something less pronounced and more delicate. Maybe it's happiness. Whatever it is, it stays with me most of the day in the gallery.

After a full day at the gallery, I am driving home, and Dad's constantly on my mind. I don't know why, but I decide on a visit before going home. He is sitting just as I pictured him, in his room, staring out at the Ochil Hills and becoming all nostalgic with the past, him as a young man walking up Dumyat and through the Alva Glen. Quiet and content, I am more like Dad than I am Mum. It wouldn't be unusual to visit Dad and for us both to park the conversation and drift into a scenic, melancholy whimsy, like we are doing right now. Sharing the beauty there is in the variety of autumnal colours, the static purple of the heathers and heavily foliaged branches of the trees. The light dims towards early evening and there is a sadness. We know the colours will change, first they are green and in a few more days there will be orange, yellow and red and every combination of these. We don't know how long the season will last, or how long it will take for the leaves to chronicle the start of winter. There are days when the colours are bright and vibrant, fending off the season's end. We don't know when they will fall, but we know they will eventually fall. And fall they do.

* * *

November embraces the chill of winter into December, and with winter comes a serious chest infection for Dad. Always cheery during my visits, but this time it is hard to ignore the sight of him failing and giving in to the infection. The low full tone of his rasping voice is a contrast to his greying, pasty complexion and dark shadows around his eyes. I can tell he's struggling and his breathing labouring as we chat away as best we can. Not even his lovely Ochil Hills can draw his mind back to being healthy. Our quiet contemplative times during our conversation hang heavy over us.

'Dad, I'll leave you to rest up now, eh, give those horse pills the doc gave you a chance to work.' I lean over and kiss his warm forehead.

'Come back soon.' It's as if he knows something and I know too. I cry on my way out, head bowed and trying my best to be invisible to staff as I exit the nursing home.

It has been less than six months since Mum's horrific assault, but at 1am on 11 December, John and I are sitting either side of Dad's bed after phoning the priest to see if he can manage through an early fall of snow. There is nothing we can do for Dad except talk and make sure he knows he isn't alone. His last few breaths are noisy, clutching onto as many moments as he can. John tells him it's okay for him to go to sleep and that's what he does, quietly and peacefully, taking his last walk in the hills. I've never felt so devastated and utterly lost to my heartache.

A broken heart, further wrenched as Jenny and I sit over what's fast becoming bereavement cups of tea. The suddenness of it all, Dad's decline creeping up on us.

'Why didn't we see this coming, Mum?'

'Papa was a good age, Jenny, and I suppose behind his jolly moments, he was quite fragile.' And we smile, recalling the fun they had, her papa playing the big kid again the moment she walked into the room.

'What's Nanny going to say?' And I actually can't answer her straight away. It was the first thing that sprang to my mind before I even left Dad at the nursing home.

'We all just need to rally around her, Jenny. She'll be upset and maybe even mixed up at bit.' I'm not confident at all about her lucidity and ability to take in such serious information, but I try not to let my anxiety shine through and become apparent to Jenny. I'm her rock right now, the one she draws on time and time again for comfort and explanations, explanations I'm quickly having to conjure up like rabbits out of perpetual magician hats.

'I'll miss Papa, Mum.' Her huge tears come tumbling down, taking mine with them.

* * *

I head briefly to my gallery the next day to put up a notice saying it will be closed due to a family bereavement. Leaving the closed gallery behind me, I'm slipping on stubborn frost as I gingerly make my way towards where I'm parked. Skies darken in winter and a seasonal gloom hangs over everything. There are things to do, pick up the death certificate and register the death. The funeral director is also calling on us later to make the arrangements. Dad wanted to be buried. Walking, deep in thought, I look up to re-establish my bearings when I catch sight of Julian approaching, our eyes capturing and holding each other's stare. As he closes in on me, my sadness seems to billow out from inside me and it's as if I'm suitably positioning my grief, knowing that he will be a trusty recipient, one who, on revealing my news, will help me, give me comfort and hope. But it's Julian for heaven's sake, a man I hardly know and yet someone who holds such immense and as yet uncharted trust. I'm in tears before he even reaches me and then I tell him about losing my dad.

'Grace, I'm sorry. I wish there was more I could do.' And I truly believe he means every word. Despite very little to connect us, it has upset him hearing my news. Right now I want him to embrace me, to wrap all he can offer around me and take the edge off my sadness. It isn't likely though, I know that, but I still can't shake the idea that, given the chance, Julian *can* make this less painful. I don't know how long our conversation lasts, but I remember not wanting him to go, not wanting him to leave me there and then. Eventually, we part.

As I'm walking, I'm picturing his face, recalling his expression and features as I broke the news. Maybe it is just how I am feeling, I have no idea, but my recollection is somehow adrift and hazy. I cannot recall his face or presence. Instead, I have a sensation of utter loss, not only loss for my dad, but a moment or opportunity that should have happened but didn't quite get off the ground. I feel rejected and disappointed that he didn't embrace me, he hasn't stemmed this wild flow of sorrow. I stop for a moment to pull a paper tissue from my handbag to wipe tears which are pouring down my face.

I turn to look in a shop window, playing for time to recover myself. The shop is empty, closed down some time ago, with dark screens pulled down to evade prying eyes. I see nothing but my own reflection staring back, and I'm stuck firmly to the spot, unable to move, tears streaming uncontrollably now. The background noise of the city disappears, and I am still standing gazing at my reflection. It's then that I suddenly don't feel alone. In this dark moment, Dad's come back, no longer missing in my heart but trying to fill my life again, glancing through a window and watching over me and telling me to keep going. And then the void is filled by something new, an inexplicable strength that lifts my spirit.

# – 11 –

Overnight there's been intermittent snow. It's been like that since we lost Dad. I'm looking over at the rows of Norwegian spruce trees in the forested area opposite my cottage. White laden branches sparkle below a departing moon. We prepare Mum as best we can for Dad's funeral, and the funeral director prepares the logistics of excavating the lair at the cemetery against a forever-changing pattern of snowfall and frost. It seems you can never predict the weather, just like you can never anticipate the ideal timing of a funeral. Mum's fully aware of what's happened, and although she hasn't spoken much about it, I can see her disappointment over time passing by too quickly for her liking.

'I never got to tell him what happened,' she says. She is bearing the full emotional strain of the assault. We are there for her, but we are not Dad. 'Maybe,' she says, 'it's for the better.' And I admire her strength and humility.

The long black funeral car picks us up to take us to the church. We are all in black and must resemble a box of Black Magic. I'm also wearing a hat, my only black hat as it happens. We stop by the nursing home to get Mum, who has chosen to wear navy. Insisted, actually, according to Leigh, the nurse who has agreed to accompany Mum throughout just in case. I double-check she is warm enough, given the likely temperatures at the cemetery later.

I sometimes disappoint myself and I am certain I have been the source of a few disappointments to Mum over the years. But for Dad's funeral, I took particular care. Mum instructed, or rather ordered me, to pay attention to the flowers for Dad. I knew this before she said it since flowers were their weekly connection for many years. And it was here that I failed terribly. I began to plan out floral tributes for the altar and coffin and even spoke to our local florist, listing ideas and an array of different flowers that would have the altar look like it had been tastefully invaded by a rioting mob of flower arrangers. However, I was warned against this by the funeral director, who suggested I speak to Monsignor beforehand, so I did.

The General Instruction of the Roman Missal (GIRM) is a church document that offers guidance on the subject of church décor but didn't seem to be interested in stipulating the part flowers had to play. I suspect it is one of those things that grows with the tradition and custom of the local church, but I don't know for sure, given I am rusty in most things Catholic. I meet with Monsignor to enquire, and he tells me during the feast of Advent, there are to be no floral tributes on the altar. I don't want to question this too much, as I have been forewarned by John, who is more of a devout Catholic, that I am to be nice to Monsignor and not cause any ill feeling. Bull and china shop are muted. Monsignor, however, will permit flowers on the coffin so long as they are subtle and removed when the coffin is brought up to the altar, a very plain GRIM altar.

Not wanting to upset Mum, I choose not to tell her this. After all, I didn't write the rules for GIRM, and I assume she won't really notice. And that is my mistake. We make our way to our seats near the front of the church and there is a respectful quietness in the congregation. I sit beside Mum with the nurse to her right. That covers all angles, or so I think. They bring Dad into the church.

'What have you done with the flowers?' Mum more or less shouts from her seat. I grip her hand gently to try and quieten her, but by now at least ten rows behind have heard her. 'Is that all you got? What have you done with them, where are they?' she continues as a beautiful, albeit subtle spray bouquet is lifted off the coffin and almost discarded to the side. You can't even see it now and my stomach tightens, thinking this is more ammunition for Mum. I clearly haven't managed the flowers well.

But we get through the church service with just the cemetery to cope with. Outside the church, we are all ushered into the Black Magic box again to take us up to the cemetery. The hearse pulls out slowly in front of us respectfully with the funeral director walking in front, leading us in his black herringbone coat and top hat. Unusual nowadays, but he knows our family. Like the reverend in Gilead, with his congregational steps, so measured and hypnotic that you can't help but be consumed by this palpably good person almost haunting the street and hill up to the dual carriageway.

'Is he gonna walk all the way up to the cemetery? I mean, it's a dual carriageway ahead,' asks Rose. And at that, he turns and heads sedately back into the front passenger seat of the hearse. 'Ah, he's back in the car now,' Rose notices.

'Aye, spared us the roadkill,' I mutter under my breath.

# – 12 –

The hearse and accompanying car disappear out of sight, and people standing outside the church start to disperse, heading to their cars, ready to follow the path of the hearse up to the cemetery. Lifts are negotiated and a steady stream of filled cars drive away from the church. The steps leading into the church are empty now, empty apart from a lone figure of a man in a long dark coat, his scarf wrapped around his neck and lower face. He pulls out a black knitted hat from his coat pocket and pulls it down on his head, stretching to reach the scarf, keeping the cold air off his face. With a sad, post-funeral expression, he walks off in the opposite direction of the cars on their way to the cemetery.

Sitting a sensible distance towards the back of the church, and on the opposite side from the family, Archie Connell could see Mrs Fallon, a short, round figure safely surrounded by Grace, looking towards the altar and the coffin where her husband lay. What was she thinking at this time? Coping with the funeral and still bearing the scars from her assault those few months ago. From his pew, he could see Mrs Fallon side-on, imagining what she had gone through. Her empty sad expression was one that felt all too familiar to him.

It has been over a year since the break-in at the Connell farmhouse. Since his dad's voice had been robbed, leaving long periods of quiet, blank conversations. He never wanted to talk about what happened that night Darren Rodden broke into his home. Despite special police personnel on hand to help him speak about it, it was an impossible task. Nothing, he said nothing that would help them understand why Darren had been found in bed beside him. Or what had led him to the remote farmhouse, a place by all accounts he'd visited before. Creeping around the back of the farmhouse to an old outhouse where the police had found some of his personal belongings in amongst a makeshift den. He couldn't sleep that night, so had gone for a walk, he'd told the officers. 'Saw a light on and the door was open, didn't think anyone still lived there,' was his only justification according to the police at that time. The cold frost brought a sudden end to his nocturnal walk, and he'd gone inside to keep warm.

The funeral brought further troubled thoughts back to the fore. At the time of the break-in, Archie was prepared to accept Darren's account of things. But the recent television reports on the assault on Grace's mum made it hard not to connect the state of his dad's current behaviour with some heinous, sinister motives that night in the farmhouse. Police believed Darren though, let him off with a warning, citing it as housebreaking.

What was he thinking about coming to the funeral today? Initially, Archie had made his mind up after hearing the news about Grace's father. Obsessing about whether or not it would be a mistake attending, ruling it out the day before had only led to one of the most restless nights he'd had in a long time. Drawn towards an addictive desire to see things for himself. And now, witnessing the falling apart of Grace's family adds to the tension running through his veins. Quickening his stride, and with his hands thrust deeper inside his coat pockets, he checks to see if the note is still in there, and it is. He has no idea what will curb and dull his angry mindset. For now though, with Grace and her family saying their final goodbyes to the old man, he follows what is becoming a new regular route for him, an obligatory route past Grace's home, one that's almost punctuating his daily routine.

# – 13 –

My moon is at its fullest and I can see it big and bright over the Christmas tree forest. I wonder if Mum follows her moon too, lying awake, staring up at the night sky. Hauntingly perfect, its surface albedo swirls and draws you into its beauty. Despite its optimistic glowing halo, there are dark bits too, gaps or rushing water on the surface, and the longer you gaze at it, the more it lets you see into it. But I take nothing away from this moon tonight, no answers or comfort, so I turn away and wait for the big white spot effect to remedy itself in my vision. The moon's synodic period is laughing at me, unfaltering with its seemingly never-ending cycles of triumph.

I slip my makeshift bookmark into the book I'm attempting to read tonight. As I close the hardback, I slide the utilitarian railway ticket, hiding the station names with just the journey's logo peeking out the top of the pages. I tuck my chilled feet under me and pull my cream Witney blanket up over my shoulders, folding over the cool satin edging away from my neck and instead breathe in the warmth of the wool.

I haven't really taken in the last few chapters of the book. I can't settle, so I head through to the kitchen, pausing at the bookshelf en route. Reaching for the row of art books, I slowly remove a book about the artist Louise Bourgeois, a book titled *A Woman without Secrets*. The book provides a new covert internment for two notes I've now received. After the terrifying delivery of the first note, the second one had appeared quietly and silently just after Dad's funeral. Closing the front door, I'd nearly missed the folded paper. With insufficient weight for it to drop to the floor, it had stuck in the bristle interior of the letterbox. In the same handwriting as the first note were the few words. *SORRY FOR YOUR LOSS. YOU ARE NOT ALONE HATING DARREN RODDEN.*

I can recognise the handwriting now, penned unnaturally in small block capitals, their anomalous roundness disguising the author's own writing. I remember taking a strange comfort from its tone when I read it for the first time. The rawness of losing Dad clawed around me for several days. Discovering new ways to break the cycle, gently easing me back onto a sense of what daily life is meant to be. The note, a handful of kindred words, propping me up, nudging me to take the drive into Edinburgh, and to show face at my gallery, coping with the infrequent customers popping in that day, most oblivious to the fact my dad was gone. It helped that they didn't know, in the same way as the second note helped because they did know.

* * *

It's been almost a month since Dad's funeral. At lunch today at the nursing home, I notice how Mum's stepped down again due to yet another small transient stroke. I call it her staircase of decline. Her hair is thinning, or has she lost weight again?

The features in her small face are drawn in below a taut shiny scalp. I make a note to check her weight chart in her records on my way out. They've dressed her nicely today with one of her many dress scarves picking out the purples in her cardigan and tweedy skirt but mismatching her pale-yellow blouse. I help her with a tartan lady bib, red for the girls, green for the boys, tucking it under the edge of the dining table.

'Push yourself up a bit, Mum, or you'll spill your soup.' It's not as if she is able to exert the necessary adjustment, so I am plumping up and pushing down a cushion at her back as she reaches out to pick up a slice of her buttered bread. They've cut it into visually attractive triangles, two per slice, and as she pinches a corner and picks it up, it droops down towards the plate of soup prematurely. Her eyes widen with her surprise at how that could possibly have happened when she never instructed it. She intuitively juts her chin out as she opens her mouth and takes a large bite of the sodden corner of bread. I'm still midway through adjusting the seating position. It's as if she is oblivious to what I am doing as she tends to her hungry palate. Having things done for her, chipping away at memories of her staunch independence.

After lunch, I help her walk with her Zimmer into the TV lounge with the promise of a cup of tea on its way. Finally she reaches *her* chair in the lounge and drops into it, pinning about a third of her crocheted blanket under her bottom. I'm not sure if a slow tug might send its colourful stitching pinging in all directions. She won't be cold though, since the room has reached that temperature where it is hot, and it feels un-fresh, so we decide to leave it be. I can always retrieve it at the next toilet break. I pull up a chair beside Mum, careful not to knock over the vase of carnations on the side table. My aunt had brought them over yesterday, plenty buds of impending blooms, just as Mum likes them.

It doesn't take long before my conversation moves from marginally one-sided in my favour to more of an afternoon soliloquy. They look at me with both delight and suspicion, the other residents sitting in the lounge. They are the same as Mum but with a different family, although I'm the only visitor this afternoon. Time and decline have narrowed their variety, with residential care indoctrinating their beings into this arbitrary visual blandness. Cups of tea are half finished, biscuits and cakes picked at and lying on inappropriate standard issue white side plates. Hard to tell whether the pitiful lumps and crumbs are discarded through sparrow-like appetites or after clumsy, abortive attempts at the hand, to plate, to mouth formula. There is so much waste in this room, and it makes me sad because I think they notice.

Moving myself out of the room of dense blanketing malaise, I take the opportunity, whilst Mum is having a nap, to check her room and toiletry supplies in case they are lacking and need me to top them up. I glance back at Mum in her chair as I head out the room and see she's sort of slipped to the side in her chair, her head tilting in the same direction and her mouth slightly wilting. When I was sitting, I never noticed, as I slid sideways with her.

Wandering down to Mum's room, I leave her in the lounge in the mute company and amidst the articles of her day-to-day living. Bits of Mum meddle the route down to her room. Photos taken of her sitting out in the nursing home garden are on the residents' noticeboard and one of her ex-vases of flowers sits on a window ledge. They join the dots along the nursing home's huge footprint. Pausing at the door to her room, I reach up for the door key on a brass hook, high enough that I have to stretch, out of reach of the stooped residents. I fix her plastic nameplate on her door; it's slipped slightly out of the reusable railings. Then I unlock her door, replacing the key on its hook. Mum wears *her* key on a lanyard around her neck so that she doesn't lose it. I step into the domestic order that is Mum's room and check her supplies, which appear to be in order.

The interior of her room has changed and it's funny, but Mum never said anything. They've moved some of the photos onto the neat little coffee table, which has also moved to a different corner of the room. I see the wicker chest is still in situ. Of course it's all very laudable, making best layout choices, but it's the lack of engagement that is troubling for her, or is it just disturbing for me? The latest stroke steals away more memories and it would be nice to halt the degeneration by having the interior of her room static. I'm being overly sensitive, and the logic is crazy and panders to it. I need to accept there are only so many stairs and it's a one-way system.

# – 14 –

Next day, I feel nervous and can't seem to shake the feeling. I have a meeting with the Crown Prosecution to update me on progress, in particular the QC will be there for part of the meeting. I agree to meet at the court, since she is in court on another case. I'm early, so I park up some distance from the city centre and walk up to the High Court since it's a lovely day, a touch of frost but a hint of winter sun periodically. I decide I have time to take a different route up to the High Court and, out of curiosity, head up through the New Town, passing the office of Julian Brodie. Whilst he hasn't ventured into the gallery again, our paths have crossed, literally with him heading into work and me on my way to open up the gallery. Our encounters are fortuitous and happen as a consequence of mutual timing and random parking. I've worked long enough in the city to know where the most likely availability will be, for a variety of times of the day, and figure he's equally talented in Edinburgh's static version of The Knowledge. I stole his newly found parking space on one occasion, since I happened to be on the correct side of the road whereas he was midway through an illegal U-turn after passing it on the opposite side of the road. As I recall, he was mischievous yet gracious in defeat. We walked together that day, taking our time, accompanying the rich architecture with intelligent snippets of conversation about our lives, nothing too heavy. We arrived at his office first and I had to retrace a couple of paces, since I had developed a brisk walk to match his pace and hadn't realised he had reached his destination.

'I've enjoyed your company, thank you.' I was only being honest.

'You're good company too,' was his response. And then our separate days began.

But today the heavy black storm door of his office remains closed. I feel disappointed that his presence should be else-where. I slow down to look closely at the building, trying to glean something more from it, as if the building would embel-lish what I already knew about this thought-provoking man. I glance in the window, raised slightly above the street level. I can still make out heavy oak bookshelves with neatly grouped volumes of leather-bound reference books in various shades of distressed gold, dark green and burgundy red, their spines ornately barrelled with black labels and gilded lettering. A blackout linen roller blind is pulled a third of the way down, its brass toggle catching the odd ray of sun. And I can just see the top of his Gainsborough desk chair, the polished cognac leather beautifully worn in places. I wonder at the artworks that adorn the other walls. My nosiness is disturbed by the inner realisation I look a tad suspicious standing staring in at his office.

I move on, heading up The Mound, resting my eyes on the gothic splendour of St Giles with its imposing Crown Spire and stained-glass narratives. The gradual climb has started to labour my brisk walk, but my pace is constant, my heels more pronounced as they meet the pavement and echo against these lesser but still grand buildings. The steadiness of my walk once again restores a sense of well-being within. At the High Court, I slowly enter the glass doors and steer through the security checks, placing down my handbag and collecting it after screening. My name is on their list, so I am expected and told to take a seat on the first-floor atrium. Before long, I am taken to an office and wait for the QC.

My nervy feeling has returned, and for a fleeting moment, I'm reminded about the as yet undeclared notes I've been sent. The first note was so long ago, how is it going to look, the fact I've hidden it from them? And I can't help but think there is little detail given in the notes, so there is not much to go on. They would probably just humour me by telling me it's just prank notes and not to take it seriously. Last thing I want is to come across as being some sort of super sleuth, announcing the unwanted arrival of these notes. Closer to home, I also think Pamela is enough of a drama queen without fuelling her any further. And so the notes get pushed to the back of my mind as the QC is introduced to me and various caveats are listed about what she can and cannot discuss.

There's good news.

'A date has been set for the trial to begin, 17 March.' I acknowledge this and try and work out how many weeks away that is. 'You will be called as a witness for the Crown, as will your brother and possibly sister-in-law. You will all get an official summons, but for now, some advance notice that you will all require to be available then.'

'That's good then, isn't it, the trial? Hopefully he'll get locked away for good.' It was what had been keeping me going the last few months. As Mum slipped progressively, there just seemed to be yet another delay with bringing the trial to court. Another delay with Darren still free, a thought that never seems to escape me as it shifts from anger to concern. He knows who we are; he perhaps knows about Jenny. Justice and its slow wheels threatening me with its complacency.

'Grace, you need to remain realistic about the outcome. It's obvious he's evil and shows no remorse for what he's done, but it doesn't take away from the fact it will be a difficult case for us. Ordinarily in cases like this, the victim is in court to give her account of what happened. As you know, we fought hard to ensure your mum didn't have to go through with this, which is in her best interest, but does complicate things. I can't go into detail about the evidence we have, and of course your account of what Mum told you is important.' The QC is quick to dampen the optimism of a positive outcome for this case.

'Would you rather force her to go to court then? Put her through more trauma? Especially with her current mental state, I mean, she's still terrified and gets flashbacks.'

The QC adds more dampeners. 'Your mum's mental state is key too in all of this, not just since the assault but prior to it too. The defence will want to focus on your mum's already fragile state and use it to dismiss what actually took place.'

'Mum's mental state was fine. She lived on her own and independently, now all of a sudden everyone thinks she is just another old, confused lady who clearly doesn't know her own mind. Or more to the point, cannot be relied upon to give a clear account of what happened.' I'm shocked that suddenly the evil bastard was turning things around by saying Mum, what, imagined it?

'We are doing all we can, I can assure you. It's just that it will be a very difficult case to bring to court. I'm not in any way saying for one moment the assault didn't happen, it's just proving it beyond all doubt for the jury,' she adds.

And then it occurs to me, the vileness and nastiness with this whole thing. 'Has it occurred to you that's *why* he picked on her? They target the ones that can be easily dismissed. Who cares? No one bothers to question it, another old person, ripe beyond reliable cognitive recollection. I can just hear them scrape up all manner of mental misdemeanours. Oh, remember the time she turned up at Tesco at 4am and wondered why it was shut? Some youngsters spotted her and called the police, who took her home when she eventually remembered where she lived. However, forget about how she remembers to ask us about insignificant aspects of our lives, aspects mentioned in earlier conversations. Forget how she used to hoover and tidy up on the day the daily help was due to come, so that her home wasn't too messy. Forget how she remembered to buy Milky Ways for her two granddaughters and put them away in the *same* spot, in the *same* drawer. She lived independently, she shopped, she cooked, she cleaned, she cared, and she *functioned*, and she was, *is*, our mum!' I'm crying in a very messy way now, tears water falling down my face, and my nose seems to be joining in. What a state. The QC slides over a box of man-size tissues.

'Grace, please believe me, we are and will do absolutely *everything* to convict him. None of us for one minute disbelieves your mum. It's clear what went on. I know these things take ages, but we are doing all we can, doing it properly to ensure he's put away.' And for once I see it in her face, witnessing the lives of families falling apart, bundled up in beige files and silk legal ribbons. How does she manage to keep putting herself through this?

I'm bracing myself for venturing back out into the city

and down to the gallery. I'm back in the atrium of the court building sitting and overthinking and becoming angry inside at this whole mess he's left behind.

'Hi, Grace, how are you?' I recognise the voice straight away, Julian. Suddenly I wonder if my face looks as puffy as it feels. It's probably devoid of any replenishing makeup; that's been rubbed off on the handful of the QC's tissues. It's hard to know how to answer him, since here I am again, in what must appear to be a habitual court visit. 'Just out of a meeting with the QC who is dealing with Mum's case. She...' And I pause, unsure what or how much to say and knowing that severe brevity will have it all sound a bit odd and unbelievable. 'My mum was violently assaulted last June, and the trial will be starting shortly.'

'Let's go for a coffee.' There is no shock or surprise in his voice as I try and sequence events around the day of the assault. I try not to highlight the monstrous nature of the crime and the accused. I want him to think I am sensible and not someone who overreacts.

Picking up the tray with our coffees, Julian makes his way over to a table at the far end of the room. He places our cups down on the table, opposite each other. After fidgeting with my coat and handbag, I look up and realise the lack of depth of the table; we're sitting remarkably close, close enough to feel a faint brush of air as we lift and sip our coffees. I can see my hazy reflection on the lenses of his glasses, my gaze reaching beyond it, finding his eyes and resting on them for just a bit too long. It's hard to look away, even as we speak.

'You don't have to explain to me there are dangerous people out there.' He interrupts me as I'm explaining what happened to Mum, sparing me the horror of reliving events for his benefit. 'And I'm familiar with Mum's case.'

'Oh, should I be here speaking to you then?' I say jokingly. By now I'm well versed in the rules. After all, it seems every meeting I attend with either the Crown Prosecution Service or the police begins with a series of caveats.

'Well, we are just having a coffee, are we not?' he replies. I feel glad as I stir the thick, tarry espresso he's just bought me. His is a regular black coffee, with cold milk specifically on the side, I hear him ask the girl. 'I hate my milk hot,' he shares with me, and this simple preference seems to enhance the unusual oddness about him. At the same time, I'm heartened he's let me in on this splinter of domesticity.

Julian doesn't say too much about the impending trial and neither do I apart from a short rant about *his* lot wanting to force Mum to give evidence in court. To which I stupidly respond about plans I have to steal Mum away and hide her since I wasn't about to let *them* put her through that.

'I think you'll find that's highly illegal,' he says in a light-hearted way. And at that, I think it best not to share my humble opinion about the morality of how the mafia handle such heinous crimes. He may get the wrong opinion.

Our conversation over coffee is warm, not simply questions and answers like the boring people do. We are acting out a shared truth in a play of our minds. As we talk, we look at each other, and the longer we do this, the more it seems we are lost in each other, dissolving some pain in moments of pleasurable anticipation. I can smell Julian's coffee on his breath, my cup inches from his mouth, his thin lips parting and smiling, strong yet almost nervous. And I know he's looking too, inching his way down my face and neck, halting at the lace edging of my black camisole top. I should draw the sides of my fine wool cardigan over, but I don't want to. I'm comfortable sitting here, second guessing what thoughts are going through his mind. I feel like we are the only people in the room.

'Well, I best not keep you any longer. When do you have to be back?' I ask him.

'About 7pm,' he replies, almost flat. I see and feel the sadness in his eyes. I'm meaning back to his office, or back to the case he is in court for. But it's as if no one cares about his daytime schedule, and 7pm routinely bookends his days.

'Take care then.' And I want him to take care.

'You too, look after yourself now. You have a long way to go yet with the trial.' And I wonder, in that moment, if you put two broken souls together, might they just mend?

# – 15 –

How bad must it be when you are a couple of days into the trial and Darren Rodden's original defence team announce they can no longer defend him? Eight months after the assault and suddenly now he needs a new team. I get the phone call from the Crown Prosecution Service to advise me or rather relay the news. I'm not told the reasons why; I ask, but they can't tell me. Could be for a number of reasons. I make up my own mind. It's going to take him a bit longer to come up with a believable story. The first group of witnesses are un-summoned and told they will be re-summoned. Three of them have already given their evidence to the jury and will now have to go through it again.

Just over a week later, his new team are on board. He found someone daft enough to believe him. Nevertheless, they are granted additional time to play catch up. And this team seem to be hanging in there, and so it all begins again, with a new date for the trial.

I spend the first few days in the witness room that's been set aside for us. For the first time I'm given a hint of how the trial will progress. There are numerous people known to Mum, neighbours and carers as well as the paramedics and police officers. And then there are expert witnesses, the doctors and psychiatric experts. And of course, us. We all have our letters telling us when to come in, so everyone turns up sequentially, religiously acting out the order of the trial. The paramedic looks strange in a suit that for once isn't regulation green. We all make small talk but not about what we all have to say at the trial. We can escape the doom of the witness room by heading down to the small café. Instead, I opt for the small coffee bistro not far from the court building, the same one Julian and I went to. It gives me a break from the heavy misery of waiting and waiting in the court surroundings. After a few days, at a certain point in the afternoon, we all begin to get a feel for whether we've just sat through a wasted day. Preparing for a return trip the following day, in the hope that our time in the witness box will be over. There's a tentative half hour around 2.30pm when it can go either way. Intuitively we all check our phones and watches for the time. For some reason, there is no clock in the witness room.

It's 10am the next morning and I'm to be called as the first witness that day. I haven't been in this particular court, so I only have a generic appreciation of the layout and where Darren Rodden will be sitting. I'm called and accompanied in through a door and a few steps forward into the witness box. I glance over at the jury, just briefly, and then turn to the judge, who takes me through the oath. The judge looks kindly, somewhat slipper-faced, which mocks the grandeur of his wig and gown. He's comfortable in the large oak and leather throne-type chair, sitting regally under the coat of arms on the wall. And I swear to tell the whole truth.

I look straight at whoever is talking to me, following advice that was given as I prepared for this day. And it works. So far, I've responded to the judge and am now facing the Crown QC and, by default, the jury at one o'clock in my vision. They'll decide, after all. She settles me well with straightforward questions and I reply simply without fuss or additions. My hands shake slightly as I put on my glasses to look at a book of photographs that's been handed to me, all numbered. There is some surface noise and rustling in the courtroom as the judge, jury and defence all get their corresponding book of photographs out too. I'm instructed to look at a selection of the pictures taken, mostly in Mum's house. I answer her questions, slowly and carefully. She smiles as she goes back to her seat and then the defence QC stands up. For a few seconds, I lose my concentration as it brutally occurs to me that he is representing Darren Rodden and taking instruction from *him*. I have to restrain myself from looking over towards Darren Rodden. There are no simple questions to begin with. The defence QC moves straight towards his key questions, referring immediately to the book of photographs. I cannot recall now if I am looking at the same photographs or different ones than before. I just try my best to listen and respond. The book of photographs is then removed and replaced with a copy of my statement to the police. Once again there is rustling as everyone else in court is experiencing the same exchange. I stumble a bit at the questions, in relation to a pink blanket and various articles of clothing. This is difficult for me. I'm trying to relay this to the jury, as if to apologise for my slight stumbling, only I don't say so much, I just imagine I'm standing looking incredibly strained.

One and a half hours later, those welcome words from the judge, who thanks me for giving my evidence, and I am now finished and can go. There is one more thing I need to do before I leave the courtroom. It's at this point that I turn to *him*, to see for the first time who Darren Rodden is. I have never felt such hatred and repulsion for another human being in all my life. I am led out the courtroom and take a few minutes down in the café to get a cup of tea and wait for a suitable break in proceedings. I can then go back into court and watch the rest with John.

They're playing Mum's video to the jury. I've seen it. I'm in it. And I remember sitting there that day in the hospital room in utter torture as Mum tried to recall and tell them what happened. She doesn't know it because she hasn't seen the video, but it's painful to see her bruised, swollen and bloody face, with the words coming out of it. I know she struggled that day, but her features are so battered and damaged there isn't any sign of this struggle. It is like she doesn't realise how bad she looks. No one's told her that she looks awful, and I feel more comfortable knowing she is oblivious to this. But it is the first time John has seen it and he's crying; Pamela is holding his hand. His face is drained and filled with complete devastation. He leaves the courtroom after this and is violently sick.

Proceedings end for the day shortly after this and I am grateful for the timing. I don't think John can take any more.

## 16

I punch in the security code at the entrance to the nursing home and sign in the visitor book. It's quite an empty day so far, weekdays usually are. Mum's sitting, napping in her chair in the lounge. Her crocheted blanket is showing some slippage and her stocky fingers curl into her palms, grasping a blanket in her dreams. I quietly pull up a chair and sit beside her, not wishing to disturb her sleep but be there for her when she chooses to wake, usually startled, I'm told. She's on her own here in the lounge, the other residents preferring to nap in their rooms after lunch. The nurses tell me Mum's frightened to be in her room right now.

She's wearing a fine, white cable knit cardigan and contrasting top with a flecked coral yarn and of course a scarf in wispy swirls of yellow and orange. She looks like an advert from an old Patons knitting pattern. Slippers appear to have been swapped in favour of a pair of chunky bed socks. Although I see her flat shoes are parked under her chair. And it's in this quiet room, I know far better the taste of each day. Mum's misunderstood, sleeping face shows her calm but masks the solitude within her. She hasn't spoken about Dad since the funeral, and I wonder why that is. Does she still think of him fondly but just not speak about him? The staff have commented on her being quieter than usual. Her days are not filled like mine, and with Dad gone, it's left a further void and she has nothing to fill it with. There's no capacity there for new hobbies and challenges. It's like she's given up and I feel sad for her. She shudders a bit when I rest my hand on hers, trying to reach under the tight knit of the cuffs of her cardigan to see if she is as cold as her hands appear to be. She stirs and her eyes open slowly, small dark pupils open up for a split second into a mad stare and then settle when she finds me.

'Oh, it's you, Grace. Where's Jenny?' I try not to feel too redundant. It was always about the grandchildren with Mum, and John and I somehow slipped by the wayside. 'Ah, she's fine, Mum, busy with her studies. Look, I've brought you some fresh flowers. I was going to get a vase from the girls, and you can help me arrange them?' And with little response, I head off to get a vase and water.

All credit to her when I return, she seems much brighter. Maybe I woke her too quickly. I position her trolley to her right side and place the vase close so that she can use her better arm to reach. I remove the polythene wrapper and pull down the elastic bands, which seem overly taut, almost garrotting the stems. There's a mix of pink and yellow carnations and some greenery, which I have already placed in the vase to get things started. I pass the carnations to her, one stem at a time. She plonks them in the water. She manages about eight stems before there's an issue with over-crowding in the vase. It will need a bit more vigour placing the remaining stems in, so I distract Mum with the ninth stem by asking her to see if it smells nice. Inhaling the faint perfume, she looks at me as if she isn't overly impressed. It's allowed me to put the rest of the flowers in the vase though.

'They don't seem to smell as strong as the old-fashioned

ones, do they, Mum?' I wonder where in the human senses 'smell' sits in terms of what you lose first when you get older. I ask her to have another sniff, but not before I jokingly bump the flower head under her nose and laugh at her reaction.

'What?!' she laughs back, and I hope she remembers she used to do that to me when I was very young.

One step forward and two steps back, that's what I think as I walk down to the car park. I'm battling against unachievable odds with Mum and can only hope that paltry efforts at re-seeding her memory reap small bursts of reward. It's a futile attempt at replenishing the void Dad's left behind, new paths that entice reminiscences down them for a stroll. At times an unwelcome visitor comes by though, that's the problem. I wish Darren Rodden would just do us a favour and lose *his* way.

\* \* \*

I avoid the main supermarket, preferring for the time being to keep out of everyone's way, thereby defending my day of drifting. Not the best idea I know but try stopping me. There's a late afternoon lull on the local high street which pleases me as I head up to the butchers, thinking the heavy pastry of one of his famous steak pies might doorstop my disconsolate state by tea time. I'm stopped halfway up the high street by a kind face from the past, a considerable time in the past.

Our family lived in a block of flats on the top floor when I was very young. John and I played with James, whose family lived in one of the flats at the other end of the block. I only really remember the close I walked down from our flat to reach the path that ran along the front of the block. Two flights of yellow wooden painted stairs from our attic flat, then onto a further two flights of concrete stairs. Then along the draughty hallway on the ground floor that connected the rear drying greens to the front of the building. The doors were never closed for the majority of the day, which was why there always seemed to be this howling gust present. Changed days now with security entrances and their buzzers connecting those that live inside to the outside. I try to think back when that change happened but don't come up with a timeframe. James's close had no doors, which made it ideal for hide and seek. No clattering latches to give away the direction of the hide but awkward for ball games, with no doors to halt footballs we slapped about the place. I was never particularly good at the kicking, so tended to throw the ball up and slap it with my hand. John and James used to get bored with me after a while and I'd go back to sit on my painted yellow stairs.

As I approach James today, I know my memory is trying to help me here, help me to connect him with the past and happier times, detracting from our other heartaches. He lost his daughter at the school shootings. Standing right in front of him now, we are both thrown to the horrific connection, and I don't know what to say.

'Hello, Grace, I was so sorry to hear what happened to your mum. Your brother also mentioned your dad had passed away.' Quietly, he just stands and looks incredibly sad, not expecting any further response or anything from me at all. I know it must bring back tragic memories for him. James continues. 'Just because of what happened to Darren, it's still no excuse for what he did to your poor mum, it really isn't.'

I think I thank him, but I'm not sure what I say. Dumbfounded and close to tears, I walk on because I know if I burst into tears, I'll have no way of telling who those tears are for.

## 17

Today is brewing up to be a short day in court. I have a funny feeling when I arrive that something isn't quite right. The QC seems to be rushing about, and when I take my seat in court, there is talking amongst the defence team, albeit their expressions are buoyant. When the judge takes his seat, you can't really tell what his expression shows. He always has this stern, agitated look about him anyway. I wonder if he ever laughs at a comedy show.

Darren Rodden arrives in his usual morose grey suit, flanked by two officers. I've grown accustomed to the steady smirk adorning his face at every opportunity. Beady eyes behind silver-rimmed spectacles, peering out insect-like, watching what's going on. There is this strained pull of his mouth, a habitual facial tic that has the effect of extracting himself from proceedings. Clearly not wanting to be there, yet happy to be the object of inconvenience to the security company who are tasked with watching over him in court each day. I feel such revulsion towards this evil bastard.

'I need to bring something to your attention today, my lord,' announces his defence QC, who is now standing looking at the judge. Coupled with the slight delay to the start, it signals something is happening. Darren Rodden just sits there, as if it's nothing to do with him. 'You will be aware that my client suffers from attention deficit hyperactivity disorder, or ADHD, for which he takes daily medication. Due to an oversight, it seems he left to come to court today and hasn't taken his medication.' His defence continues. 'My client will therefore be experiencing the effects of its absence and, well, it is regrettable this situation has arisen, but there are implications for him if he were to give his evidence today.'

'And just how did this situation occur exactly? Can he not take his medication now?' the judge asks calmly, but clearly he's livid.

'Well, normally he takes his medication at a specific time in the morning and today, for some reason, that didn't happen. He forgot, essentially.'

'Yes, yes, we've established that.' The judge now struggles to hide his agitation.

'He left to attend court today before it became apparent at the oversight. In fact, I've only been made aware some 15 minutes ago,' continues the defence team.

'And at the risk of sounding like I am repeating myself; can he take it now and we'll adjourn for a short while?'

'Well, the form of medication he takes is a slow-release version, so the improvements won't be immediate. I'm aware there is other court business later today that you will be in attendance for, and given the logistics of accessing his medication, which is in his home, and timing of the latter business.' He pauses, as if to allow time for everyone to mentally put together the flawed timeline.

'Well, it's unfortunate that we will have to delay proceedings.' Announcing this, the judge looks over at the crown QC, who acknowledges the current predicament, agreeing that the only course of action is to delay.

I want to scream, 'Like hell he forgot, he didn't take his fucking medication because he knows he's giving evidence today! He's not that bloody dumb that he doesn't know the importance of his medication that he takes every day.' But to do so would have them throw me out of court. I'm visibly shaking with anger, and given half the chance, I'd gladly reach over and punch his beady pinhead eyes into his head, one by one.

And so we are sent home for the day. It'll be Monday now before we hear his evidence.

* * *

Mum's in hospital now following a terrible week for her at the nursing home. First there were the sleepless nights with her screaming at the flashbacks and John being called to sit with her to try and calm her. Her mood became very low during the day, and she was refusing to eat and drink. Seizing her failing health, a chest infection got a grip of her weakened condition. There was an urgency to give her antibiotics intravenously to speed up any recovery. Being sent home early from court today provides the opportunity to spend time with her and to try and coax her into eating something, anything, just anything. We are all becoming increasingly concerned she's slipping further.

Reinforcements by way of Jenny and some small pasta with a light homemade cheese sauce are called upon. We both arrive with high hopes of encouraging Mum on the road to recovery. Jenny's visits to Mum have become less frequent and it's clear Jenny isn't coping with her gran's decline. I'd began noticing it especially when she gives Mum a cuddle before she leaves.

Gone are the full-blown, yet somehow careful, delicate bear hugs. They are replaced by her extended arms, as if distancing herself. She'll sit across the room rather than beside Mum. During visits, Jenny is forever 'just nipping out' to check on something, phone or text. It seems she would rather be anywhere but here, witnessing this slippage and despair that just fills the room. That of course is when she chooses to come with me for the visits. Quite often she'll have an excuse not to and I never push it. I doubt my mum notices, but I do.

For today though, Mum's staring up at Jenny as she spoons in another mouthful of pasta. I tried earlier, but she wasn't taking any of it from me. Then Jenny stands up and insists she gives it a go. I'm not overly optimistic. 'You need to eat, Nanny, or you won't get better. Its macaroni cheese, you like that. It's still warm too. C'mon, eat some more.' Jenny is adopting her best encouraging tone of voice. I'm just utterly relieved Mum is taking in some nourishment, and after 20 minutes, she's eaten the full bowl as Jenny blethers away in between each spoonful, as if distracting Mum from her fate of eating. Earlier on in the day, Mum had told the nurses she just wanted to die.

Back and forth, Mum's army drive to the hospital, and between us all, we manage to continue her eating and fluids to the point that the doctors and nurses are much happier she's heading back up. She's taken her fight to the next level, whilst Darren Rodden's fight lies firmly ahead of him. I can't help but think she's somehow unwittingly won this contest.

In a way, I'm relieved when Monday arrives. I'm sitting in court with John and Pamela, ready for today's proceedings. Over the weekend, they had bombarded me with questions about the injustice of it all. From the initial delay at the start of proceedings, when he had to get a new defence team, to

Friday's banal act of duplicity with the medication oversight. It isn't as if I am disagreeing with the unfairness of it all. I certainly didn't have answers or remedies. This whole business is constantly unloaded at my front door, from where it is inevitably sprouting arms and legs.

And so Darren Rodden is escorted across the court, the witness stand his delusional stage. I'm ready for the onslaught of bile that spits from his mouth. But I'm not ready for this as he begins his evidence on the witness stand.

'I was walking past her house and the light was on, her front door open. I thought it was my chance to save somebody. I always wanted to be a superhero,' Darren Rodden utters with a bizarre self-belief that cloaks the true vile bastard within.

Does the nutter get a kick from the absurdity of what he's saying? Once again, taking up the slack of his mouth into that strained facial pull. How timely and fortunate for this modern-day hero to be passing her home and drag his predatory sexual needs into the safety of her front room.

'I thought something bad had happened and wanted to save someone inside,' as he unleashed his fists and feet again and again into her soft body and face. This delusional sick man, character acting to the most unbelievable degree. And I'm listening to the painful lentissimo of court proceedings playing a sadistic version of the Tichborne trial. Like a bad joke, that's what it is. Not worthy of all the pain and suffering Mum is going through. Surely Darren Rodden never spent his extra weekend conjuring up this? And more to the point, he must surely be getting advised by his defence team. And they let him take the stand and spout this? I'm terrified because he isn't laughing. It isn't a joke. He truly believes it, or more to the point, he wants the jury to believe him.

## 18

'You look terrible, Grace. Are you alright?' By this stage, Julian has ushered me off the street and into the hallway of his offices. My face is flushed after walking for what seems like miles in the rain. My raincoat is soaking wet, and Julian is struggling to fold up my unruly umbrella, so decides it's better served left open to dry out a bit. He pushes the mechanism forward and, with a click and ping, the rain droplets are propelled onto the worn oak floorboards. I feel embarrassed I'm incapable of managing this simple task, opting instead to just stand there and let him do it.

'Here, give me your coat to hang up. Come through and take a seat.' As if reinforcing my ineptitude, he takes my raincoat and adds it to his coat stand in the corner of his office, beside his own quilted jacket that's been placed neatly on a coat hanger. I sit on one of the two ample chairs in front of his desk and breathe in his office. It looks reassuringly familiar from my voyeurism a couple of months ago.

Julian heads towards his own chair behind his desk. He strokes the sides of his chin, pulling imaginary folds of skin to a point and wondering what he should do next with me in his office. 'Can I get you something, a glass of water or maybe tea?' He realises, given the interminable rain outside, something warm might be preferable. I'm still rubbing warmth into my fingertips. The chunky silver atlas ring spins loose on my middle finger, skinnier now due to the cold.

'Can I have a sip of your cup of tea here?' I pick up and cradle his pottery mug, cupping the glazed roundness in gentle warm sweeps, taking what warmth I can get from it. Julian searches my face, I'm not sure what for. With an admiring expression, he simply matches my smile as I brazenly drink his tea. It's a rare occurrence for him, this feeling; one that emits an inner release of gentle and unselfish nurturing from within him. Our dialogue beginning there and then. 'Would it make any sense if I said no one is listening to me?' It's more of a statement than a question I'm asking. I hope it lacks any sense of self-pity. But I know my words sound full of sadness.

He's aware of the impending decision on the trial, with the jury out now making their decision on the verdict. Timing again was against us, as we were sent home and told the jury would not make the decision at this late hour; it would now be tomorrow. I had hoped the verdict was a foregone conclusion, but his defence seemed to ignore the insanity of Darren's recollection of events when he took to the witness stand. Instead, they focussed on questionable evidence, reminding us of the fact Mum could not identify him from the computer photo fit exercise carried out whilst in hospital. Add to that the extent of Mum's dementia and cognitive functionality prior to the alleged assault; well, at one point they had made her out to be a silly old woman. And their overuse of the word *alleged* registered loud and clear this was a crime they were loathed to apportion against Darren.

Sitting in court, I grew more and more unsettled and

frustrated as the scales kept tipping in his favour. *Our* QC showed great dexterity in attempting to steer the evidence back in Mum's favour. I recalled how the defence QC almost left DC Bain tearful and red-faced by undermining her actions on that day. I began to wonder if we as a family had done enough with giving our statements and evidence. But it was never a free for all in court, we were given precise boundaries within which to respond to the questions being asked. The law clearly being given precedence over any sentiment surrounding Mum's tragic condition after the assault. I even sensed a tinge of resignation as the judge summarised for the jury, with the witness support official doing her best to maintain hope by reminding us how the law can appear callous and factual and therefore unforgiving at times. My brother felt relief that Darren's background and involvement in the school shootings didn't feature anywhere at the trial, since this would unquestionably have given his side a healthy injection of sentiment for the jury to latch on to. To say the whole family were distraught by this point would be an understatement.

Sitting now in Julian's office, I can't even utter words that express my despair. I'm caught in this perpetual cycle of doom, and with each hour passing, it pushes me further down. I'm crying now and can't stop as I deposit Julian's near-empty cup of tea next to some papers on his desk. Not that he grudges me it for one minute.

'I wish there was more I could do, Grace, to help. I am sure the jury will reach their decision early on tomorrow. That will be another chapter finished and you can draw breath for a bit.' His heavy oak desk is laden with medical reference books and client files, their height and quantity an unwelcome barricade between us.

'You know it was my birthday recently and I'm not sure what I did to mark the occasion. Can I get a kiss for my birthday?' I'm looking directly at him. My flagrancy doesn't shock him as I expected it would, especially given how very obvious and contrary to his professional standards my request is. Surely the same thought is crossing his mind.

'I don't see why not.' And at that, he stands up, meeting me halfway at the side of his desk. And then, without any hesitation or doubt, he pulls me close to him and into a full deep kiss. 'Fucking Jesus. I'm so sorry, Grace.' He withdraws, relieved but shocked at the immeasurable need for one another. 'Sorry, so so sorry. Grace, I shouldn't have done that. I could lose my job. Jesus fuck.' He's now pulling back his hair and sorting the sides where my fingers must have been exploring. He feels flushed and overwhelmed and angry at his physical urge.

'Hey, quit with the swearing. It's fine, don't be sorry. If anyone is to be sorry, it's me. I'm not going to give you any hassle. I wanted this too, have for a while. I guess I've had, how can I put it, inappropriate feelings for you for some time now.' I'm feeling the heat too in his office and glance over at the low-level cast-iron radiator below the window, pumping out more warm air towards us. I sit silent for a while, we both do, the desk between us, listening to the noisy steam plinking away inside the metal columns. Julian feels the tension lift and relaxes.

'It's been a long time since I've done that!' It isn't an apology for the expanse of time lessening his enjoyment, far from it. It was some embrace that's for sure, and a kiss that he wants to repeat. 'Let's have another go.' And with that, he stands up and we kiss again, both aroused, our bodies close and joined, neither one of us wanting to stop. 'The receptionist will be back from the post office soon. You best go, Grace, before we regret anything.' We stand close, not an ounce of awkwardness, just looking quietly and holding hands. And then a tender parting kiss.

Walking back to my car, I am tingling, thinking of nothing but our embrace, the reckless spontaneity of it all and about the total lack of ambiguity between us. It wasn't as if it had cropped up in any conversation we had, but one thing is becoming clear, how we both simply want each other.

* * *

At ten to seven, Julian turns his key in the door of his house and steps into their front porch, shaking off as much of the rain from his jacket as he can. He stands briefly, looking beyond the stained-glass panel of the internal door, turns the handle and steps in.

There's a chill in the hall. He calls out to say he's home and can tell from the acoustics of dishes and cutlery clanking she's in the kitchen preparing dinner.

'Got us a nice bit of fish from the fishmongers today. What veg do you fancy with it?' she yells out, hoping tonight's menu will reach him in the front hallway. And then the heavy surge in his chest, reminding him of his own culpability, the stain of disloyalty and its secreted damage.

# – 19 –

John and I pick our spot in the public gallery the following morning; we've got here early and, as such, have a good view of the steady stream of faces taking their seats. In the front row the Press are sticking together, clasping their regulation spiral-bound notepads and pens. Two of them have been present throughout the trial, but shame on these new ones turning up for the juicy bits only. I don't know about the gentleman in his fifties who sits at the far end of the row behind us; he's familiar, I think, from the original trial, but I can't be sure.

The Crown Prosecution and the defence team take their positions for what will be closure on another case for them. Desk tops remain stacked with files and documents, the occasional one being pulled and opened even at this late stage. At one point the 'opposite sides' start speaking to each other, business-like and equally not giving anything away. We almost feel like the forgotten collective in the public gallery, eye witnesses to the repetitive nature of the business heard within the court walls. Two members of the defence team move closer and privately discuss some matter, with one approaching Darren to speak to him, but we cannot hear since we are too far away. One of the defence team looks up into the public gallery and takes in all our faces, pausing, I sense, at me and my brother, who are both nervously waiting on things to begin.

I dare not start a conversation with John because I am fearful of all the worried thoughts I may end up sharing with him. Having been through most of the *'what if'* scenarios, I am back at the start for yet another re-run. Of course I am wishing for the word *guilty* to echo within these four walls and to take in Darren's long-awaited reaction. I'm also second guessing what I will feel too. The impact of the trial has pushed me to an almighty, nervous level, one which I rose to unwillingly at each and every step along the way. Those early optimistic and practical strengths blown away with what must have been ease, since I don't recall my fight against losing them. There's one thing about losing a fight, but another about being mentally absent to the moment it takes place.

I spin around to see who is behind me, to see who might be looking at us for our reaction. A couple of police officers have come in and are sitting amongst court officials, who seem to have multiplied where once we had one, perhaps two officials. There are also completely new faces and I guess they are here for one of the next cases being heard today. And then there's that man that looks vaguely familiar, staring not at the proceedings but with his head bowed down, examining his feet or the floor. There's activity in the front court area now, with a court official checking details with both sides. Things are about to begin, and a hush settles on the entire room. Darren Rodden is sitting in his usual spot beside two police officers, who anticipate the arrival of the judge as a rear door opens and a court official signals the entrance with those all too familiar words: *'All rise.'* Darren stands too, his arms crossed in front of his body, one hand gripping the other hand, just above the wrist.

The judge sits then glances over towards us; perhaps it's important he knows we are here for the verdict. He begins writing on the few sheets of paper, their volume strikingly out of balance with the masses of files lower down the courtroom. The jury spills in from the side, filling the three rows in the same order, always the same order. I have grown accustomed to spotting them, their shapes and sizes and ages and features.

I look around them randomly, their faces not telling me which way this is going to go. They are probably relieved the trial is about to conclude, returning to their lives and jobs without the inconvenience of factoring in another day in court.

We are not kept waiting long before the judge firmly asks Darren to stand, which he duly does along with the police officers on either side. The court official stands and looks directly at the jury, asking the spokesperson to stand up. My heart is jumping in my chest now and I can't stop my hands from shaking. And I hear the reply.

'*Not guilty.*' By a majority.

John raises one hand over his mouth, but I can still hear the faint strain of disbelief being uttered. Tears are falling down my face, but I'm not making any sound. I just make out the judge telling Darren he is free to go, but I don't attempt to move. Even John's usual bravado doesn't surface; instead, he's being comforted by Pamela, who is also crying. The court official approaches and tells us the QC wants a word, if we can make our way to our usual side room when we are ready. There's a sudden internal buzz in my head, the tension moving and shifting in my veins. And then the cold, a shiver running through me as the people leave the courtroom, pinballing round the magnetic draw of the press, always with their eye on me, now hoping for us to talk to them, their patience and respect up until that point repaid with a story. But I want none of it, no talk about it, no sharing of my feelings.

The jury has decided Darren Rodden did not commit this crime. We've missed out on the prize; that's what it feels like. It's what my mood was alluding to yesterday as I took in the summaries by the crown, the defence and the judge. All acknowledging what happened to Mum, but the defence in particular at pains to highlight their overwhelming doubting of the evidence. There's a disappointment that such a momentous milestone as the end of the trial isn't bringing a hint of elation as I hoped it would. Instead, I'm left with Mum in ruins and we've let her down, we haven't got who did this to her. And yet, Darren Rodden did it, I know he did, I've never been so sure listening to his lying. And if he didn't, why have the police stopped searching for the perpetrator? They must know too. But it's failed the true legal test, beyond reasonable doubt. Oh, they believe the assault, they just don't have enough to believe Darren did it. Some of the jury thought he was guilty, but not all of them. How can it be so divided? All of this I am relaying to the QC, who listens and expresses how sorry she is too, citing her previous concerns about the difficulty in getting this proven. She doesn't go into details and, quite frankly, I don't feel I can listen to any more excuses.

* * *

Archie Connell stands outside at the side of the court building, staring, shaking his head from side to side, recalling watching Darren Rodden, defiant to the end. How the hell did he get away with it again? His anger fuelled by the judge's passing remark, describing Darren as *odd* and some of his actions as *not normal behaviour.* How abnormal do things have to be before they realise what they've done is essentially allow his paltry track record of petty crime and antisocial behaviour develop into deeper, more evil tendencies? Darren will be feeling he's got away with it again. Oh, he's going to be loving this. Breaking into the old man's house, was that his taster? Pushing the boundaries like a spoilt child, seeing what he can get away with? Archie feels the bile rise, and then a nauseous taste, and turns and walks down the hill, not before a momentary thought about which court exit Darren Rodden will be coming out from. He's just in time to see a prison security van pull away from the court building rear entrance and head off, empty. It's closely followed by a blank-faced Grace, driving out the car park, staring ahead, with none of the emotion and relief he hoped would come her way. It's time for him to remove himself from the vicinity of the court building. He quickens his pace. Pesky press are still hovering around, on phones and with cameras swinging heavy around their necks. Yes, best get the hell away from the place.

# – 20 –

I'm not long off the phone to the nursing home. Mum had woken terrified from one of her nightmares during the night and the staff were letting me know. The flashbacks had been quite distressing for her, and they wondered if I would be free to pop in and see her at some point during the day, they think it will help her. The psychiatric nurse has been trying at each visit to work out her mental state since the assault, but Mum shared very little except during the flashbacks themselves. And it all seemed a terrible jumble for her now. I will go and see her over lunchtime; that way, I can feed her and chat to her. For the rest of the morning though, the court papers and judge's statement are available and I'm reading through them.

Darren Rodden was born in February 1991. His pre-school years were strained due to his behavioural difficulties. In 1996, as a five-year-old schoolboy, he survived the school shooting, during which a gunman broke into the school and fired indiscriminately at teachers and pupils, killing many and wounding others. He was shot and wounded.

On Sunday 13 June 2010, when aged 19, he spent an evening with friends. He drank a considerable quantity of vodka and beer. In the early hours of Monday 14 June 2010, while under the influence of drink, he was walking near the house of an elderly lady aged 76, who lived on her own. She had a close family and carers who visited regularly to look after her.

Seeing the door of the flat ajar, he entered the insecure dwelling house to offer assistance since it was unusual for a door to be left open at such an early hour. He found her in a distressed state, lying on the floor and crying, but he couldn't say with any great certainty what her injuries were. He panicked and ran out the rear door. When asked why he ran off, his rationale for this was he thought it would distress her more seeing him and he didn't want to frighten her further.

I was punishing myself by continuing to read extracts from the trial. During his *first* interview with the police, he gave an account of his movements which in effect denied any involvement in the incident. In his *second* interview on 14 June 2010, he gave a statement which was noted as follows: 'All that stuff I said did happen, I went into town to see if any pubs or clubs were open, but everything was closed. Then I wanted to walk to clear my head, so I turned right at the bottom of the main road, then left past the phone box, past the old lady's flat. The door was open. I went in, had a look, a woman started screaming, coming towards me, I can't really remember, then I went out the back door.' He was noted by the trial judge to have said that he described himself as being pretty blitzed, saw a house door open, so he went in to have a look and some woman was there who just started screaming at him and he panicked. She was quite old. She started to try and push him, so he pushed past her to get out of the way and she might have fallen over. He wasn't sure because he quickly ran out the back door. He denied having been in her bedroom. He dropped his packet of cigarettes in the house.

He denied having removed any of the lady's clothing. He denied having dragged her to the bedroom or having said he was going to have sex with her. The judge went on to further recall that he said he didn't know what clothing the woman was wearing 'probably coz ah was blitzed'. He denied having removed her underwear.

He headed straight home after running out the back door and, when he got home, put his clothes in the wash because they were dirty from sitting in the field with his pals, drinking. He felt pretty upset about seeing the old woman in the house. He claimed that he said sorry to the woman for pushing past her. He could not remember if she said anything back to him. He strongly denied that there was any sexual reason for his going into the house. At the conclusion of the police interview, he was taken to the charge bar and cautioned and charged. He replied, 'It's not true.'

I remembered at the trial how it was continued lies and excuses from Darren.

He admitted having been with his friends in the woods on the evening of 13 June 2010 and having subsequently entered her house at about 0345 hours on 14 June 2010. He had gone out for a walk, as the medication for his ADHD had worn off. He saw a door ajar and thought he would have the chance to rescue somebody. He did not know who lived there. He had always had a childish fantasy that he was a hero.

He was half in and half out of the door, and when he turned around, she appeared from the living room and was screaming. She came up and pushed his right arm so that he was turned around and the door shut on his arm. He barged the door purely to release his arm and, as she was behind it, she stumbled a bit and lost her balance, causing her to 'sort of sit down on the floor and fall backwards'. He didn't believe losing her balance would have caused any major injuries. Seeing her lying there, he tried to help her. He said, 'Calm down, I don't want to harm you, I want to help you.' He was positive that he did not say that he wanted to have sex with her. Panicking, he headed back to the front door. On opening it, he saw someone coming down the road towards the flat, about 20 yards away. He then went to the back door. On his way, the old lady grabbed his left leg. He jerked his leg to try to get free and it might have struck her. He then ran out the back door, went home and felt sick. Thinking it was because he hadn't eaten and had drunk so much on an empty stomach, he ate two packets of microwave chips.

I remember at the trial on the stand he was swivelling about, very animated, performing his movements at the front door, as if to help illustrate the innocence of it all. A slightly different account of going into the house and finding her already lying on the floor. I can't stand reading the court papers any longer; they are upsetting as I try and piece together the wording on the court script, matching it to his pathetic excuses and claims of innocence during the trial.

I head out in the car and, after half an hour, park up for a walk over the Forth Road Bridge, a walk I've enjoyed over the years. The bridge rises sleek and majestic, unlike its paunchy oligarch railway twin with its sickly red, sucking up its bellies to span the Queensferrys. The road bridge's chameleon grey beams dance with the passing clouds. I'm almost halfway across when I stop, pressing my rib cage into the railings. Like an impatient child, I'm wishing for the biggest, heaviest articulated lorry to go by and allow me to savour its vibrations through my entire body. My brother and I walked the bridge when we were young, with Mum and Dad. 'You have to press hard to get the biggest vibration in your stomach,' my dad would shout, above the noise of the flowing traffic. After a short wait, I'm rewarded with two lorries and a bus. Feels the same as it did all those years ago. I lean over and look down. The dark murky green waters below the bridge draw me in. The waves are breathing back and forth, hypnotically capturing my imagination. I visualise the prophylactic cocooning of the waters around my wet clothes and body. I don't remember feeling this all those years ago.

I step down, turn and continue my walk and remind myself to make the next few minutes a continuous stroll. Well, best not to alarm the CCTV operators with my stop-start-stop-start and vacant gazing. Crying is best avoided too. Weariness is setting in and it seems the wind has cottoned on to this and begins to crank up the knots and aim for me. I smile at how feeble it is when there is a bigger target for it. Tonnes and tonnes of metal, cables, tarmac, not to mention the constant array of rush-hour traffic. But I'm safe, hiding in its midst, the bridge like a close friend. I bid it farewell and leave behind its secrets washed away in the estuary's seasonal light drizzle.

Walking the bridge today reminds me of the permanent dour mist hanging over me these past few weeks. There's no trusty equilibrium. Lately the path leading there has become overgrown. I've neglected it, given permission for *things* to lurch over the edges. I haven't been able to bat them away. Some turn up as vague temptations disguised as normality, whereas others have swaggered in like they own the place already. I'm left with this untidy muddle. I have no idea if indeed this is my path anymore; it could very well belong to someone else. There's nothing familiar about it. No warm smell of baked scones, just a harsh existence that gains its right to own me, smacking my face and running away laughing down its own happy path.

I'm struggling as I head home exhausted and decide on an early night to try and forget about things. I don't think I have been sleeping for long when I wake from a familiar nightmare and pull myself out of the bed, but I don't make my footing and my leg gives way. I fall on the bedroom floor, and I burst into tears, unexpectedly, because I thought I was already crying. Calm, calm down. I wait for the rush to calm me, if only to give me a moment to realise it's just a dream. I sit, cold, my head in my hands and I cry, deep surging breaths releasing my pain. Feeling freezing cold, I roll myself back under the bed linen chaos and pull the covers up tight and around my body, rocking and tucking to make a snug fit against my back and legs. Feeling I just can't hack these bad dreams anymore.

But there is no clarity or insight at 3am in the morning. Thoughts turning in my mind, churning worn-out unoiled reasons why, each one more confused or circuitous than the last, and it's never ending. I get out of the warmth of bed, hoping the frosty pang against my skin will waken a new way of thinking. I grab my blanket and sit on the wide window seat, avoiding the cold of the glass. There's my big moon reflecting my condition on this earth, why I'm here, because, well, I may as well be here. I want it closer to let it whisper into my soul as I wake to the slowness of a new day.

The next morning, I decide I want to go and see Dad at the cemetery today, see how he is getting on and let him know how Mum is doing. He still doesn't know about the assault; I haven't told him. Oh, I don't talk out loud to him, it's all talk in my head, hoping he receives my news. I break the early morning silence over the graveyard by lifting the latch on the rabbit prevention metal gate. Only huge rabbits would fail to infiltrate the generous gaps in the bars. I imagine their deep aubergine globe eyes and giant furry ears dripping down the sides of their faces. My hand absorbs the full vibration of the latch as the *ding* peters out into the air. The generous tarmac path snakes up the incline and soon I've arrived at Dad in the top section, second stone on the right. It's a lovely bit of pale grey granite with just a hint of sparkle in the grains. A bird has played a bad joke on him with a plop of crusty cream and dark grey matter, hardened mid-slide down the polished section of stone. Dad would have laughed at that. I tidy up around the stone, not bothered where I stand because I don't believe he's still there.

As life goes on, so does death, and in the newer top section of the cemetery, new arrivals of grannies and grandpas put a protective arm around the special children's section, the children that lost their lives in the school shootings. Dad is close by it because he chose his lair years ago, recalling the discussion with Mum over which one to choose. Lair 95 is on the brow of the hill, with sweeping views and the added benefit, as Dad put it, of no draughts or noises from the front gates. I take the short path leading up to the children's section and sit down on the semi-circular memorial bench. A continuous trickling sound comes from the gentle water feature, soothing over their innocent names, lovingly engraved in the stonework. The liquid tenderly recycled then reappearing as if renewed, telling them it hasn't forgotten them and never will. I look through towards Dad again and wonder if in the depths below, or some other place, they share this intergenerational sanctuary of strangers, taking comfort from each other, learning, guiding.

Seeing James the other day brings things back to me and

I am sure to him as well. There won't be a day that goes by when his mind doesn't connect to their little girl, the girl I'm sitting close to right now. The raw, hellish cruelty of it all fills my heart and I want to sob. Does James think what I think about, the selective taking away, too soon? There is no all or nothing choice; it must surely be all of them allowed to fill this world with their laughter, handing out their daily smiles and love tangled amidst their childlike needs. That's not what happened though. Some were taken away without thorough deliberation. Some were spared. Darren Rodden was spared. His evil going undetected.

Archie Connell walks towards the old apple orchard at the end of the farm's big field. Wizened and crooked, the few ancient apple trees cast an almost mausoleum effect against the backdrop of young, vibrant sheaths of barley, bending in the breeze. He'd regularly sought sanctuary amidst these old trees, but today with the dampness from the overnight rainfall wafting a stale bark smell, it was all he could do to find a seat on a bundle of logs and cry.

His father's health was spiralling downwards, with each day displaying the fragile state of his mind; a mind that brings him fear and distress. Exhaustion from the constant need to reassure quickly turning to anger, piecing together the fragments of what his father could recall from that fateful evening of the break-in. And to think, in the immediate aftermath of the news of the break-in at the farm, he had felt such relief that no harm had been done. He thanked fate for dealing an almost kind criminal act. Darren Rodden had gone in to shelter from the cold, nothing else. They even laughed almost at the audacity of making a sandwich with the bread and ham he had found in his father's fridge. How lucky he had been that nothing more awful or tragic had occurred. Sickening, he felt he had been duped by the police, as if they had been too quick and complacent, not pursuing the incidents with vigour and proper intelligence. And to think he'd felt a tinge of sympathy for Darren, given his background and surviving such a tragedy at the school. Here he was one evening, momentarily lost after a night of sharing a few ciders with his friends. He had even considered turning up at his front door to offer a generous reconciliatory talk. One that would lift him out of his troubled past and not allow him to dwell on the unfortunate events of that evening. But now, wiping the tears from his eyes, the orchard comes into sharp focus, the trees hinting at the memory of rope swings his father had tethered up for him to enjoy as a child. Carefully watching him scurry up the branches with his matchstick legs, his father would stand, arms outstretched in case he fell, and then the brave launch over and grab of the rope, the sturdy knot providing the grip needed to swing back and forth, laughing at his father's relieved face that this time, no damage or broken bones had been incurred. Expertly watching over him. Look at him now, how feeble he felt with his attempts at simulating the same care and attention to his elderly father. By not knowing the reality of that night, and with his father with-holding the facts, he had become an accomplice to the potent untruth.

Back inside the farmhouse kitchen, Archie puts the kettle on to make himself and his father a much-needed cup of tea. Sipping away at his milky tea, his father seems content, happy taking in its remedial effects. Whereas before they would speak about work needing done at the farm, now they both stare intently into the hot tea, watching the surface level slip further down into the cup, leaving behind the nasty tannin staining on the china walls. Occasionally, he glances up to catch his father's eye, but it's as if his dad is avoiding the contact, for fear it will lead to yet another interrogation into the break-in, interrogations which seem to be happening more frequently of late for some reason.

'Give me your cup, I'll take it through to wash, Dad.' Walking back to the old kitchen table, Archie sits down beside the empty cups and reaches over for a sheet of his dad's writing pad next to the fruit bowl and begins writing.

*HE NEEDS TO BE PUNISHED. HE CAN'T GET AWAY WITH IT.* Then folding over the paper, he inserts it into one of the envelopes and heads out the door.

'Be back later, Dad,' he says, popping his head around the door. 'Back to check you are settled after your tea. The carer will be in to prepare you something tonight. It's Wednesday, mind.' And with that, he heads back into his car; he has stuff to do.

His usual routine was to drive past to see what cars were in Grace's driveway, picking the right moment to deliver the note. It was hard to tell what was drawing him to send these notes. Hours were spent poring over what was said in court, trying to determine where it all went so wrong. He was finding it hard to side with the jury when his own sense of balance was so hideously against every word uttered from Darren's mouth. Lie after lie after lie in his police interviews. Seeing the driveway empty, he parks his car further up the road, at the beginning of a track leading up to one of the fishing lochs on the nearby estate. From here, there is a shortcut, allowing him to head back to Grace's cottage, leaving only a short distance walking on the main road itself. It's best not to be clocked anywhere near her cottage.

Nudging the letter through the narrow letterbox, Archie withdraws his hand and turns down the garden path and onto the gravel driveway. His stomach is somersaulting, longing to get past the 50-odd yards back to the shortcut and out of sight of prying eyes, or worse still, getting caught in the act. Through the crunch of the gravel, he can just make out the distant sound of a car heading up the road. He's been fortunate so far with no other vehicles travelling along that route. By now his nerves are causing frightened shivers to run through his body and he quickens his pace, turning left on the road and breaking out into a slow jog back towards his parked car. He hears the familiar crunching of the gravel driveway as a car pulls in not far behind him. Panicking, he starts to run, heading off the road, sliding on to the muddy side section of the B road, terrified to look back for fear of showing his face, but desperate to gauge if he's covered enough ground not to have been spotted. Finally he rushes towards his car, quietly shutting the door behind him. He's unsure what to do. If he's been spotted, then driving out and back down the road leaves too much to chance. Manoeuvring his car around, he opts to head north up the road rather than risk passing the house so soon. This way adds 12 or so miles onto his journey back home, but the additional miles are worth it, he decides.

## – 22 –

I'd read the note several times over since it was delivered yesterday, each time putting it back inside the book with the earlier notes. The few words didn't alter on each reading; all it did was wind me up with more worry than I needed right now. Thankfully, Jenny was still at college when it was put through the letterbox. I'd seen him run up the road when I got home yesterday. Of course I couldn't be sure it was him, but then why else would someone out walking suddenly break into a sprint as soon as I got there? I was too slow to go back outside and check further up the road. By the time I had gone in and noticed the note and read it, I was more interested in ensuring my front door was locked, in case he came back to the house. I kept going over to the front window to check, but there was no sign of him. It was too much of a coincidence though, the man passing my house. But who is he, and what's his intention with these notes? My thoughts are disturbed by the sound of a door opening and Julian's receptionist approaches me. I blush, feeling secretly guilty. She recognises me, but I'm glad she can't mind read, glad in more ways than one.

'I'll see if he is free to see you now, if you want to take a seat.'

The receptionist heads back to her desk after appearing in

the hallway, alerted by a hidden buzzer system that belted out as I opened the front door to Julian's offices. The old oak seat creaks as I sit down, pulling my raincoat neatly across my lap. Placing my feet side by side with measured precision, I glance at my two-tone brogues and note how well they co-ordinate with the scraped antique floor and distressed-looking Persian runner. Familiar plinking sounds come out of the old-fashioned, low-level radiator. I figure the entire system needs bleeding to get rid of the trapped air that is rife throughout the internal plumbing. I can smell polish, essential given the excessive oak panelling, flooring and furniture.

Sensing it may be a few minutes yet before I get called to go in, I make the most of my time by browsing the framed prints on the wall. The few Max Beerbohm caricature prints are impressive and catch my eye. I scrutinise the thin pen lines and pale watercolour tints of the dandified costumed gentlemen, with what seems like overgrown foppish-haired heads tapering down towards skinny ankles and pointy feet. Surely not originals, I'm thinking, but a welcome choice from the usual sombre hallway landscapes. There is limited furniture in the entrance hall, not surprising considering the long wooden bench takes up most of one wall. Below the prints is a rather battered trestle table, with an equally neglected chipped Delftware pottery tub, hosting an oversized aspidistra, clearly well-tended judging by its large dust-free leaves. I sit down again, repeating the ritual of feet placement and neatly draping my raincoat.

'He'll see you now.'

The receptionist shows me into Julian's office. I could have found it myself. Then again, she isn't to know, is she?

'I wasn't expecting to see you, Grace. Come in and take your coat off.'

And with that, I help myself to his coat stand, noting his longer raincoat hanging up and a striped Hackett scarf. 'Can I interest you in your own cup of tea this time?'

'No, thanks, I'm fine really. I just came to give you the latest update on things.' He had asked to be kept up to date with the trial, but he'll know the jury found him not guilty since I think he's been quietly following the court progress too. This of course has escaped my knowledge, and instead, I'm finding favour with the preferred option of seeing him and telling him myself. I don't seem to be able to spin out the update to any great extent, as I find myself running out of further things to say. We both begin a sentence at the same time, and stop at the same time, half laughing at the overlap but both sensing an awkwardness on the horizon. There's a pause and more plinking from those bloody radiators.

'Grace, what happened between us before can't go any further. It has to stop.' His eyes are soft and almost bursting with apology. Jumping to begin this new conversation feels too hasty, too callous. I swallow, fighting to hide my sinking heart, with one side knowing this and the other side refusing to give in just yet. I shiver as a chill hits me from the wind outside, battering against the equally old windows in his office.

'But it felt kind of right, didn't it? It takes two, they say. Our minds think alike.' I just don't want our conversation to end, well, not like this. I'm tracing back his apologetic stare, trying to find the common ground that not so long ago had us so intensely drawn to each other. I mean, we kissed and he asked to do it again, and if I am not mistaken, the second time took *lingering* to a whole new level. But now, standing on the threshold of some liminal stage of our rituals, an unwelcome opportunity has turned up, offering us time to step away. The truth is the kiss is still constantly on my mind, and his too, denying any weakening fissure to come and fracture its arousing effects. Right now I can think of nothing more than the restorative warmth we offer each other, our mutual capacity to take the edge off my anguish and his as yet undefined anguish.

'Grace, I'm *married*. I'm so so sorry.'

'Well, of course you are, why wouldn't you be married? I mean... Julian, this just doesn't feel fair. I don't know how to put this, but... Sorry, I so didn't want to hear you say that, but at the same time, I guessed you probably would be married.'

'It's complicated.'

'What, the way I'm pathetically seeking your affection and wanting you, or is your marriage somehow unorthodoxly complicated?' No sooner have I said this than I listen on virtual playback and know just how pitiable I'm sounding. Thankfully his kindness sees through the tragic fog I'm filling up his office with.

'I feel bad, Grace, that I let this happen. It's not your fault. I mean, you have enough on your plate. I, I should have acted... Oh Christ, I feel the more I say, the more I'm causing you hurt, Grace.'

'Julian, I know the hurt that's hitting me right now. It's hearing the verdict yesterday and knowing there is fuck all I can do about it. I've no say, Mum has no say, our family has nowhere to go with this.' I'm thinking that by discussing the trial, it will somehow reduce the likelihood of us straying towards an ending that's inevitable but one I can't take in right now.

'The trial and court business is like a form of cruelty. Must be hard for you, Grace.' And with this, he makes to stand up from his chair, moving from behind his desk.

'Julian, this isn't helping me, and deep down, I know it's

unrealistic of me to... to adorn you with this task, this task of helping me. I'm not your responsibility. I just feel as if you care, or have I got this all so horribly wrong?' Our conversation is flushing towards an impending gloom I for one don't want to hear about.

Julian doesn't trust himself; that is blatantly obvious. Standing up when sitting behind his desk was the more conventional meeting layout with officials and clients who come into the office. I look up at him as he comes closer to me, wondering what his next move is, wanting him to approach me, yet he's got an expression that is bordering on terrified. Sitting back down, he does his best to switch on his habitual dour expression, his hand once again stroking his chin in a pointy motion, straining the sides of his mouth. Christ, it's as if he is on the verge of a personal undeclared contest for impenetrability. I'm weirdly savouring his pernicious and enigmatic aroma as he sits behind his desk. Clearly, I'm not about to be chucked out his office yet. Perhaps he'll buzz the receptionist and have her evict me.

We had kissed that time, drugged on an unforgivable impulse, when instead stepping away would have been the sensible move. Now his jotter has been blotted, stamped by a transgression which thankfully remained beyond the reach of the medical disciplinary panel. Convincing himself he had gone into the gallery for a conversation, nothing more than a few words. But there's more now, a desire for some kind of greater meaning. He can see that surely, me saying one thing, yet so expressive of a guileless longing. It's impossible not to feel moved.

It's getting to the stage now I feel like a smell in his office. If I stay much longer, I'll seep into the walls and lurk there. A communicable disease building incrementally then getting set to creep nefariously up his nose. This meaningless conversation about the verdict must be almost oppressing him with its weight. There is a knock at his office door and the receptionist walks in, whilst apologising for the interruption. I think we are both relieved, to be honest.

'Have you any mail to go, Mr Brodie? Remember I'm leaving sharp for my anniversary dinner.' She whispers the last bit, aware it's not really appropriate to share with a client present.

'Yes, yes, I remember.' And at that, Julian hands over a small bundle of signed letters.

'If that will be all, I'll head off if that's okay? I'll lock the outside door on my way out.'

We're not sure what still needs to take place in our meeting. Clearly there isn't much more to discuss with any true purpose and drifting into thinking about the previous embrace wouldn't be wise. Well, the reality is we are not likely to just shake hands all business-like and notate a date for the next meeting in the receptionist's diary, when there isn't a requirement for any future meeting. You couldn't script what is going on in our minds as we scan the medical reference books and beige folders on the desk. Pathetic. One of us has to make a move; we are both pathetic.

I watch Julian stand up again and pause at our spot at the side of his desk. Using the waistband of his suit trousers, he adjusts them with a pull, inhaling and standing taller, bringing comfort to his interest below. I stand to meet him as he sits on the corner of his desk with a homely sigh and smile. For me, I feel expressionless and catch him looking at me as if I am a spoilsport, ignoring the opportunity, yet feeling the vitality of second guessing each other's thoughts. Those unsaid delicious temptations hanging around us and, for a moment, eliminating any sense of us drifting into unfaithful territory.

And then, with ease, and without any ambiguity, we take our clothes off.

## 23

S he's eating and staring intently at me. I think she wonders who I am, who this chatty lassie is that's feeding her today. 'Lentil soup smells tasty, Mum. Making me hungry. And I brought some of your favourite Italian loaf.' I think *lentil* and *Italian* might ignite a tiny memory spark, to break the expression on her round puzzled face, but it doesn't. I've fallen into the trap of layering too much information one after the other. The discipline will come, but it's hard to break a lifetime where Mum and I fought over airtime during our blethers.

She loved to chat with everyone, the neighbours especially as I vividly remember as a young child, standing helping her hang out the washing in the back garden. 'Teresa, are you winning with that washing?' her next-door neighbour would shout across the fence. I'm standing in my dungarees, clutching the peg bag as Mum struggles with an out-of-control billowing bed sheet she's attempting to peg onto the washing line. Mum's staggering on the drying green, the wind splays the sheet to form a comedic ghost-like apparition around her plump body shape. I'm reversing further back, for fear the sheet might also swallow me up, and of course, the very important peg bag. She deflates as she is finally rescued, undraped and grabs the pegs

I've been holding out for her to pin the unruly sheet onto the line.

'Pass me two more pegs or we might lose this sheet from the line.' Obediently, I dig down into the floral bag and pull out a further two pegs, one of which is hastily held between her teeth, and it looks like she's snarling at the washing. 'Another two.' And once more, I pass the pegs over. She continues with this double conversation with the neighbour. I say nothing and just wait for the 'another two' order directed at me, midway through her chat. I stick my head almost into the peg bag; there must be hundreds of pegs since we never seem to run out. Finally she smiles down at me and lets me know we are finished now; she just needs to go and get the wash pole. She passes me the empty wash basket and tells me to drop the bag of pegs in and leave it on top of the coal bunker for later. From the coal bunker, I look up towards the drying green and watch her stab the pole into a gap on the washing line, causing the sheets and pillow slips to jut upwards in unison. Heading over to the fence, she resumes her chat with the neighbour as I head back into the house. I might manage to get to the biscuit tin and back out to sit on the plastic garden chairs before she notices. They look like they might talk for ages.

The plastic garden chair she was so fond of has been replaced today with her special plug-in chair, currently unplugged. A huge elephant of a chair that's greedily taking up floor space in the compact dining room. Mum's not walking anymore after a period of stumbling confidence. Plugged in, the chair generates a pleasurable, grinding hum that manipulates and reaches the parts other human contact can't reach. The chair is green too. It's the king of chairs, what's not to like about this chair? It makes Mum look tiny and frail. Its superb manoeuvrability starves her of trying to walk again. Its green upholstery has a hint of lime, veering towards a lurid shade of jaundice. And she just sits in it, she's become it, she is this hideous chair moved from room to room. It punctuates her decline, down, down and further down.

Great, the sausage casserole has arrived, and I begin feeding her. Mum's not looking at the food, she's still staring at me, buried deep in a private mental domain. She hasn't spoken during the starter, and I'm thinking the entire three courses will be in silence. My running commentary continues, taking me back to the days when Jenny was a baby and the health visitor encouraged you to talk to your baby and tell her what you are doing. Babies have no idea what their new mum is doing, so the benefits are plain to see; Mum has spent 76 years eating, so I think she is somewhat well versed. But I get the same new-born look.

One of the nursing staff comes into the dining room. 'Teresa, you look like you are enjoying what your daughter's giving you today?' Mum's eyes startle and move to the sound of the new voice, then back to this person who is sitting feeding her. I am not sure she knows it's me and I fight back the tightness in my throat that wants to open up and just cry. Before all of this, if I was cooking one of her favourite dishes, I'd take a bowl of it down to her in her flat, since she didn't always fancy going to the bother of cooking just for herself. She'd phone me after tea saying she liked the fiery paprika or sweetness of the shallots in the goulash or stew, mentally dissecting the ingredients, as I had grown to expect from her lifelong cooking talents. Today, the sausage meat is undefined, the feeder a kind stranger. She hasn't a clue, so I continue and hope that whoever she thinks I am, my company pleases her.

* * *

The beautiful afternoon weather keeps me outdoors and I want to walk and fill myself up with the goodness of it all. I park in the car park in the centre of the forest trail and pull on my walking boots. Before long, I settle into the damp, odorant pine of the walking trail. The wide path sponges and buffers my steps, the rhythm broken with the crunch of twigs and pine cones. Nature's goodness binds me into a more relaxed state, and I can breathe well again. I look up to feel the warmth of the fading sun as it weaves through the tall waving pine branches, the warm rays falling on one side of my face. I continue my walk, savouring this gifted earthshine, waxing like a new skin. The forest is immense, its density broken on either side of the path with pine tree trunks pegged bolt upright in the undulating mulch terrain. The distant coastline welcomes the sounds from the migrant grey plovers arriving from colder climates, getting ready to nest with their new young, gorging on the forest's berry feast. They will baton down during autumn and wait out in the kinder winter of the east coast. Spared from the harshness of their homeland, with renewed vigour, I know they will leave as the season begins, for the time being, stealing from nature's pro bono service. I take a right spar, crossing the coastal path, and follow the signs down to the seashell walk. The musky forest and its weighty canapé are behind me now and the light and air lift. My face stretches and tightens, and I draw in the medicinal sounds and smells of the estuary. The tide lolls inwards and I know it will soon be high tide. My quickened pace and seaward gaze invigorate me in equal measure. Sea foam rolls over the sand, its salty spit sinking into the grains. Nature's ephemeral body clock, reliable and never failing in its endeavours, somehow escaping an old age. If only it was prepared to share its secrets beyond its selfish evolutionary cabal.

I have time to head to my gallery and pick up the mail for the day and check what there is in next week's diary. Timing wise, I've missed the parking curfew times, which will make it a quick in and out. I've promised Jenny I would pick up a pizza on the way home too and I am just waiting on her text confirming her toppings; she was pondering when I spoke to her. We had negotiated a deal whereby she could have free rein on the choice of toppings if I could opt for the thin and crispy base. This was instead of her favourite stodgy mozzarella stuffed crusts, which claw in your mouth no matter how much you chew and swallow; they just sit like lead weights in your upper intestine waiting for the pink dyspepsia bus.

Unlocking the gallery door, I reach down to gather up the mail then punch in the code for the alarm, shutting the door behind me with my heel. Sufficient light streams in from the front window display, so I forget about more lighting and head straight to the back office for a swift sort of the mail and check the diary. A handwritten envelope simply addressed to 'Grace' catches my eye in the bundle. These days my post seems to be laced with the odd surprise. I anticipate the need to install pigeon holes in my office to assist in compartmentalising it all. It goes without saying, I still have Ms Bourgeois' secret stash, furtively slotted into its position on the book shelf at home.

I open the letter.

*Sorry I missed you today. J*

I liked the J.

The following morning, I park the car and step out into the fresh air, heading in the direction of my gallery. I'm so tempted to swing by and see if Julian is in his office, but I don't have an excuse other than to acknowledge his note. It's a very straightforward detour, so internally I'm persuaded. A few streets down, I turn when suddenly I'm caught and spotted some metres from his front office. He's just exited his office, but he is with another gentleman. Foolishly, I'm thrown into acting like some sort of reduplicative hallucination as I attempt a coincidental walk past which looks wrong on so many levels. There's a hopeful forgiveness in his smile as he concludes his conversation with the man. And he's alone.

'I got your note, Julian. Sorry I missed you too.'

'Were you coming in to see me just now or heading for your gallery?' Thanking him personally for his note will seem exaggerated and over the top, but why else am I walking past here when my gallery is the other way? With a free hand, he reaches for mine, hidden in the folds of his coat, and leans in towards me. I'm inches away from just drawing in further for a full kiss. 'Don't open up your gallery, just wait for me there. I won't be long, just dropping off these papers then I'll come and see you.' He releases my hand and slides it down, just skimming the side of my hip.

I potter aimlessly about the back office of the gallery, glancing out at the door every now and again until I see him. I shut the front door behind us, and he grabs hold of me and I'm grateful for the privacy of the inner porch. He looks beyond the front exhibition space and registers the light in the back office. 'C'mon, let's see you properly, Grace.' And with that, we move to the security of my office. He's enjoying me, every reckless inch of me, taking in the urgency of it all. I'm about to attempt redressing, but he's still kneeling, kissing the side of my knee, making his way gently down to my ankle. 'I like your feet,' he says as he places his lips gently and kisses the sensitive skin at the side of my ankle. 'You have dainty feet.' I smile up at his strong eyes and wonder at his enthusiasm and what lies behind his wicked smile. 'You're perfect, Grace. If there was any way I could make this work, I would. It would break so many hearts though.'

I say nothing for a few seconds, since I don't have an immediate response, his words timed awkwardly, too close to the intimacy of it all. 'Then why did you come back here, Julian? I'm not complaining, but I'm getting the feeling from you that you're regretting it now.'

'Being with you, Grace, is amazing. I've forgotten about all things to do with intimacy. It's been so long, months since...' He breaks off mid-sentence, clearly not wanting to share or divulge his very private *other* life.

'And being here again, sharing our second bout of intimacy, has suddenly sparked this... what... compunction?' I'm aware that my voice is getting louder, yet I feel the immediate urge to tone it down or I sense he'll just walk away, and I want to talk to him more, not end as soon as his conscience catches up.

'You've a way of putting things, Grace, you really do. I felt disloyal that day I kissed you and I know I sound like an old record saying this again, but *this*, what we have, has to stop. There's nowhere it can go, you must realise that?'

'Then why did we let it continue? You can't believe it's just me, I mean, Julian, the things you say when we are in the *throes of it*, are they just mutterings in the heat of the moment?'

'When I say I want you, I mean it, Grace. I want you, more than just *those moments*. Truly, you have to believe me. It's just that I'm caught in the middle of this... I mean... I still love my wife despite *this*.' His eyes are wide now, staring at me but not in an angry way, in a, well, quite undefinable way. There's an obvious reply here, but fortunately or unfortunately I can't tell him just how lame those words are. I had this long-standing belief that loving someone was stronger than *this*, but clearly, there's a middle ground that for years has escaped me. 'I need to go, Grace.' And with that, he almost scoops me up, wrapping me in a tight embrace, his kiss leaving my mouth and walking to my forehead and side of my head, through my hair, taking in the smell of me. I wish I could just slap him, and I mean a good hard slap, but his actions are utterly invalidating my slap compulsion. There's no way of continuing the conversation well without the futile slide into despair. After, I will think of a hundred things I could have asked him, or told him, but for now I'm mute again.

## 24

Today I've shaken myself out, let the dead dust settle and grab hold of some focus. I decide to open up the gallery early and rehang a few works. Four new works came back from the framers, and I am keen to incorporate them on the walls. The back office is overwhelmed with bubble wrap from the new works. I fling open the small window and nature's essence fills the space. There's a round hollow in the cushion on the sofa taking me back to yesterday with Julian. I pick it up to trace his smell and hold it on my lap as I rediscover the room, my desk chair still out of place, spun round, quickly as I recall, and facing the corner of the office. I pick up some bubble wrap and stroll back into the front of the gallery and sit down at the small desk. As I plan the re-hanging in the front exhibition space, I amuse myself and pop some of the bubbles.

For the rest of the morning, a few people venture into the gallery and I enjoy the banter with them. One is a regular customer, never bought any of my works, but I like her. Today she asks how Mum is, and it quickly reminds me why I avoid socialising with friends these days. I attempt to be as upbeat as possible, refraining from tumbling towards Stygian gloom by turning the conversation around before her body language and expression deflates. Embarrassed to have inflicted such an effect, I reel off my happy questions about her holiday and family and work, and before long we're galloping back to jolly land. It's exhausting, but solvable, I'm sure, with a 15-minute tonic of Julian. After that, I would live and feel again.

I close the gallery early after lunch to attend a review meeting at the nursing home. John's there too, to agree Mum's palliative care plan. Today she has decided to have a nap in her room after her lunch. John and I sit in the conservatory room for our meeting. A pot of tea and some biscuits are brought in, but we don't have the appetite, so just begin the meeting. The nurse reads her notes out loud, her face and words resigned to the picture of Mum sadly in decline. It's read out almost as a pre-requisite textbook for evidencing ultimately what the best course of action would be 'if something were to happen to Mum'. It's hellish speaking about her when she is only just up the corridor from us. It isn't right we are here deciding her fate, but that's what we have a duty to do. There doesn't seem to be any way of thinking about it in my head that somehow makes this seem a normal progression. Up until now decisions seem to be hemmed into the living and the prolonging side of things, but this, well, this is crossing the line and it breaks my heart and John's too.

'Well, Grace, we need to do all we can for Mum, we can't just do nothing.' John's looking at me and sitting on the living side of the scales and now anything I say not only shows my opposite feelings on Mum's fate, but there's this added need to bring him along into that way of thinking. I feel I'm at the head of the death march, rallying round other followers, and the weight of it burdens me to the point where it's hurting. 'I still think of Mum as she used to be, when she was herself, always doing stuff and busying herself, and can't get away from wanting to decide on "things" as if she was choosing, in those days in the past when she was better. Do you think she would want to be the way she is?' John needs to know how I feel. And I realise that it's as if I have drawn her timeline now and I've decided where the line ends. Who do I think I am deciding on the end of this road? I was also the least religious in the family and what I say is so heathen-like, I now know why I am the oddity in this family. 'Always wanting something more or to be different' were the words launched at me, pushing me to the side-lines all the time. I tried hard to be a part, to conform, honest I did.

We're not getting anywhere at the meeting, the meeting to decide if the DNR note goes on her records or not. It gets more and more upsetting because to decide, we have to have described to us what's involved in resuscitation and the underlying violent act that it can be to get someone alive again. 'Oh God, what if she thinks she's being attacked again?' And now I've compounded everything by bringing up the assault again and linking it to keeping her alive. The senior nurse has her view, and she is doing her best to stay impartial but arming us with the details. John's eyeing her up with having some statistical agenda for ensuring every bed counts in this nursing home. Now we're ganging up on him *and Mum.*

'There are days when I can have a laugh with Mum, you've seen that, the way she can still talk and joke.' John's scoring the ultimate point now, because when I visit Mum, she doesn't know who I am. It isn't her fault; I don't mind really. What started off as me going to see her for her benefit has gone full circle, and now I go and see her so that I can stay part of this circle. It doesn't mean I don't want her to stay with us for longer.

John doesn't judge me, but we end up agreeing to DNR on her records.

* * *

It's 3am and the witching hour, the one that savages the meagre few hours of sleep I manage these days. Wrapping up warm, I quietly pull the cottage door closed behind me and venture down the road. I want to make sure I don't wake Jenny. It's eerily quiet as I lurch through the dark inkiness, my arms swinging, sweeping away the heaviness of the night. I take the short walk to the bridge over the river and find the rocky outcrop waiting for me on the embankment. I pull my coat down under me and sit, huddled in a cornucopia of bracken and gorse. Watching the night dance of the stars, veiled with passing gossamer clouds, whose speed defies the sleepiness of the hour. I start to cry, ashamed to interfere with the symmetry of the night. I'm the guest they have to invite to the party out of pity and now I'm letting the side down. There's nothing to cling on to, I'm swamped with endings, ending after ending with a big fucking full stop at the end of it all. I'm even further away from Mum; she's pulling away, escaping the cocktail of disease in her mind. All the time running away from the evil memories he's branded in her head. I don't know what's worse for her. Just go, Mum, just let go, please.

# − 25 −

I make a point of never wasting time thinking about Darren Rodden, because he truly is not worth the effort. That is until a day like today, when an accumulation of worry and anger leads to this damaging preoccupation. Naively, I thought that over time I'd be able to leave it all behind, stop going over the things said in the trial. But no, it sticks to me like a fungus, reeking in the pits of my mind and general unease. It's driving me crazy. I've barely opened the gallery when already I'm dismissing the front exhibition area in favour of pottering around the back office, aimlessly looking for something, I don't even know what. Perhaps I'm hoping it will find me. Deciding today is a lost cause, I pull the gallery door shut behind me and head back to my car, beginning a journey I've resisted for so long, but one which for now is sitting noisily in my mind, so penetratingly agonising that ignoring it further is impossible.

I spot Julian as I leave the gallery early today, but he doesn't see me due to the exactitude of split-second timing and the confused warren of side streets close to where we regularly park our cars. I'm heading back to my car and he's just collected paperwork from his car. Perhaps avoiding him is deliberate; I'm afraid propinquity might lead me into temptation, and so for today, I am grateful for fate's sliding passageways of time severing the streetscape.

I begin the one-hour drive home, thinking and convincing myself my next move is wise when on the face of it, it's clearly going to add to my woes. I want to see Darren Rodden's flat; I want to see if he still lives and breathes there. After the assault, it wasn't difficult for John to establish where he stayed. I went to great lengths to warn him to stay away from the place, not trusting my brother's hot-headed temper from spilling over into an ugly scene. Come to think of it, I am sure that's when the idea first entered my mind, stupidly assimilating my brother's hypothetical plan to stalk the place with my own, more sensible plan... of stalking the place. Once the idea was there though, I couldn't rid myself of it. Even times when my sensible brain clicks into gear, there is always this strange hope that by doing this, it will eliminate whatever it is that's eating away at me.

I stop a few streets away from the flat, planning my next move. There really isn't anything more to plan since I've gone over this a hundred times. At least I'm driving past his flat and not walking past it, the latter feeling too conspicuous and liable to have me caught in the act. I admit though, it briefly held some appeal a week ago. I indicate, drive forward and turn into the street, slowing down since I'm not familiar with this small housing scheme; it's not an area of the town I have ventured into before.

I'm a couple of doors away from it, well, if I am to believe the house numbering. Leaning over to the side, I steer but look over intently at his front window. No sign of anyone through the maroon curtains, but I can't drive any slower and spend too much time looking in or people living close by will spot me, maybe take my number plate. I straighten myself up just in time to swerve and avoid a grey wheelie bin hanging precariously over the kerb in the house next door. This is such a bad idea. I put the car quickly into second gear and accelerate out of this situation.

\* \* \*

Hastily, Archie Connell heads down the side street and runs up towards the main stretch of road outside Darren Rodden's flat. He is sure it was her in the car but needs to see for himself. Turning right around the corner, he halts, taking in what feels like his first breath in ages. Steadying himself against a low-level, cold sandstone wall, Jesus, it is her car, coming back down this way, and he's going to be seen. Spinning round to avoid facing the passing car, he hunches down and pretends to tie an imaginary lace on his right shoe. Bending only increases his thumping heartbeat as he waits for what seems ages for her car to disappear out of sight. Standing up, he feels lightheaded and sits down on the wall to steady himself, quickly, he hopes, so that he can get as far away from his flat as possible. It would just be his luck if Darren himself came out the flat and saw him.

Feeling disappointed and stupid, Archie realises just how futile these frequent walks are past the flat. And for what, some desperate, illogical need to check he's still there? It's like a spell, an addictive madness that shows no sign of abating. What's he to do to end this torture? I mean, it's his right to live here, that's what they'd say, his right to live freely. What about everyone else's rights? And Grace and her family having to take it all in, and knowing what he now knows happened at his dad's farmhouse, that Darren is an evil bastard that's got away with it *twice*. Seeing Grace now, he gets a sense she's experiencing the same madness as him. Why else is she driving past his flat? Archie thrusts his tightly balled fists deep into his pocket, not because of the cold, but to stop himself punching a wall.

## 26

Julian paces about the bedroom, looking for his jumper; his wife Lydia sighs in the background as she applies something out of a shiny purple bottle around her eyes. 'For Christ sake, Julian, you are like a demented animal stomping about the room. What have you lost that's *clearly* so important?' she snaps at him vigorously, no doubt praying for him to leave their bedroom so that she can slam the door behind him.

'My lamb's wool jumper, the moss-coloured one? Wore it the other day and it's not here on the chair where I left it.' Julian swivels his head from side to side, polluting the air with his impatient spit that seems to be uncharacteristically launching out of his mouth.

'In the wash! It's in the wash!'

'Who put it there? I only wore it once. You know it goes all bobbly if you wash it too often.' And at that, Julian petulantly strolls over to the wash basket, seeking to retrieve the garment.

'It's in the wash, Julian, because it reeked of perfume, and not mine either.'

'Not this again,' he mutters under his breath after opting for a clean jumper from the wardrobe. He makes his way down the stairs into the hallway and, grabbing his coat, heads out the door to his work. Julian turns the key in the ignition of his car, glancing back at the front door he's closed, imagining his wife calling him all the names under the sun then bursting into tears and sobbing for hours. He feels guilty that her crying episodes have little or no effect on him now. He thought even she knew he wasn't interested in providing comfort and talking her out of her gloom and perpetual trail of upset and ruin. Heading out the house today, he had picked up an overnight bag and was heading to Edinburgh and to the small flat above his office. The flat has denied him a tidy rental income and has instead been vacant most of the time but provides a bolthole for him when he needs to get away from it all. Today he is truly bolting. Stopping at traffic lights, he glances down at his mobile phone sitting on top of the passenger seat. He wonders where Grace is right now, and what she's doing. Was she suffering on her own too with this shocking business with her mum? Putting the slow lamenting progress of the trial behind her, a trial that had cruelly attacked her day after day as yet another pathetic legal excuse was thrown at her. What a strong woman she is seemingly absorbing it all yet still being able to delicately flaunt her happy disposition and get on with living. Yes, that's what he wanted to do, get on with living and not be rubber-banded back to his misery.

Arriving at his office, he flicks on the switch of his desk lamp, just enough light to curb the empty feeling inside. All he can think about is Grace, and her warmth. He pours himself a solitary cup of tea, smiling as he recalls her drinking from his cup a few weeks back. Delving into the few case files sitting in a neat bundle at the side of his desk, he attempts to draw on some professional capacity to get through them, but it's difficult. He picks up his mobile and dials her number. 'Grace, it's Julian. Fancy some *conversational* company tonight, over dinner?' He can't help it; he just wants to see her again.

* * *

On the way to the restaurant, Julian asks the taxi to stop a couple of streets away, after checking if I mind getting some fresh air before dinner. Stepping out of the taxi, we walk side by side, close enough but not touching, and I wonder why, but know why in a way. It doesn't stop me wanting to reach over and take his hand, but I'm not sure it's a permissible activity and enquiring about it will sour the introduction to the evening. As we turn the corner, the restaurant comes into view. Industrial and stunning, this gothic red-bricked block rises up, up into the sky. Its impenetrable robustness softened somewhat by metallic filigree tower tops on each rooftop corner. Their delicate lace-like ornamental outline against the wispy cloudy sky, surrounding the building's wonderful top-floor lantern viewing room. Picket hedges, snipped to perfection, contain the hotel's vegetable and herb garden. I'm aware of Julian staring intently at me, not saying anything, taking in the beauty from my expression.

'I don't even have to look at it, Grace. Your face tells me how perfect this place is.' It's then that he takes my hand and I look at him and know he has somehow come home.

The girl at the reception desk warmly greets us and shows us to our table. Menus and wine lists are distributed, and we are left alone. Sitting like two anonymous people in the restaurant, it's our first chance in a while to relax in the wave and confusion of strangers. I'm studying an old, framed black and white photograph hanging up on the wall beside our table. 'It says here the restaurant is a converted water tower. Where did you stumble across this, Julian?' I'm excited and encouraged by his choice of restaurant, unusual and quirky and of course appropriately out of town, just in case.

'*Traveller Magazine*, I think, a few months back. Well, I've been thinking about coming here and was fed up getting to the stage of almost booking it before something cropped up, putting a stop to it. I just wanted to remind myself what good food tastes like. The menu's vegetarian, but it's had great reviews.' There was almost an apology from him due to the absence of meat dishes.

'Glad you did. I like it here, such a nice atmosphere.'

'Aye. You deserve it too.' And I marvel at his face, the long-awaited straining smile, buffered by tension, then his facial muscles gently lapse and ignite those eyes. At last, alive.

Amidst the sea of crisp white table linen, we both agree on the ten-course taster menu. Early signs are that this dinner will not disappoint. Julian is staring at course three that's just arrived. Courgettes, some hot some cold with the most delicate smoked beetroot chutney sitting on a bed of chicory ribbons. The chef manages to make even nature's stranger and less attractive vegetables sit up and look amazing. 'It's like a work of art, Grace. I don't feel I should eat it.' Julian can't help but compliment the chef for taking such simple ingredients and displaying them so artistically.

'I'm lost for words, never seen anything quite like this. You have to taste it, such talent in this kitchen.' Each course arrives, surpassing the previous one, and we are both taken on the most delightful culinary journey. Course seven's hot morel mushroom consommé with cubes of celeriac root sits erotically, the hot juices swirling below three protruding, firm baby parsnips. I've never felt so engaged over food and with

Julian's easy, mellow companionship. Course nine is definitely the ladies' dish with its perfectly formed timbale mound of quince jelly, sticky and draped over melting goats' cheese with just a hint of a wobble and quickly brought back into focus with homely, sharp-tasting strips of Granny Smith apple.

'I'm hoping the espresso will curb the hard sensation I fear that might behold me when they bring us the dessert.' Julian's laughing and relaxed playful humour now in full flow and I've never felt so happy to be in a place and to be with him. And yet, as I take in the finishing touches of our meal, I know there are things we haven't spoken about during the meal that need to be said. Bracing myself, I'm half listening to Julian whilst playing about with a few sentences in my head, sounding them out before I have to utter them.

'Julian, is this just dinner we are having tonight?' And it's maybe not my best choice of openers, but the others used words and phrases that hint at the evening leading on to something more. I'm using a careful tone to ensure there is no suggestion of a lack of gratitude, especially seeing as he's just paid for the meal.

'I wanted to see you tonight, Grace, to spend time with you and, well, I thought having dinner is public enough for us both to behave.'

'You must know by now though my feelings for you are difficult to just set aside. We've been holding hands for the last four courses; I mean, it doesn't feel like a dinner for friends, well, not for me.'

'And I'd be lying if I said I saw you as simply a friend, Grace. I think about you a lot, and not just in *that way*. You are so special to me.' We both smile, both aware of the not-so-hidden desire we can't seem to extinguish.

'But we can't ignore the fact you've said this can't go any-where. Sounds like you want it all, Julian, with no intention of upsetting your wife but at the same time content to tinker with my own feelings. I'm sorry, but I don't feel *special*.'

'It's hard to explain, Grace. I'm not really living my life right now. Lydia is...' And he drifts off without explaining it. It's also the first time I've heard him say her name. It cuts right into me because I'm not daft, I know right now, for whatever *unexplainable* reason, I can never be his priority.

There isn't much said in the taxi from the restaurant back towards the city centre. Stopping outside his flat, he pays the taxi driver and for a moment we stand, unsure of what's next. 'I don't want you to go, Grace. I want to chat away to you right through into the early hours.'

I'm staring at the darkness at the end of the street. It's the way to my gallery and to where my car is parked. I'm not wanting to risk looking at him. And then the silence is broken. 'I don't trust myself though, Grace, with the way things are...'

'And how are things, Julian?' I don't let him finish the sentence. I'm at the stage where I have tried to accept his reluctance at even attempting to explain how things are. Either he tells me or this whole shit is just going to go on and on. Then slowly, his hand settles on my shoulder and my eyes level with his mouth. 'I need to go, Julian, before I begin to convince myself that staying at your flat is a good idea.' Reaching up, I kiss his cheek before turning and heading in the direction of my gallery.

'I'll walk you back, Grace.'

'No, I need the fresh air, Julian. Honestly, I'm fine.' I know he's watching me as I make my way to the end of the street. For about the third or fourth time, I'm forcing myself to get to the end and out of sight. Only then will I fully resist turning back to be with him. After all, he lifts me out of my pit of heartache, no matter how wrong or immoral it is, he makes me feel better. As I turn the corner, leaving him out of sight, I start to cry, crying for myself and this utter emptiness and crying for my mum, knowing she will have broken down at some point today as well. Where's the goodness, where's the way out of all of this?

The drive back home seems automatic, as if I haven't taken in any of the passing motorway traffic. I'm sitting in my car, in the driveway at the cottage, have been for a while, still thinking of Julian. It takes every ounce of energy left in me to head inside. After a shower, the crisp, precise cotton sheets clash then warm my freshly showered skin, and within minutes, I breathe in the nourishing scents of vetiver and donkey milk. I imagine an intense artisan sitting outside a hut, at the base of the Massif des Maures, talking to his doughy-eyed four-legged companion as he blends the exquisite liquid in his homemade pestle and mortar before setting them into new bars of soap. For now, I drift into its earthy amber tones, intensified as my body temperature heightens under my duvet. I drift off to sleep.

* * *

The following day, I head out to the local delicatessen to buy something nice for lunch; Jenny is joining me, taking a break from a college essay. The bread is always utterly amazing, and I opt for a full sandwich option from their takeaway menu. I watch the girl behind the counter make up two sandwiches for our lunch. She lovingly places the prized flour cog loaf onto the marble counter top, sawing off four chunky slices.

She smiles as the knife blade is expertly ground through the shiny tough crusty outside, then the blade is almost poetically dragged through the bubbly, porous loveliness of the internal, crafted dough. I never want to pull a slice of bread out of a plastic wrapper again having witnessed this. Once filled with hummus and fresh roasted vegetables, each sandwich is cut in half and wrapped and taped into waxy sheets of paper and into a compact brown paper carrier bag.

I walk out from the delicatessen, pleased that today's lunch offering has lifted me, especially after leaving Julian following last night's meal. He is never far from my thoughts. Back home, Jenny and I lift and bite into our sandwiches, our lips floury from our delicious doorstep bread, quietly contemplating the rest of the day, back it seems to the bittersweet months ahead. It's so hard to see a future, other than one that lacks a few lucky breaks, filled with an inevitable gloom.

'Mum, do you find some days you wake and just want to cry? It's just that I never see you cry and yet there's been so much happening.'

'I try and just get on with it, Jenny. It's all you can do. You're not at home much these days anyway, so we don't really see a lot of each other?'

'I don't find the cottage a place I enjoy staying at, Mum. Oh, nothing to do with you, you've made it all nice and that. It's just there are no memories here anymore, like Dad's things.'

'I haven't removed the few photos that are here though, they're where they always used to be, Jenny.'

'Oh, I'm not explaining it well, Mum. It's just that I used to feel Dad's presence, but since what happened to Nanny, it's as if that's been wiped away. Do you know what I mean?'

'Not sure I do. Certainly with what happened to Nanny, it's

put a hellish dampener on our memories in general. Maybe that's what you are feeling?'

'Suppose so. It's been ages since I visited Nanny at the nursing home.'

'I know, but you said you find it hard to see her, as she doesn't always recognise you when you talk to her. She doesn't mean anything by it; it's her forgetfulness taking a grip.' I lay down my sandwich, unable to eat the second half of it now. Jenny's starting to pick at hers too.

'He's taken so much away, hasn't he, Mum? Not content with what he did to Nanny, and getting away with it, he's there in the background sucking everything else away from this family. Uncle John said he could just murder him some days.'

'Oh, you know how hot-headed he is, Jenny. Even if a car indicates the wrong way, he wishes he had rocket launchers built into the sides of his car.'

'It is true though, Mum. You can't deny it that not only has he ruined what little time Nanny has left, but he's like a rot taking away all the stuff we hold dear to us. He's still winning.'

I've run out of things to say because I'm feeling exactly what she feels and what she's been articulate enough to say.

## 27

My phone rings at 7am on what seems like a habitually difficult morning for me. Waking, I pull myself from under the duvet. I hate this time of day, and yet it stirs and angers my inner fight into a huge sense of achievement, fighting off the monkey on my back. I can eventually say 'fuck it' to it and get on with my day, proud. It's the nursing home on the phone. 'Hi, Grace. Mum's still not good after yesterday's relapse. I think it best if you come to see her this morning.'

I ring John and give him the update, and it isn't long before he is joining me sitting at Mum's bedside. The doctor has been called. All I can do is hold her hand and stroke her lower arm which is somewhat puffier today. I notice these changes in Mum but never say anything since there is no point. Yet I absorb this crumbling, shifting the accompanying heartache into part of me that remains capable of harbouring the pain. 'Talk to her, Grace.' My brother's words are demanding yet encouraging. I have nothing left to say to her. It seems futile to tell her Jenny's had her hair cut yesterday and it's looking quite different now. She doesn't care what I had for breakfast and it's bloody obvious *she* hasn't eaten breakfast. No news on Dad; he's *dead*. I don't know who I'm angry with, so I sit quiet and just tighten the screws on myself. 'We're here, Mum, it's John and Grace. We are all here for you.' He's like a maddening autocue as he leans over the bed to take her other hand. I haven't read the script, yet I'm clearly accused of forgetting my lines. I'm not good at this preamble to death, it isn't in my psyche. I only do motivational living and general geeing up. The harsher I am to myself, the more forgiving I will be later, or so I imagine.

There is a knock at the door and the female doctor steps in and says how sorry she is for disturbing. She's not disturbing Mum in any way it seems. I step aside and let the doctor check Mum then turn to us with a practised but genuine look. She tells us Mum doesn't have very long.

'Not long,' my brother recites, not asking, not seeking clarification, purely just something to say to acknowledge her brief medical visit. It seems so important and final and yet we are not in any need to question when life's light is in the last throes of extinguishing itself. We are ready for this, fully briefed and prepared and withdraw into the privilege of knowing this. Does Mum know before us? Is she ahead of the game as usual? She was always on the ball. And it comes, her last breath, and she is taken away from us. The doctor returns and confirms the ending.

After speaking to the undertaker, who has arrived to take Mum away, John heads back home to tell Pamela and Rose the news. I've let Jenny know and she's sad but manages to wrestle through her tears by saying it's best for Nanny not to have to suffer anymore. I ring Julian and tell him what's happened. He seems preoccupied, not surprisingly since he's back at home and not at his flat in Edinburgh.

I can't engage with anyone for the next few days. Well, I can when it comes to what needs to be done with the funeral arrangements. The funeral director takes the lair certificate from me, his request brief since he knows I am well versed in this process. I can still recall the number of the lair from Dad's funeral and here it is again, getting recycled and updated soon to show two places remain for the family. I walk into the church on the day of the funeral, and I'm overwhelmed by its fullness. Standing room only at the back and already folk are standing in available gaps. The church is heaving and I'm still wondering why it's so full. But they are all there, nursing home staff, colleagues, police, paramedics and local faces I've seen but don't fully know. But Mum knew them, of course. I feel small in my black coat and black hat as I walk up to collect the communion and wine from the back of the church and walk down the aisle to hand it to the priest. They've cleared a walkway for me to get to it. I can't look at anyone, I'm just so lost.

\* \* \*

At the back of the church, Archie Connell blends in with the congregation. With his handkerchief, he dries his face, the tears an overwhelming surprise to him. Carefully watching Grace's slow pace down the aisle, her narrowing shoulders tiny and pathetic as she reaches the long step, cushioned for those who will soon participate in Holy Communion below the grand stone archway of the altar. Turning, she doesn't look up, simply returning to her seat next to her daughter. The service continues, with much movement as some people take communion, leaving temporary and unwelcome gaps and spaces at back of the church. Archie feels exposed, almost visible. Sensing his condolences would be out of place, Archie waits for his moment and slowly heads out the church as the congregation settle down for the final reading. Quietly, he closes the heavy oak doors behind him, leaving behind the strains of the organ's introduction to the final hymn.

* * *

Days pass, I have no idea how many. I'm managing with the day-to-day living and spending time with Jenny, who finds herself lost too at times. Occasionally we wander around the house, the two of us independently oblivious to each other's presence until our paths cross and we drink our cups of bereavement tea in silence. There isn't a babbling of conversation. Neither of us has anything to say; neither of us can believe the rotten luck that fate has thrown at us, tossed in our direction and then she runs away, telling us to get on with it. Well, fuck you, fate! In moments when I do have the energy for reflection, it doesn't appear to be functioning. Forward, looking forward, moving on with my life, our lives, Jenny and mine. The flawed pack of cards being played once more. Surely by now all the jokers have gone from this faulty pack. The next day, I go to the gallery and lock the door behind me. I'm not in to officially open up today, as the hastily typed note on the door explains to customers that it's due to a family bereavement. I've been in touch with Julian, quite a lot it seems, talking quietly over the phone into the early hours of the morning. We agree to meet up. My time with Jenny right now is precious, our torn hearts dangling on fragile threads, both waiting on the snap, whilst clutching onto each other to pull us through this. I'm so upset seeing her like this and I worry how she'll get through it all.

Julian arrives at the gallery on time, and we are lost

together again, sapping at the draining nectar and taking what comfort we can from each other. I open the small office window as he makes a move to leave. Once again I don't say or ask the many things I want to in yet another sacred exit. As he leaves, he hands me the small pile of mail that is lying on the floor behind the front door of the gallery and then he is gone. Trance-like, I stand clutching the bundle of mail and cannot believe Julian hasn't spotted the folded-over note in what is now the fourth instalment. I also can't believe I didn't spot it when I first arrived, the A5 folded sheet and hardly the soul of discretion. The same rounded, capital letters but a longer note this time. It's more personal now, like a comforting hand on my shoulder; it tells me the evil bastard won't be allowed to hurt anyone again. Oh, and he or she is sorry for my loss. It's as if I have become numb to them, in the same way aspects of my daily life drift by, leaving no noticeable trace. I have no idea who is sending me these notes and I want to run out into the street and call Julian in again. But what's the point? I'm not sure what he's doing here anymore, other than waiting for a break in my despair that will bring an end to our mutual weakness and restore what we know to be the only way forward. It's something I never ask, when will I see you next?

## 28

After a jaunty waltz from Strauss, I'm glad of a rendition of 'Pie Jesu Domine' from John Rutter on Classic FM. The voices in the choir veiling over me. I lean into it and remain still for the few minutes, shifting the shape of my day to make it complete again, a new routine after a dignified withdrawal from my visits to Mum at the nursing home. History repeating itself again, this relentless remoulding to fit into all corners, in case a gap left unattended would tear open into a seeping wound. I'm not sure about closure, but there's infantry-style barricading going on.

Today I'm restacking the books on my bookshelf. I carefully replace Louise Bourgeois according to its correct height alongside other books. I don't want it to jar, especially after I placed the latest note alongside the others. I decide not to get rid of them but to hold on to them, a catalogued memento mori, although for now they strangely sit in a state of purgatory. There's an as yet undefined connection to Mum, that much I know, but not enough for me to do anything about them. So they sit, pending and largely forgotten.

What's also been forgotten is Julian, forgotten in the sense of me to him, since I think about him most days. There are the telling signs of precipitation retained in storm clouds, heavy as udders, bulging from above, radiating this oppressive stench of another ending. Nothing's been said, just a verbal abridgment to one of us stating the obvious that could spawn our disuniting. It's become apparent how much we adjusted our daily patterns to accommodate each other. The logistics of his office and my gallery forging this narrowing as we arrive and leave work on some telepathic synchronised body clock. It should therefore be easier to simply operate in different time zones, but we tweak and nudge it a bit this way and that way, but not to the extent we cannot inhale the addictive bonding. We dip our toes in classic one-liners that read like they are from some literary guide to ending destructive relationships. There's no punch or determination behind them though, just a bittersweet dangling of words. It's as if we haven't got the balls to just end things. I've fallen for him. I feel love for this man.

But do it we do. We de-harmonise our co-ordinated timing, intently rescheduling our daily routine and trying to gaily ignore the blatant absence from our electronic inboxes too. I struggle with my already diluted day-to-day living, resenting how life had already performed a callous decluttering. I mean, it's fucking barren right now, with little creasing to provide my variety. It's all become so singular. I abhor my spirited determination that sees it as a white canvas, like I'm meant to feel it as some gift from above. Doors flapping open, enticing me with the smell of opportunity. Give me a foot hole, just something to help me.

'Hi, Grace, how are you? Are you okay?' We screwed up the timing today, me late setting off from the cottage and Julian back from an early appointment. I say I'm fine and try not to appear too interested in how things are with him. I want to reassure him that bumping into each other today is simply that. There's nowhere for us to go anyway, since I can see my car parked up and Julian is within diving distance of the storm door to his office. 'Have you a cold or sore throat, Grace?' My chest infection isn't shifting quickly, run down the doctor tells me, so my voice is croaking in a sick baritone way, around the middle C if I were to guess.

'Yes, I can't seem to shift this pesky chest infection, another one this year. I know, I'm falling to bits. I need a chest transplant.' I try and make light of it.

Julian glances down at my chest. 'Oh, we can't be having that now.' His smile recalling them, rather than a suggestion for medicine from the pharmacy to help clear it. We walk together to my car in a quiet pilgrimage way, and as I unlock the door, he reaches down and gently takes my hand, holding on and not letting go of my pinkie and ring finger. I lower my eyes down, aware he is looking at me, and I get in the car and put my seatbelt on. It twists slightly in the upper buckle. It won't correct itself until Julian splays the offending fold and gently checks the mechanism. I don't know if the belt is the cause of the pressure on my shoulder or Julian; either way, I look up to meet his gaze, his eyes saddened where once they danced, alive.

I can't face the rest of the day. I'm agitated and can't place a stake in the ground that will bed me down into normality and routine. Giving precious time to my thoughts only contributes to the unravelling. This isn't me; I'm better than this self-pity. Only it's not pity. Pity brings with it other people in your imagination looking in and helping you savour your devastation as you see the sorrow on their faces. I can't see anyone doing this, so my pity is really heartache. I wonder about taking myself into the other world where I won't feel this constant sense of utter loss. There's no way out. I'm not impatient; if this were not so prolonged, I'd give it the time so many people kept telling me about at Mum's funeral.

I drive into the centre of the city to meet up with Jenny for a bite to eat. She is there with friends, which pleases me because I imagine in their company, she can unburden some of her grief, grief she doesn't want to share with me since it will only add to my sadness. It's hard to find an outlet for it these days. We have a laugh and I chat with her friends, then off she goes into the night, her delicate, light aura following her. I decide to savour the city air and not head home to the cottage. Instead, I head back up to the gallery to sort through stuff and I can always bed down there for the night on my office sofa, having done it many a time.

In the office of my gallery, I lift out Mum's wedding album from a box. It's been sitting there for months now, part of her treasures we carefully chose to put in her other treasure, the wicker blanket chest at the nursing home. She enjoyed looking at old photos with us and we did too. I was determined to root her back into happy times, an antiseptic for the cruel brandishing that bastard inflicted on her. Whilst I lacked the intellect to understand the wiring in her memory, I had the creative edge to come up with ideas. The flower arranging was another one albeit my skill was laughable, clearly illustrated on one occasion. I veered off buying Mum's pink and peach carnation sprays and picked up gaudy sunflowers, with their mutant heads too heavy for their stems, with some bright daisies softening and balancing the bunch. It was like Coco the Clown performing a circus act with a vase. Even Mum's face had a hint of 'is she winding me up?' Floral electric shock treatment that went horribly wrong. For five further days, the nursing home tolerated the helianthus from hell, with much comment about how it could reasonably be a trigger for a wave of anthophobia amongst the residents in the lounge. I still buy sunflowers and they do make me smile, but for all the wrong reasons.

Mum is stunning in the black and white photographs of her wedding day. The scalloped lace edges around the sleeves and neckline of her dress framing the beauty of her buffed, round smiling face and the precious glint of her eyes. Beyond the wedding party, bay after bay of rich, polished oak pews edging the aisle reaching upwards towards the clerestory windows. With the wedding guests below, the giant space opens upwards to the airy, vaulted ceilings. Dad standing proud, film-star-like with thinning, gelled back hair and a wonderful grin. Mum's hand is placed on his cuff, and he's brought his other hand over to rest near it. Dad loved Mum right up to the end but still she couldn't tell him what happened. I love the way he holds her hand just as I love the way the angels carved into the corbels are watching over them.

The wedding album had inspired me to begin stitching some artworks using the collection of old and vintage lace and embroidery samples I had been foraging for and storing over the years. A simple black and white pallet was the basis to stitch together a canvas that could capture Mum's frail happiness, the lace a flimsy coverage and fragile cohesion to her life. At 16, she came to Scotland from Italy and couldn't speak the language. Taking a job as a 'lady's' assistant, she was able to adopt the culture into her daily routine, building interest, but more importantly she'd mastered the art of filling the gaps, and with strength and confidence, she strode out to make a future for herself.

I'm wanting to know how she managed it, since I am in

desperate need of her inspiration. And it dawns on me how much I didn't know about her. Upset at being left with her latter years, sharp and clear and which include the hell she faced in the attack, like a frenzied mad woman, I leaf through more photos in the box because my memory of her must go further back beyond this. Crying, I find I didn't spend enough time with her, in the way you see mums and daughters out together, for coffee, for a walk, at the theatre. They are the smart ones, weaving a close stitched tapestry that can be rolled out and hung up for clarity and trips down memory lane. No point blaming anyone now, but I just can't work out what stopped us doing that? Did all those people at her funeral spend more time with her and share her life, filling the gap her wayward daughter left? Like the empty Pringles tube the police found in her wardrobe, where she kept her money safe. *I gave her money each week* in tidy sums, so she didn't need to go *hiding* it. Fucking hell, I couldn't even get that right. And there's Jenny out with her friends who are helping her with her grief because her mum can't provide that. Suddenly no matter if I look back or look forward, I'm seeing the shoddy coating of ineptness that is tarnishing my shitty perception that I am a good human being.

I head through to the compact toilet in the gallery to splash some water on my tearful face and the light from the office illuminates a runway through the gallery front, right to the window. I jolt as I see his face at the window, his scrunched-up face pressed up close to the glass, hands cupping the sides to tunnel his visual interrogation inside the gallery. It's Julian and I'm relieved it's him, because standing in the space between the doors of the office and toilet, I'm like an exposed backlit rabbit.

'I saw the light on and wondered why you were here so late?'

Julian squeezes into the gallery through the small space I've left as I open only one half of the front storm doors.

'I was out with Jenny and her friends and just didn't want to go back home to the cottage. Never mind me, what are you doing creeping about the streets at all hours?'

'Oh, the usual shit, been at the flat last few nights. Wanted some fresh air, so took a wander, heard you'd put up new work in your gallery, so thought I'd have a nosey.'

'Guess you know these aren't my normal opening hours.' I laugh and inside I am so pleased to see him. Whether he notices I've been crying or not, he doesn't say anything except pull me into a lingering kiss.

I never ask him about the shit that brought him to his bolt-hole flat for the last few nights. I know him well enough to know Julian can be brief to say the least with back stories on how things are. We spend an hour chatting, with Julian looking through Mum's wedding album. I gather up the lace offcuts and samples and sit them carefully onto the desk beside my sewing basket and rolls of heavy linen fabric. They make quite a visual treat and I feel more able now to begin the new works over the coming days.

'I'm thinking my flat is comfier than that sofa of yours?' At 1am, we wind our way down the New Town and towards Julian's flat. I look up and see he has left a small light on. He makes me a cup of tea and places it on the side table by the sofa and sits down beside me. 'You shouldn't be upset and on your own at the gallery, Grace, not healthy being on your own when you are so low.' Gripping my shoulder, he tugs me repeatedly, drawing me close to him, my head making a puppetry wobble after each tug.

'And is that why *you* are here? I mean, look at us, it's not as if you can be here when I need you. And anyway, I'm not your responsibility.' I am aware my tone is verging on ungrateful and mockery as if it's his fault. Julian doesn't respond, just stares at the rug in front of the blackened cast-iron fire surround. I should shut up, but the lack of response prompts me to dish out more of this reality check through my inscrutable expression. 'I have no idea what I want from you, Julian. We've been doing our best to avoid each other, ignoring each other as if we've had a major fallout or argument, and here we are again. You said it yourself, it's going to have to stop.' I'm about to burst into tears but tighten my throat since there's still more to come out. 'I hate him, Julian, *hate* him for what he's left behind, I... I... I just wish he'd fucking hang himself in his flat, die slowly and painfully, hanging there, suffering the rotten shit that he is. And I'd watch him, watch him die slowly and tell him what he's done and send him on his way to *hell.*'

'You're upset, grieving, Grace, after your mum died. I get that.' His voice lifts theatrically at the end, as if a fuller emphasis will make it sink in and mean more to me. He tugs me and I keep my head rigid this time, since the wobbling looks stupid and childlike and lends itself to us both smiling about how stupid I'm being, and Jesus, I don't want that.

'*That* was the easy part, Julian, *yes*, dying, *that* was the easy bit believe it or not. For over two and a half years, she suffered, and I'm not meaning her losing her faculties because of her dementia, I mean, *that* in itself would be like any normal old person's decline and I'd get that. Her head was so fucked up, all over the place; one minute she was with me and she knew who I was, next she was terrified with flashbacks of what the fucker did to her and she's looking at me, staring like I should have stopped him, where was I... in fact... no... no... it wasn't even that... She didn't *know* why she was so terrified... as if she'd forgotten what happened... as if she *could* forget it... feeling so scared and she can't even pin it on a moment in time because all that wiring business in her head is broken, doesn't work anymore... I just... I just can't begin to understand where she was half the time with it all. *How could she possibly forget?* Where was good old fucking dementia when it was needed to scrape out that memory, eh? *No*, nowhere in sight and *that's* what *he* did to her; *that's* what *he doesn't even accept was wrong. What kind of human being does that?*' My expression is now no longer ambiguous. I'm angry, I'm upset and just can't place myself into a moment in time that's at peace anymore.

'Well, if he accepts what he did was wrong, then he's got to face the reality. That's probably why he denies it to himself, Grace. He won't be able to handle the truth.'

'What shite is that, Julian, something from the bloody medical jargon crap you read? Yeah, pin it on a reason because *there always has to be a medical reason* for all of this. I mean, it's not as if he's maybe just an *evil, inhumane fruitcake bastard.*'

I try and get up and in the process shove Julian back down on the sofa as he attempts to stand and follow me at the same time. I wander off into the small hallway and haven't a clue where I'm going since I don't know the layout of this place, tears streaming down my face. I petulantly return to the lounge annoyed with myself because I'm lost in a one-bedroom flat of all fucking places. Julian grabs me in a bear hug to ensure I don't wander off again and rocks me back and forth and I just let the tears soak into his jumper and I don't care about the mess I'm making. And I know if he could, he'd get rid of him too.

We spend the night together. And I don't know why he wants me to stay because I'm a mess. This madness that I have been holding as wisdom for so long, I mean, in the right context, it can seem like wisdom, but suddenly having spent the last few delusional months with it, it's reappearing like the nasty stranger it always was from day one. Then they grab me, Julian's tunnel eyes, his dark pupils that encapsulate loss, dread and sexual confusion.

# – 29 –

My morning coffee is savoured today; tastes different for some reason as I check the label of the coffee jar, wondering if on her travels Jenny has picked up an unusual brand from some deli. Her friends I know are huge tea fans, with tea bags being tugged out of handbags and back packs when they come to visit. But there are no clues as to why today's coffee is fundamentally better. Seeing the early morning sun breaking through, I head out to the front garden with my coffee, hoping to expand on the wonder that I'm tasting in this cup.

I sit on the old wooden bench, with its dry, flaky wood desperate for some linseed oil. It seems to forgive me today, granting me permission to just enjoy my morning coffee. Fresh, damp, earthy tones rise up all around me as the sun heats and dries out the cut grass. That was another outlet for this newfound energy yesterday, starting up the petrol mower and taking my time back and forth until the front and side lawns looked pleasingly carpet-like.

Swept up in nature's growing season, I'm garnering strength and putting it to good use. Friends turn up at the gallery, relishing this invisible announcement that things are starting to get better for me. Buoyed by my enthusiasm, one of my close friends introduces me to two local artists and together we hatch a plan for an exhibition of our work. Small pieces are brought in to my gallery and we all sit and begin to select the artworks for the show. There's a boldness too, and we choose a few larger scale works they've completed, ones we think will complement my new textile ones, whose vibrant colours demonstrate a cheerful split from my retrospective love of mute and natural shades. There's a touch of the Carmen Miranda's about a few of them and we end up laughing at the prospect of an opening night in gaudy fancy dress. I do, however, agree to serving fresh fruit in the nibbles department.

Jenny arrives on cue, having agreed to put together posters and invites, for which she's developed a flair, although I'm not sure she knows quite what to make of our selection of works for the show. 'Are we providing sunglasses for our guests, Mum? There's a touch of the Frida Kahlo about them, with a hint of exotic colour?' We all sit and scan the works again, clearly sensing Jenny has captured something else from our selection. I'm proud she has a recollection too from our visit to London, when, at just six years old, she was so engaging, wandering around the Tate Modern, taking in Frida's works. I'm confident she will come up with some fantastic samples of posters and invites for us to choose from. Floating on this creative wave, I begin to feel alive again.

The rejuvenating effect of planning my exhibition is fuelled by Julian's continued presence in my life. He cultivates my emotions with such care, offering my heart a perpetual safe refuge. I imitate his, at times, industrious silence, drinking from a silent confidence. A collaboration of love and support we both thrive on, with neither one of us prepared to deprive ourselves of it.

But gone are the futile moments, settling instead into a steady rhythm of companionship and heady, arousing liberations. This could last forever.

Today, Julian sits examining Jenny's final posters for the exhibition and smiling, happy for me, I think. The works are carefully numbered and bubble wrapped, safely stored in my office away from prying eyes. There's no room in the office for Julian's advances. Standing in the front gallery, I playfully remove his hand from my breast, replacing it with his personal invitation to the Preview Night.

'People will see us, Julian. Behave.'

'Who cares?'

\* \* \*

Julian's wife opens her husband's sock drawer and places the newly laundered items inside. Reaching across, she opens her own top drawer and pulls forward the contents and rummages in the back, pulling out Grace's business card she found in the bottom of the wardrobe a few months ago. It had been troubling her of late, that and Julian's buoyant mood, a mood she couldn't defend based on anything attributable to herself. Bloating does that to you though, makes you render yourself a puffy, unattractive object of desire. No amount of standing tall and breathing in can remedy the effects of a generous muffin top when lying sideways in bed. Cruel gravitational forces were at work in those opportune hours in the bedroom at night. And there was clearly nothing opportunistic on the menu of late.

After showering, she pulls on her favourite Betty Jackson dress, ready to head out. Quite slimming, she thought, worn with an added heel, and the dark green fabric providing an equal amount of tapering effect as her well-worn black number. She had frequently memorised the address of Grace's gallery in Edinburgh and, parking up a few streets down, she couldn't help but warm to a slight smug feeling that was festering nervously in her veins. Grace greeted her warmly, welcoming her into the Aladdin's cave of Julian's favoured framed delights, it seemed. She had no intention of entering into any conversation with Grace, for fear she'd somehow taste the visceral aroma from this purely fact-finding mission. Potential mistresses didn't embellish themselves with a dishonourable badge or brooch. Fifteen minutes later, and after picking up a flyer to her forthcoming exhibition, she politely said her goodbyes and vacated the gallery. But not before a final glance at Grace's shapely figure and classic attire, and then a walk past that was noticeably too close but provided her with the ammunition of a passive sniff of her perfume. Damn it, she couldn't place the smell or have any way whatsoever of capturing it to satisfy her insatiable, fixated imagination.

Two customers came into the gallery as she headed out, and she stood across the road, staring at Grace engaging with the two people, browsing and talking through one of the artworks. For her though, this visit hadn't achieved anything; seeing Grace, and a tentative link to her business card found in their home. But still, it was the first card she'd ever found in the bottom of their wardrobe. It was enough for her to spend the next futile hours at home, squeezing her rotten memory back to the brief conversations with Julian, when in fairness, he was quite open about Grace's artworks. She hadn't given his words the acute attention though that the last few months had now convinced her was required.

'Why couldn't her gallery be in ruddy Glasgow?' she muttered as she measured a distance of 0.4 miles between her gallery and his office on Google Maps. Her knowledge of Edinburgh streets was pretty good, and she knew it must have been close. But it was important to understand *what* the exact distance was, and in her mind, it was too close.

'Jenny, did you dust the tops of the frames on the walls last night?' It is just one of what seems like a hundred questions I have thrown at her as we prepare the gallery for this evening's Preview Night. Fending off my nervousness with yet another worry about a missed task, she has been a great support with her youthful bullishness towards my exhibition.

'Calm down, Mum, we are not putting a man on the moon here.'

But I am nervous. Eating my way through a large packet of Basset's wine gums has served no purpose, other than to cramp up my stomach as it continues to fail in its best endeavours at breaking down what must be a jellified globe the size of a melon. I remind myself the exhibition contains a combination of works, with my two artist counterparts clearly demonstrating their ability to take it in their stride as they dance about the gallery with such grace and casualness. Perhaps their work is better than mine.

'You'll be fine, Mum, as soon as folk start arriving, and you will be no doubt blethering away without a care in the world.'

'What time is it?' Jenny pauses to check her watch and then

verify it with her mobile phone in her pocket. 'For God's sake, what time is it, Jenny?'

'Oh, it's midnight, Mum, and no one has turned up!' She bursts out laughing, clearly at my expense.

'And oh how we'd all giggle at that, eh?'

I gulp down the last few mouthfuls of water from my glass as the first guests start to arrive. And Jenny is right; the relaxation comes as I stand there thanking my friend who had suggested the exhibition in the first place and introduced me to my fellow artists. She had refused a sneak preview yesterday, and instead, she's helping me along here by walking around the show with another guest and sharing her surprise and delight as she views the works for the first time. It isn't long before the large vacant space fills up with noise and laughter. I catch Jenny's eye at one point, and she beams me one of her magical smiles.

An hour into the show, I excuse myself and head through to the back office, just to contain my excitement and to take a couple of minutes quietly reflecting. I eat the last wine gum from the bowl on my desk; it looks lonely. A quick dusting of powder on my face and I'm ready to head back out and enjoy the rest of the evening. The red dots have come out for a few of the works, and I'm chuffed to bits that all the preparations and nerves are being rewarded. No one seems to notice my brief absence as I reabsorb myself in amongst the guests. A pang of discomfort hits me after about a minute as I raise my head only to spot Julian on the other side of the room. It's hard not to meet his usual wonderful stare, but tonight his stare meets my eyes like a bolt. He's turned up at the show with a woman. His wife.

Protocol, my cool head and thumping heart are all telling me, avoid him. Once the split-second decision is made, it is hardly dampened by an almost instant crumbling of mixed feelings and thoughts. On any other occasion, I would have a warm flutter and joy at him being here for me. I daren't look over again in his direction; I can't deal with this surprise. Instead, I stand beside a guest who is pointing and talking about the sixth artwork on the left-hand wall, one of my own, a piece called *Bellissimo*.

'Hi, Grace, how are you? What a great show.' I turn and come face to face with Julian, forcing myself to visually dissect who I presume is his wife standing beside him, holding out her hand.

'Hello, Grace, I'm Lydia, lovely to meet you.' There is nothing I can do except take her hand and shake it. And that's when it dawns on me, I've seen her before, a couple of weeks ago when she came into the gallery. I gulp and am convinced I have just re-swallowed the last wine gum. My facial expression is now beyond my control, and without any lingering look, I gauge what Julian's face is doing right now. And all of this under the pretence of appearing casually normal.

Jenny approaches us with a tray of canapes. My hands are shaking so much I doubt I'll be able to even pick one up. Christ, I see we are now onto the sweet nibbles as the dusted, mini Cranachan shortbreads come into view. Surely their entrance must signal the near end to this evening. Jenny's arrival and accessible positioning does have the effect though of Julian and Lydia moving back a bit, away from me, giving hope that my newfound, oppressive halo will shortly dissipate. Lydia takes a canape and, with full gusto, knocks it back enthusiastically with her near-empty glass of wine. She delicately wipes her mouth and panoramically takes in the gallery, wondering if a fresh tray of wine is imminent. Oh God, she knows. I can't help but feel she knows about Julian and me. Thankfully, our conversation is short-lived, as Julian steers his wife away, suggesting they take in the works hanging on the other side of the gallery. She turns quickly, much to Julian's surprise as he feigns an apologetic shrug before joining his wife as she swaps her empty glass with a full glass from a convenient passing tray. Well, it certainly isn't the art on the walls that's grabbing her attention tonight.

'Please, I can explain later,' is all Julian can secretly offer me in the few seconds open to him without risking being caught or held in suspicion.

Whether our avoidance of each other, both physically or visually, or the rapid effects of her wine consumption are at play, it's hard to tell, but I feel an immense relief seeing the pair of them leave the gallery an hour later, without compromising us or indeed causing a scene in front of the guests.

\* \* \*

It was easier just to return to his flat in Edinburgh, a place Lydia never usually ventured. It doesn't take her long to fall into bed, and with the duvet loosely draped over her, she falls into a deep sleep, her mouth slightly agape, revealing her red-wine-stained teeth. Julian takes his queue and heads outside on the front street to ring me on his mobile. Earlier my face had registered mortification he hadn't seen in a long time. In the gallery, tidying up after the successful preview, he wants nothing more than to walk the few streets down and see me. Having explained it was Lydia's idea to attend the event, for some reason, with her paranoia in full swing, to refuse would be a clear admission of his guilt. Julian is, however, convinced she knows nothing about our affair.

'Julian, I can't do this anymore. It's not fair on all of us and once again you leave me devastated, just like all the other times you leave me to go home.'

'I thought it was worth it though. Christ, Grace, have you any idea how I feel about you?'

I can't reply; there are no words to break through another ruinous pit. The back office of the gallery is screening my crumpling face from Jenny, who is still tidying up, and I know if I'm caught upset, she'll want to know why I am in such a state.

'I love you, Grace, honestly, I don't want to lose you like this.' The silence from his mobile is, I feel, the best way to just end this.

'I'm sorry, Julian,' is all that comes out as I hang up and head to the small toilet.

* * *

After the exhibition, Christmas came and went and did nothing to curb this buzzing pain and yearning that flavoured each passing day. On 28 January, Mum's one-year anniversary, I head up to the cemetery. I wish I had put on gloves as I pull down the freezing metal latch on the cemetery gate. I decide to come down early, so it's quiet as expected and the *clunk* of the heavy gate shutting resounds in the frosty air over the graves. I check the pathway for slip-free sections then carefully walk up the hill. The wrappers on the flowers crunch every now and again, and I get a faint perfume from the flower heads. Carnations, of course.

When I've visited Mum and Dad before, I've noticed it tends to be singular visitors to the graves of loved ones. In the immediate aftermath of passing, people descend in clumps, usually in twos. I like to come alone here, always have; that way no one can put me off my private contemplations. And staring at Mum and Dad below the ground, I can stay for as long as I like.

For a while, I am not sad as I unwrap the flowers I've brought them, filling the metal vase with water from the nearby tap. I gather up the small bits of stems I've broken off to fit the vase and the wrappers and elastic bands then stand back to check it all looks in order, and it does. It's like a one-way conversation in my head. What do you think about when standing in front of a grave? There's the whole argument about just what is in the ground. I remember back to the day of the funeral, as Mum's coffin hovered over what seemed to be a hole that was way too deep. The priest turned to me as I sobbed and said that's not your mum in there, her soul has left this world now. Like a bad taste magic trick, what was I supposed to take from that? Was it to take away the edge from the real process that was going on? In that wooden box, whether I liked it or not, lay Mum's body in all its glory. There wasn't a bit cut out of it for the *soul* to get out before facing a lifetime of solitude in a box buried beneath heavy earth. I clearly don't understand or *get* death in the way that true believers do and once again I'm found lacking. Because it would be a nice thought knowing that Mum, and Dad before her, had fooled the people that box up the cadavers, and run away to somewhere better than this draughty cemetery.

So I take what I can from this visit. I tell Mum and Dad what flowers I've brought them today and hope they like them, even though they can't see them. For the first time, I don't selfishly ask them to give me something, some strength to go on. That feels harsh since they know they're kind of out of the equation now and I'm the fortunate one above the ground. Be a bit of a cheek to ask. Today's visit is timely though; it's my last-ditch attempt at harvesting strength and support from beyond the grave.

With January nearing an end, it marks a healthy distancing from Christmas only a few weeks ago. It was a Christmas that hacked away at me, still feeling the loss of Julian and not able to shift into another gear to steer me out of it. He'd rung me, of course, and we'd met up in full view of the public, as I recall insisting on. I didn't trust myself; he didn't trust himself. It was too soon to be alone together. Marking an inner boundary, deliberate in its method of defining and justifying retaining our contact. It was a dangerous, empty hollow space. Delicate and best left to heal, but I'm helpless to this craving. My visit to Mum and Dad at the cemetery leaves me knowing how they must be so disappointed in me today. But I just cannot be without Julian, not now.

# – 31 –

Darren Rodden pulls the glazed door shut behind him, ignoring the dirt and cobwebs on the wired glass panel. He'd picked up his rucksack to take along with him for the day.

The old lady's flat was just a few streets away. Tempting though it was, or curious to see if it had changed, he'd better not be so daft. How would he justify a return there if word got back to his folks he'd been seen hanging around it? They'd take it as his weird obsessive nature getting the better of him and the questions would follow too. What was he doing there? What did he hope to get out of it? And more importantly, at least a few of the 9,000 or so residents are bound to have long memories. Bit of a change, being known to folk as one of the kids spared at the school shootings, but now he'd be the one that they secretly believed did that to that auld woman. Looking back, he was an idiot playing the big man during the court appearance, smiling as the press took his photo outside court.

Sitting down on a bench next to a car park, it feels safe to hang about here for a while. He unzips his rucksack and takes out and tears open the Mars bar he bought at the newsagents earlier. Never really one for being out and about during the day, he looks around at the nearby houses, imagining the different take he'd have if it was dark. Can see a lot more in the dark, he reckoned. Gives him the advantage, huge thick stone houses with lights on and life being played out in kitchens and living rooms. They think they are invisible to the outside world as soon as they shut that door. They treat the outside as invisible, so it's perfect for him to have a good look. He liked it outside at night, if it wasn't too cold. Easy to get shelter in a shed. Once slept in a makeshift gang hut under a tree. Nobody clocked him; why would they? Hundreds of different places out there for him. He could always go back to the flat if he wanted. What was it they called it? Wandering, aye, nocturnal wandering, that's what he liked to do.

He looks down at his watch, drawn to it because the plastic strap is cutting a bit into his wrist. Resting on the ball of his foot, his leg bobs a bit up and down, and the watch strap's rubbing the side of his wrist. Nerves, impatient nerves, either that or his meds are running low in his system. He had a review with the doc recently, but they kept the same dose whereas he felt he needed a tad more to take the edge away and stop him being irritable in the evenings. Wasn't his fault, he had too much spare time in the evening. His folks bothered him all the time, not major, just hassle, pissed him off. Same all his life, they never listened, he knew, but they never listened, so really what do they expect of him, just to get on with it? Easier said than done. Fuck the lot of them.

For now though, it's best to move on, get warmed up a bit. He clocks the old slats of wood at the side of a gate, and it pleases him. Thrown out, odd shapes and lengths sitting squinty and splintered where they'd been pulled away from a wall or something.

Could make something out of that, easy. What a waste, he'd take it off them no worries. Nowhere to put it right now. Nothing had changed though; habits folk had putting stuff out in their sheds and gardens. Idiots, the lot of them.

Around 9pm, he heads back to his flat. He sticks two boxes of microchips in the microwave. They're still a firm favourite because wandering makes him hungry, and his stomach is growling now. With no clean plates to hand, he just eats them out the box. He empties the chips from one box into the other, easy for carrying it back to the living room. Flipping open the swing bin to toss out the other box, the smell of rotten food, sweet and pungent, makes him recoil. It puts him off his chips.

Being out tonight reminds him of the night he met Becky. They were heading home in the same direction after a house party earlier, but he never spoke to her there. The mate he was with was chatting to her, think he had a wee thing for her. Said they'd worked together at the motorway café, and they had hit it off. He didn't, he couldn't hit it off the same way as he did with lassies. Didn't know what to say to them, and by the time he'd necked a few beers and got the courage, it was obvious they weren't interested. He'd glowered at them for a bit, working out the best time to approach them. Last time some bitch walked up to him, black eyeliner eyes like a panda at the zoo, low-neck top showing herself off, said he was staring at her. Well, he was, but not for as long as her potty mouth made out there and then. Weirdo, she called him, cheeky cow, and he would have bought her a drink too. Her loss. Suppose when he thought about it later, she had a point accusing him of being weird. But he didn't know when a return look meant a lassie wanted to talk to him and so the more he watched for their response, the weirder it must have seemed.

Becky was different. She liked attention and so it wasn't like he was playing interested since it was all the same to her. He thought she didn't see him as being a bit different. Friend of his mate and all that meant he defaulted his way into the crowd around her. She left the party and spoke to him as he followed her out into the street.

They were both a bit drunk. Sat on a bench just out of town and she pulled a bottle of beer out of her handbag. So funny, she'd stuck the top back on and kept it upright in her bag since she left the party. Hardly a drop spilt. They shared it. He noticed she had small hands, with a variety of silver rings on them all clanking on the bottle, as she held it claw-like, as if hiding her stumpy fingers. Her pale skin looked mottled under the streetlight. It was a cold night right enough; he could see that in her wraithlike, veiny ankles with strappy sandals that afforded no warmth.

He put his arm around her, easy enough since he was a lot taller than her. She laughed when he did this, and he looked at her and felt a rush of impending awkwardness come over him. It was exciting though, felt turned on by it and wondered if her laughing meant the same for her. You could say one thing led to another; it was as if she understood him. She reinforced the damage within him. She was just like him, and she was happy to give in to a long kiss. Pair of them were just talking rubbish after that, but they managed to make it back to his flat. She kept falling over against him as they walked and, in the end, took her sandals off, so now her feet would be filthy and really cold.

They ate chips too that night at the flat, but she didn't finish hers. They sat cold still in the box lunchtime the next day when he returned to his flat. Police had picked him up after Becky left. She told the police he'd taken off her clothes when she didn't want to. His clothes were off too; he remembered how cold it was because the boiler hadn't come on. Needed to reset the timer on that. His bed was still a mess, and the duvet was creased and there was dirt on his pillows. It had started when they were outside, he told the police, well, as far as he could remember, since they were a bit drunk. Couldn't believe she was upset, clowning around the pair of them were. She bit her lip, but she told them he had scratched her when he wouldn't stop. That's why there were spots of blood on his bed then. Need to put that in the wash, kind of needed doing anyway. In the end, she dropped the charges against him, I mean, charges? What was that all about? They were both a bit drunk surely and despite trying to think back, he wasn't sure if he even managed much. Was embarrassing the way she was taking the piss when he stumbled trying to get his shoes off. She said she shouted then at him to stop, but it wasn't like that at all. His mate hasn't spoken much to him since that.

For tonight though, he best clear his head and get some decent sleep when it's quiet, before the pubs close and the neighbours in the block of flats wander in making noise. The walls in the hallway inhaled briefly every time the front door opened then rattled and pulsed as the spring on the door pulled it shut again. The vibrations went right through the block. Eventually he will switch off and fall asleep.

* * *

The close by the industrial buildings provide the ideal backdrop for Archie Connell to follow and hide, follow and hide. It's easy to wait until dusk arrives, then slip addictively into the black of the night. Nocturnal wandering indeed, like an illicit hunter. Places appear bigger and more accessible and there's a pleasure knowing that the pure open space can be so readily left undisturbed. For a moment, Archie's anger had subsided, and instead, he felt strong, having secured the advantage over the evil bastard, and following him home to his flat. Play him at his own game, the dark looking into the light. Life returning to normal for Darren Rodden. Thinks he's invincible, does he?

# - 32 -

I'm not sure why, but today I find myself sitting on the big oak bench in the entrance hallway of Julian's office. With his medical background, maybe I want him to examine my 'being' and advise me which side of the wall of sanity I currently rest at, since I'm not sure myself. The happy aspidistra watches over proceedings in the hallway. Witnessing a regular stream of individuals visiting the office, and Julian's receptionist's trips to the photocopier, it probably just waits for its next watering or dusting. Simple easy living, and I think how wonderful to be an aspidistra. I'm getting stiff sitting on the hard oak bench, so I stand up and pace a few steps up the hallway. My heels are musically tapping on the wooden floor, a strolling heartbeat before turning and facing the other direction. As I pass the trestle table, I ping the china bowl the plant is sitting in and it gives off a low, resounding 'ding' to indicate a substantial water intake in the soil, but also suggesting a less than crack-free container. I imagine giving it another, harder ping and the whole lot collapsing into broken china and the soil avalanching out of the breakage. Wonder if good old Mr Aspidistra would survive that little disaster. I don't honestly know why I'm annoyed at a pot plant, but it's just an opportunistic inanimate object that I can vent my annoyance at. It's there.

Bored, I sit down again and neatly line up my feet on the floorboards. The door opens and his receptionist smiles down at me. 'Mr Brodie will see you now.' And she ushers me to follow her into Julian's office, escorting me right up to the chair in front of his desk and offering me some fresh water, which I decline. Julian thanks her, and with that, she waltzes out the room. I feel like a client.

There's even more books and folders on Julian's desk since last time I was in. It's hard to tell whether that's because he's fallen behind with work or if his workload has increased beyond what can be achieved by one person. He's not looking at the paperwork; instead, he's staring at me. 'This seemed like a good idea when I made an appointment to see you, Julian.' And at that announcement, he shrugs and pulls a sort of granny-like grimace. I suddenly feel a desperate fool, with it dawning on me that this now has to be my battle. This long sorry saga is just sucking the life out of anyone who comes into contact with it, and like a contagious illness, I'm the diseased carrier. 'How are you anyway, Julian?' And it's then I notice once his facial muscles return to a waiting expression, he hasn't shaved today, he looks in need of a good scrub.

'You are my only client today, Grace. You will no doubt observe I'm not feeling great.' And at that, I look beyond the day-old stubble and see the sleep-deprived dark around his eyes.

'So I'm a client now? Sorry, not sure why I said that since you don't know why I am here. What's wrong with you, Julian?' And as I stand up to make my way around to his side of the desk, he half raises his arm as if to halt me on my travels.

'Let's just call it a late night with not much sleep.'

'You weren't doing another midnight art appreciation wander?' And I laugh, trying to draw him into my humour, but it's not working. I'm also reversing back to my side of his desk.

'No, not much art on display from what I can recall. I was out, trying to clear out the misery in my head, to work something out.'

The time isn't right to tell him about how lost I am feeling, and despite my appointment with him, he isn't in any mood to actually ask why I'm here. Having spent hours last night reflecting on my feelings for Julian, I'd anticipated my meeting with him today and pre-played how things would go. I am sure there are numerous questions lined up in my head, all set to justify seeing him and to somehow nestle myself into a gap in his life. Instead, I turn up at the wrong time and reel off the wrong questions and end up essentially a spare part in his office. I can only guess what misery he's talking about. Maybe somewhere in the mountain of stringed binders, there's a troublesome case or home life is becoming unbearable. So I never ask. If he wants, he can tell me, and clearly the only thing I feel he wants to tell me is to leave his office. What possessed me to ever think this was a good idea seeing him again?

'Do you want to head out for a coffee somewhere? Something to eat?' I just can't work out what's troubling him.

'Grace, I'm really not best placed to head out. I've a couple of case files to look at then I shall be heading home, I think.'

'Not staying at the flat then?'

'Nope.'

I can't quite describe the embrace we share there and then. He sweeps me up fully into his arms and folds them around me, holding me strong and for a long time. I'm thinking he isn't going to let go. I think he's going to say something. But we part, and I'm at a loss as to what more I can say. It's as if this is his last embrace with me.

* * *

The following morning, I prepare myself for a quiet weekend that lies ahead. Jenny's away for a few days with her friends and the opportunity for self-indulgence escapes me. My usual skill at forward planning is lost somewhere or switched off for the time being. I'll be walking, no doubt, miles and miles of walking but not sure where to. I don't want to re-walk places I've already been to in case they hold undesirable memories. I want a fresh newness with surroundings that will lift me into new uncharted territory. My past suddenly lurches over me, like a dark enemy ready to ambush me if I so much as catch a glimpse of it. It's everywhere though, the vast overwhelming size of my world reduced down to this horrible patch of land with no obvious exit. It's suffocating.

Julian never seems far from my thoughts and never far from a life that I had, for a fleeting moment, thought we could have shared together. The moments we shared when no one else mattered, we were blessed in each other's easy companionship. Why did he not want that too? Why had I read him so utterly wrong? Was there laughter in their home and he hadn't told me, since he kept that life respectfully private? He never elaborated on it. Or was it as I truly felt, a burden he could not get out of with still signs of an earlier love he held for Lydia, a love that drip-fed in sufficient quantities to overcome the storms that seemed to happen with amazing frequency. Storms strong enough for him to dash out and over to his flat in the city. Storms that led him to me. Is that all I was, an outlet for the emotionally draining shitty parts of his life? But not in sufficient quantities to eradicate his true love. He'd said he wanted this every day, well, what was stopping him? Was he afraid at what he might find, something stronger and better?

'I'm not a bad person, Grace.' I recalled him saying this, but what did he mean? That's the problem, we never had the time together. I guess you never truly know someone. I'm devastated at how heartbroken I am to him, when all he offered was the meagre scraps of aspects of his life he wanted to dowse with joy to alleviate the sorrow he felt. But no matter how hard I tried, I could not get rid of the sense of loss at having to put aside the love I hold for Julian.

For today though, it's an early start and I wrap up warm for a wander around a new town for me. Feeling stupid, I'd pulled out the road atlas from the boot of my car the previous night and just let my eyes wander over the central belt of Scotland and see what might appear new and interesting. Consequently it might also be a lacklustre town with nothing obvious of interest, but that wasn't important. I wanted a new place. So a new place I got. With my thermos and two filled rolls sitting expectantly on the passenger seat, I've set off at about 5am. It takes me just over an hour to get there and park up, and early indications are I've chosen well. Spoiling myself, I pour out some of the steamy coffee and munch through one of the rolls, having missed a breakfast earlier. The air is fresh when I step out the car and I set off to explore what the town has to offer. Highly residential and coastal, I follow the road that runs alongside the waterfront. My view of the water is rhythmically halted as homes in various styles line the waterfront. Some with gardens overlooking the water with garden seats and benches placed intelligently to enjoy the full views.

Traditional stone houses line the other side of the road. Some displaying the billowing grandeur of bay-windowed lounges overlooking the water, others cut up into flats with one lucky person the resplendent owner of the bay window. The homes seem to gradually rise up from the water line, raising up their rooftops proudly over the road, escaping the lazy pull of the waves below. They nestle safely behind sloping lawns and bushy hedges with the odd manufactured garden resembling the brochure from a DIY store. Not sure why they bother when I like the uncomplicated freedom nature's garden can frugally conjure up. I like this place.

A structure from a bygone era appears in my path, Moorish and ornate, the thickly painted Victoriana cast-iron canopy delicate against the backdrop of the estuary. Predominantly creamy coloured, with a splash of red and green showing off the more elaborate detail they are keen should not go unnoticed. Cemented firmly onto a concrete plinth, a strong sheltered arm protecting it from the sea winds that risk dragging it into its depths. I step inside for a moment and move to the curve that looks out over the water. I lean over this imaginary helm, engaging with the sounds of the sea and the Saturday traffic over the bridge into the more densely populated city across. Filling my lungs with the goodness I'm served up.

And then it's gone, and the lack of direction returns. I turn around and see families in the big houses. Families returning from supermarkets with bulging bags of shopping to last the weekend and beyond. Routine nourishment planned out and including, no doubt, visits from Granny and Grandpa, the more able independently arriving in small cars, and being welcomed in through the glass porches. Excited grandchildren whooping up the prospect of banned sugary treats. Suddenly all the houses are availing themselves to this bustle, this filling of their weekend days.

I envy them with all my heart. Family connections joining the dots on their map with no fear of revisiting the same towns and places. Their mileage and roads leading to pleasurable things, things that make them complete and whole. Here am I, struggling to join my dots and making my journey up as I go along, with new places paltry excuses to travel down roads that, let's face it, lead to nowhere. A deathly, counterfeit family tree reaching up into the clouds and disappearing before my eyes. I walk away from this now fraudulent shelter and instead sit in my car with the window open, drinking my coffee to the sound of the water nearby. Hours pass, and the light starts to fade.

The drive home seems quicker than the outward journey for some reason. Dusk is almost upon me, and I stop by and pick up milk for what will be a late dinner on my own, one that I suspect will consist again of porridge, honey and homemade stewed brambles. I'd spotted the juicy purple berries on a recent walk close to the cottage and taken advantage of a sandwich bag I had in my pocket, filling it up until it was brimming with the succulent treats. Made a small jar of rich juicy jam out of it, no sugar, just a full, tart taste in amongst the jumbo oats of my regular breakfast. Each time taking in nature, the outside inside to replenish an appetite hinting of self-neglect.

Succumbing to a fleeting moment of poor judgement, I take a different route home. Driving, I glance at Mum's old flat on my left, new blinds and curtains hung by the new occupant. Mum's old neighbour in the flat above still showing familiar net curtains, stretched across the lower window panes, the outline of bunches of silk flowers just shadowing behind the white floral netting.

I continue around the corner and past the doctors' surgery, towards Darren Rodden's flat. Driving past, I see a light on. The road leads to a dead end, so I do a three-point turn and head back and park on a bend, one that still offers a view of his flat. There are no obvious signs of people standing up and coming to the window to see who has parked in their street. It's far enough from his flat, so I feel exonerated parking up for no apparent reason. But I'm scared, scared I will get caught interfering with the privacy of whoever is inside. I can't see anyone though, just the light competing with cloudy windows which haven't been washed for a considerable time. The curtains are an ill fit for the window, with hooks too far apart causing an untidy drooping. I can't move until I've seen the person inside. It's not fair he can just get on with it and have a life when in effect he halted Mum's life then made her live out the rest of her days in constant fear and decline. I want to kill him.

And there he is. I recognise Darren Rodden immediately from court, hasn't changed a bit. Totally unaware I can see him; he still has that stupid fucking smiling pull to one side of his mouth. The smug beastly bastard. I want to throw a bomb in his living room and watch him get my form of blitzed. A phased de-limbing, each part exploding and watching that sly smile disintegrating into the most heinous pain imaginable. I almost shake myself back into the present because I can't park up here any longer. Someone will see me. I panic and crunch a gear as I let down the handbrake, preparing to pull off. Suddenly, I see a man walking up the road towards me. Thinking the worst, that he knows who Darren Rodden is, or he knows who I am, or worse still, it's a policeman in plain clothes on patrol watching over his flat for any signs of trouble, I avoid his gaze as I drive off quickly, trying to relax and somehow make myself invisible.

Thankfully it's not that late that any traffic moving on the road would seem suspicious, so I think I got away with it. Still, I can't help but feel like I've been caught up to no good. It's still incensing me though, knowing now what I know.

Back home, I'm wrapped up in my Witney blanket again, curling into the generous armchair looking out the front window. With no streetlights outside, I once again find my moon. It's an eerie sky tonight and the moon is playing hide and seek behind the clouds. Grey and orange sheer blankets being blown over the moon and just occasionally it peeks out. Its beam getting brighter as more of its roundness becomes visible, reaching down to me with a full beam. Our conversation is a gentle rhapsody that comforts my heartache and takes control of my thoughts, manoeuvring me into a state of calm. Down the hallway, towards Jenny's room, I see her favourite chair parked in front of her desk, with her fake fur blanket hung untidily towards one side. She's absent tonight, but I imagine the back of her small head sitting in it, her hand under the side of her jawline and her hair flopping to one side. My girl bravely facing the same hell I face, with quiet dignity and showing no outward emotion, but her vulnerability in that imaginary moment cuts straight into me.

Darren Rodden has triggered this whole mood tonight, and with the arrival of yet another note, I'm like an old record sticking and sticking on the turntable. *SOON IT WILL BE ALL OVER* was all there was on the bit of paper. I don't know what to make of it really. There's a sense that so much is already over for me, and briefly I think that it could relate to this continuous turmoil and loss I'm feeling over Julian. But I know that's silly; it's all to do with Darren, just like the other notes, notes with the few words that walk side by side my prevailing moods. An invisible dual existence out there for someone, someone I'd narrowly missed seeing that day when they ran up the road past the cottage.

In this moment in time, in these late, or are they early hours, there's no obvious avenue to vent my worry or anger at this whole debacle. Even teetotal me wouldn't thank you for copious amounts of wine to numb the turmoil. Christ, it's grim. I mean, there's no one here! In the Bingo of life, I've won the wooden spoon, hah, and I laugh since it will come in handy for all that porridge I make these days. It's been weeks since I saw my brother or sister-in-law. What do they think has happened to Jenny and me? Unless John gets local reports of me acting suicidal on the High Street, all I get is a tick box phone call on the odd Friday evening, in between the first course of his dinner and his pudding, to establish my continued breathing. I move my next sequence of thoughts away from Julian because that's going to take me further down this sorry path. Why can't he just turn up on my doorstep, with a look that says he can't live without me?

Well, because he lives and breathes admirably without me.

I reach down and pick up my book, determined to finish reading the last fifty or so pages. Then closure.

* * *

Archie Connell sees Grace drive past, oblivious to him walking down the road. Still, he pulls his scarf and collar up around his neck and lower face. Grace doesn't look up though, hasn't spotted him. He'd seen her already today as she drove past him. He was heading up to his dad's house at the crack of dawn. He'd woken and was in desperate need of a shower, he had told him on the phone. Probably another accident in bed. He wondered why she was on the move so early on. It did provide him with the chance to put another letter through her door, one he knew would be the last. From now on, he needed to be discreet.

In the immediate aftermath of the court case, he had tried to take heed of the warnings in his head about staying well clear of him. Now, knowing the full extent this shared history him and Grace had with Darren Rodden, the pressure to leave well alone was wearing thin. It was the first thing he thought about waking up each morning, the first thing he thought about when he saw his poor dad struggling. And now, it has become compulsory for these daily, nocturnal visits to the outside of his flat, to just see him inside, locked up like some demented animal in what he imagines is a shitty interior of his meagre flat. In the last few days, his mind has been filled with plans and schemes to rid the town of Darren once and for all. Only then will he be able to get on with his life, only then will there be a deserving punishment. The time has also come to stop writing the notes to Grace. From now on, it is best if events remain silent and ignored.

# – 33 –

I didn't so much as head out the door; this madness in me made me launch myself out the door and into my car. Voices of reasoning bellowing at me, but still I ignore them with a virtual flick through the air for fear they might make me change my mind. Christ, it's 11pm. And yet my hasty trip out tonight was abandoned on numerous occasions as I opened and closed kitchen drawers disturbing the still of the night, which hadn't asked for even a fraction of this unmelodious slamming in the kitchen. Truly it is meant to be, well, it must be after all this haphazard planning. I turn and head back down the hall to the lounge and grab the shovel from the corner of the hearth. If it had feelings, it would have cursed back at me for messing with its habitual drunken prop against the tiled fireplace. I get in the car and head off down the road.

I haven't the slightest idea what has come over me. It's been brewing away for a couple of days at least; I keep getting upset trying to find a different way of reversing the emotions both Jenny and I are feeling. Each one turning angrier and with no escape route. I want Darren Rodden to feel as sickened as I am and to begin a preoccupation that will slowly drive *him* insane. I have no idea what event will repulse him or if he is capable of actually being repulsed by anything. Surely on the repulsion spectrum, he must tip over normal boundaries. And where does that leave me hatching up this whole plan? I'm not sure what I'm capable of anymore.

The road splits off onto a dirt track and into a field. I'm careful to avoid the mud potholes and odd large stone, wedged into the soil by the dog walker cars frequently seen in this area. On one side, brambles are overgrown and have scratched the side of my car as I try to tuck in close to them for cover. The only light on offer is from a crescent moon dipping in and out of the clouds. There are no streetlights on this stretch of road. I sit for a while; I suppose waiting for some sense to come over me considering what I'm contemplating. The road is quiet, and I haven't seen a car since I left the cottage. It is late, after all. Slowly, I walk back up the dark road, armed with a plastic bag and my shovel.

The drive down the road had taken me longer than usual since I was looking out for roadkill that I know is rife on this stretch of road. The first one I come across is a rabbit on its side next to a large blood patch. Although, a foot or so away from the blood stain, there is a visible splatter of pink and grey entrails and insides connecting it to the corpse. Dark congealed blood sticks to the fur around its neck. Careful to ensure I get the whole lot, my shovel scrapes along the tarmac, the sickening, earthy stench wafting up as I lift it into the large, plastic bag. Fresh blood smears down the inside of the bag as the weighty corpse slips to the bottom, broken limbs rounding up into a tidy ball. The next one is not too far away, slung over the kerb as it had tried to escape the headlights. Its head at a 90-degree angle to the lower body but otherwise intact. That is until I lift it with the shovel, and the bloodied flesh comes away from the side of its skull. Jerking the shovel, like I'm tossing some omelette, I manage to get the majority into the bag, and it slumps down to the bottom with the other corpse. I quicken my pace and head back to the car, my heart racing by now against a sharp, heaving, nauseous sensation brewing in my stomach.

That's the easy bit in this godforsaken plan and by now it's the middle of the night. A calmness has come over me as I drive down the road and park up. I have quickly forgotten the smell coming from the plastic bag on the floor in front of the passenger seat as I put on a rubber glove and lift it up. The more I hang about, I think, the greater chance of someone seeing me. I walk steady, just a short distance from my car, halting around the corner of the front of Darren Rodden's flat. Not a soul in sight. I stick my hand with the rubber glove deep into the bag and take hold of a handful of the bloodied corpse. I'm not sure which bit, but it doesn't matter. My footsteps are almost silent as I take a surreal stroll up to the front door of the close. Hooking the bag with the remaining corpses gently onto the close's front door handle, I then lean over to his front window, which is dark inside, and the curtains are drawn. In slow motion, so as not to make a noise, I place the bloodied corpse bit against his window and firmly turn it around, spreading the rotting flesh and blood against the cold glass window pane. It holds firmly. I want him to know he's the intended recipient of the bag of bloodied flesh.

I turn and slowly edge myself further away from his flat and back to my car.

Deed done. Take that, you *fucking bastard*.

# – 34 –

There's no denial. I'm ignoring what happened because I'm able to. Then two things get my attention.

Firstly, and amazingly so, there is no press coverage of the 'rabbit incident' as if it never happened. They got to it quickly and dealt with it, I presume. That suits me fine, to be honest. I suspect they are keeping it quiet to protect the poor soul from further distress. It also keeps the dirty secret that he is still living in his shitty original flat firmly under wraps or rather contained within the locale to prevent the rubber-neckers arriving en masse and causing havoc. I can't help but wonder if this undeserving protection is like history repeating itself, letting him off with misdemeanours because of what happened to him at the school. People have long memories though, with his own generation even venting their disgust as they talk openly about the 'Granny Basher'. Terminology which had earlier caused such horrific distress, especially to Jenny. How easy it is for some to lighten the ugliness of it all with such youthful slang.

That's the first thing. The second thing is remembering the other note that had arrived through my letterbox. Recalling now the timing of it sets my heart racing. Despite getting it, and the other notes for that matter, how reckless it is for me to go anywhere near Darren's flat let alone risk being caught outside it with a bag of dead rabbits. I'm not the only one preoccupied with the bastard, so who knows, maybe someone else hangs about too. I sit down since I suddenly feel lightheaded. I can't believe how dangerous it is to go anywhere near that bloody flat, and with a bunch of dead rabbits. The note intuitively sits, filed in my book alongside the others.

I slump down onto the armchair and break down. Scared, embarrassed, I'm not sure which, by how hellish things have become and my behaviour so calmly crazy. I have become so unconnected. Somewhere along the line, I feel I'm losing this mother-daughter connection too and becoming increasingly anxious over my lack of ability to support Jenny like I should be able to do. Instead, I'm festering away at bizarre things that are only going to prove futile. What's the point? I'm just so *lost* in all of this, but worse still, I cannot find any ledge that I can grip on to and drag myself back up. Still not learning from the blatantly obvious, I head out to the gallery, but not before a walk up via Julian's office. To see him inside, yes, to just stand there unattended and look in at him in his office. Across the road, he can't see me; there are people passing and I'm blending in with these people out on daily errands and business. Julian moves about the office, freely and in control. He picks up a file from the bundle on his desk and moves over to his computer, no doubt to look something up because he's certainly not going to be reading an email from me, one of many we used to bat back and forth with witty anecdotes and sharing reminders from days we had been together. I know this because he doesn't get my emails anymore; they bounce back undelivered. Now there's the most inappropriate cyber terminology, bouncing back, an email that simply asks how he is, simply wanting to stay in touch, an email that will lift me just enough to keep me afloat. He might as well be saying, 'Fuck off, I can't have you in my life anymore.' I know why he's done it; he wants to send softening signals that somehow gently let me go, because that's what he thinks is best for me. But I need him now and I have no way of telling him. Breaking the spell, I walk on further down towards my gallery and open up, entice some distraction into my day. Wandering around the gallery, there are still a few pieces remaining from my recent show, but instead, I examine works completed in the last couple of years. I'm not getting any sense from the past, from the time I was cutting and stitching the fabric. I lean in close to see the needlework, to see if scrutinising the stitches will trickle out a hint of familiarity. But it's all a bit flat. I'm hating this swelling that has sucked me in with no immediate way out. And if I am honest, I don't know what to do with myself.

\* \* \*

By mid-afternoon, Darren Rodden's getting a bit stir crazy, so he puts on his coat and heads out the front door of his flat, hands thrust deep in his jeans pockets. It's fair to say his neighbours do their best to ignore him. Whether it's down to bad timing, he can't recall passing them heading out or returning to their homes. He could head up to his grandparents' house and take their dog for a walk, but they've told him for the time being, it would be best to let things settle and they would prefer to come down and see him. Pity, since he likes the company of the short-legged, white Scottie dog. Probably because it's incapable of judging him like all other people are doing these days. The town spooks. He doesn't like the feeling he's being watched by folk, second guessing by their look if they know who he is. Any trouble and he'll ring the police though, and they'll have to come and help him.

His confidence has lifted recently, and he makes his way north out of the immediate city boundary and follows the narrow and neglected pavement out of town. With no tarmac on top, he is constantly watching his footing, and after an hour, he feels he's walked for miles, although the reality is it's probably only about a mile out of town. Previously, he's done the route at night but via the quiet lanes out of town, unlike today when he wants to stick to the main path. He stops at the farm road end and, shielding his eyes from the sun, he squints at the familiar dirt track and up towards the farmhouse. He knows it well; it offers some of his best hiding places. During the summer months, he can bed down in the long grass under the wooded area, but the best time is in the colder autumn months when he can be forgiven for hunting out a more robust shelter in the numerous outbuildings, with cut hay making a warm, easy bed for the night and a half bottle of vodka to take away the edge. Food is easy to come by too since the old man never locks his door. It hasn't changed and he feels a familiar surge in his chest at the flashbacks to times he spent here. He couldn't believe his luck that here he was standing able to recall the familiar place. And there would be many more, he was sure.

Darren Rodden's frame is that of a young man, but his awkward posture places him in an odd age band. A seedy slouch is evident and helped along by his slim-build shoulders giving way to a hunched bend in his upper body. Settling in amongst the long grass just off the road, he bunkers down and disappears in the overgrown corner of the field. He'll spend the next couple of hours here, driven away from the unwelcoming town. He wants his privacy and is entitled to it. Feels good in the grass, with the traffic passing every so often with cars and vans oblivious to his hiding spot.

It hasn't happened for a while, this relaxation, and now relaxing in this hidden den, he's feeling almost alive and starts to wonder what he can get away with. He creeps further into the wooded area and comes across the familiar shed in the orchard. Picking up small fallen branches and thick twigs, he returns to his den in the shed. On the shed floor, he flattens down the twigs, mixing them with long strands of wheat he's grabbed in handfuls. Makes his ground cover free from the cold damp that you get as it gets later in the day. He can now take off his hoodie and lie down, curl up a bit in his hidden den. Making it his place, nothing grand but a den where he can avoid detection and watch, the advantage with him since no one will think anything of the otherwise boring corner at the end of the dirt track. In time, he can bring more stuff here; it's far enough away from the open to be spotted. Why would anyone look here? Also, it's far enough away from his other den near the farmhouse itself. That he'll avoid at all costs. This one is good; he looks forward to making it his own. Over time, he'll get friends to come along, offering them a space where they can have a drink quietly without the hassle at home. It's as if life is starting to move forward a bit. Just needs to get a job sorted out; that's his next battle. For now though, he's creeping back to normality.

* * *

I turn the sign to CLOSED in the gallery and make my way through to the back office, tidy up some paperwork before I head home for another lonely bowl of porridge. I pick up the folded bit of paper that I'd carefully placed at the side of the shelves, where I stack my lace and fabric samples. It's the note from Julian, from the day a while back, when he missed me at the gallery. Signed 'J'. Reading the simple words gives me warmth and still the simple 'J' ignites the love I feel for him.

It was the start of our email exchanges, with me reciprocating signing off with a simple 'G' and he followed suit with 'J'. Privacy or the chaste language of lovers? Meaning from an unspoken dictionary that became more elaborate as time went on. They became almost precious, and in them, I wanted to know if he felt the same about me as I felt about him. To type the simple question and ask was never an option, afraid either way of his response. It reminded me that whilst this enduring fondness was never going to go away, to define and ratify our relationship was quite another thing. So for months, it went on, this electronic conversation with both parties taking meaning but never sure if the meaning was matched. The odd throwaway sentence would set me off on an internal analysis, one that had me preoccupied and returning to over and over again. My imagination savouring his voice enunciating the prose, with my heart lifting when it settled on meaning, then falling horribly when my reflection kicked in later.

Days would pass and my mood would dip when the sensible gene in me fought through, scoffing at my folly at even considering Julian had so much as exerted a fraction of thought as he hastily typed it in between case files and clients. I can't let go of this note though, its insignificance for now missing each and every Cupid's arrow.

I want to ring him, to hear his voice, to hear it close to me, wrapping around me in a breathable cocoon. Feeling his nose on my face, manoeuvring his mouth, then finding mine and feeling his release from the day's troubles.

'If there was any way I could make this work, Grace, I would.' Always spoken with a sadness that our being together was about to end, yet clinging on, his arms and tenderness unfaltering. 'I wish I'd met you 30 years ago.' I wanted him to be brave and make the changes necessary to be with me, but I cannot tell him this. He'll just laugh.

\* \* \*

George Connell can just make out the streetlight glow from the nearby town, the town where his son stays and is quickly on call when a scared night returns. He has them and never knows what shifts to the side and lets them in. Sleeping in the downstairs bedroom has helped, for a while anyway, passing the staircase of slow hollow footsteps every night. He dares himself every now and again to strain a look up; with his hand on the round oak finial of the balustrade, smooth and worn where once it held firm in his palm, he shunts himself onto the first stair. On these inquisitive nights, he follows the glow of the lamp on the hall table, counting up the steps to the top where it all gets a big foggy and dark. Pausing at the top, breathless from his mountainous climb, he then shuffles round to the left, to the bay-windowed room with views out towards old battles on Sheriffmuir.

Distant battles now blend into the sleepy horror that had startled and woke him that night. Alone and afraid, he shook as another shove threw him back down, his head crashing into his soft pillow, which bellowed up and out on each side, suffocating. 'What do you want here? There's no money in the house.' And he lay still, waiting for the next shove, afraid to turn and look. Minutes passed, or it seemed like that length of time, feeling the weight against him, still uncertain what was happening. Whether it was the fright of it all that led to the confusion, he couldn't be sure, but his shoulders started to get cold, and he was shivering. Fear, then intense fear as he curled up, grabbing the bed covers, his pyjamas, anything that would shield him. Crying, he had yelled out loud for someone to come, still not sure if the person was still there, young person, still a boy, never spoke just shouted stuff and smelt of cigarettes. Told him he wanted to help him and then he took his pyjamas off, and he wasn't strong enough to stop him.

This morning, he needs the toilet but can't face the darkness of the hallway, laying for another hour, listening for the front door and Archie arriving. But too much time has passed, and he never gets to the toilet. He pisses the bed.

'Dad it's just me, you not up yet?' The farmhouse door creaks then rattles the walls and pictures as it slams shut.

'I'm up here.' Then that sickly nervous feeling because he knows the mess that will present itself to his son.

'Up here? What do you mean up here, Dad?' And at that, Archie walks through to the downstairs bedroom where his dad lies in bed, his covers folded over to the side, his pyjamas soaked through.

'I'm sorry, son. I had another accident.' Then shame, shame at the piss stench hanging over him.

'You had another bad dream, Dad?'

## 35

'Are you sure you will be fine for a few days?' I'm sitting, leaning into Jenny, who rolls her wide-open eyes and puckers in her mouth, giving her this comical bug-like look. It's a joy to see and she has no idea how expensive that look would be bottled and packaged up on a shop shelf.

'*M-o-t-h-e-r.*' And she tops it off with my Sunday name.

'Sure?' There's a point at which her patience with me will turn to a 'Mother, you're doing my head in now' expression with vocabulary following suit.

'Go away, take a break, Mum, and, and... do what you usually do to chill out, some art or walking or reading or write stuff down... just *go* and *do* something, jeez.'

'Well, if you are sure, then I shall see what I can get booked up and head off before the weekend.'

'Sounds like a plan. Get you out my hair for a while. You've been kinda weird lately, Mum.' And there it is, her bug-like face, expectant eyes wide open. More frightened rabbit than bug now. And then I envisage the scene from *Watership Down*. Oh God, the rabbits.

I pack some food items hastily before leaving the house, including porridge, two punnets of greengages and a tub of

Victoria plums. I'd trolley-dashed for the plums the other day in the supermarket, having quickly spotted the last tub of the short seasonal fruits. I felt utter euphoria placing them in my trolley, proud of my dexterity with an accelerating shopping trolley in the fruit isle.

The island of Skye is only a few hours up the road, but there is nothing to dowse this sense of pure abandonment. It preoccupies my drive up to the last town before the holiday cottage, somewhere at the end of the road to civilisation. I follow the single-track road for 15 miles, generously complying with the 'let others overtake' signs, never so many smiles and waves in three quarters of an hour. I feel like royalty arriving at the small village at the end of the road. With a few hundred metres of spare road down to the jetty, this is truly the end of the peninsula. Turning in to the short hilly driveway, I stop and wrench up the handbrake and get out of the car to open the metal cattle gate, park up and make a few trips to the car to bring in all my stuff.

Wonderful how little you need to be content, so I smother myself in the sentimental frugal lifestyle that will be me for the next few days. I turn the compact armchair around to face the full width front window, and with my cup of tea for company, I slowly soak up the stunning views over towards Rum and I doubt I will ever tire of this. With the prospect of the sun setting in a couple of hours, I pull on my jacket and shoes for walking and head out the door.

I'm so close to the sea with the air carrying the smell of salty seaweed up to me. A handful of houses are positioned along the shoreline, facing slightly different directions rather than abiding by a straight line. There's a steep gradient from the house down to the jetty, and as I regulate my pace to the hill, I look over at the rooftops and chimneys of the homes below. Small fishing boats are anchored up in the harbour, bobbing about, laden down with an assortment of brightly coloured rope, fishing baskets and netting. There's nothing overly engineered in them, and I am reminded again at how simple and uncluttered living in this corner of the island must be.

The full sunset is somewhat disturbed by a low-level line of clouds that have fallen over the Cuillin Hills. Evenly spread, they float over the tallest peaks, their delicate mist in contrast to the deep purple and blackened green slopes below them. As I turn back up from the jetty, the steep hill raises my heartbeat, and the vastness of the water comes into view. Part of the setting sun is visible over the cloud cover and throws down a bright shining sphere, radiating a warm amber glow across the water and towards the shoreline below me. One of the mountain peaks is visible, nature's stretch marks scar the surface slopes, light grey trails of scree drawn down from the peaks in sweeping swathes that have been around for a long time. I stop and take out my mobile phone for some pictures that I can keep, when after a few days, I will have to leave these reliable, reassuring hills behind.

I'm up early the following day and after a sturdy bowl of porridge, I take the short drive to Kilmarie. I park up beside the cars of keen walkers who must have set off earlier and have no doubt already arrived at Camasunary, which is where I am heading on my walk. My guide book describes it as a moderate walk, done in three hours return over the Cuillin Hills. Twenty minutes in and I'm overtaken by a rambler and his two dogs, who are making the rocky, loose terrain seem like a walk in the park. My face is already glowing pink. I chat briefly to the owner of the dogs, since the energy him and his dogs are creating will, I am sure, rub off on me with renewed vigour as I aim for the peak. He's also handsome and if I had the odd picnic blanket with me, I'd throw it down on the mossy edge and quite happily spend a few hours with him. I joke about his two dogs making it look easy and he laughs, saying, 'Yeah, but they have four legs each.' And then he is gone, over the peak and down to a future on the other side without me.

I press on and reach the peak but only after numerous false hopes. The sloping path undulates cruelly, giving the impression of the peak being imminent. There's some form of mountainous mirage messing with my head. When I do get to the peak though, I can see my friend the dog walker quite a distance down the slope, his blue waterproof jacket clearly visible. He's bounding down as if this is some sort of race. I can see the beach below and the zigzag path leading to it. It's the same slow pace descending as I maintain my footing below loose scree and boulders.

There's no obvious seating on the beach. I pick up a large flat stone and place it on the ledge where an expanse of grass area meets the somewhat dirty sand. I'm the only person here with Mr Dog Walker clearly having headed further on around the coast. Familiar sounds of the sea waves stroking the beach, back and forth, relax me as I make my way through a couple of slices of Soreen fruit loaf and two of my Victoria plums.

I'm in no hurry to head back. Sitting here on my stone, there's a vast halo of nothingness and I bleed into it. The landscape has accustomed itself to my mind and keeps me static in this gap of time. If I allow myself to fall into this space, I worry about the consequences because it has been ages since I felt so undistracted. With Jenny no doubt hanging out with her friends at our home, playing music with some meaningless urban edge to it that I can't get in to, and a gallery whose hastily handwritten sign says it's closed for yet another short period of time, I can surely permit myself to wallow in the goodness of it all? It's gone quiet here, an early afternoon lull with nature soaked into the geological blocks, hiding from us all, like I am just now, hiding from anything symbolic of my life over the last few months.

The breeze picks up and the vast expanse of tall grass behind where I am seated bends back with it. Soft silky-smooth blades pushed in one direction then bounce back after a drunken dalliance with tiny yellow-headed wild flowers. Rough, dull stubble on the reverse of the blades that stick and drag on your fingertips, cutting if you are not careful. I just need to keep facing the right direction and things will be fine.

Like freshly made jam reaching the setting stage, the small surface waves are just visible and skim over the water. The sea guides me into a trance as wave after wave makes it to the shoreline, and with one final push, it dies out on the sand. I should start heading back.

The security light comes on as I get to within a few feet of the back door of the holiday cottage. Kicking my boots off, I gingerly drag my tired legs up the stairs to my room then turn on the shower to let it heat through. I step inside, enjoying the fresh scent of mimosa. Of course, I'd brought my own soap with me. With one fluffy bathrobe draped around me, I head back down the stairs, noticing my kneecaps are suffering after today's walk.

I've missed the sunset that might stretch out the day before darkness. Instead, the houses around the jetty give off domestic street lighting with some but not all their room lights on. There's enough to make out the outlines of the fishing paraphernalia stacked up on the sloping causeway. It's so peaceful and it breaks my heart I can't share this with Julian. When I return home, I will be able to recall how wonderful this place was, but retrospectively it loses its magic. Flawed Chinese whispers would use language to describe the place where, ultimately, I want to look out and share a mutual smiling pleasure. This solitary remote island is killing what's left of me. I can't even text Jenny since there's no bloody signal right now.

## 36

Darren Rodden has started drinking again and he is feeling it this morning in his head, which is throbbing a bit. Throwing in a couple of headache tablets to the mix of his other meds, he picks up the carton of milk and downs them two at a time, spilling a bit of milk on his last gulp. Wiping his chin on the sleeve of his hoodie, he's able to smell the stale tobacco smoke on his top, as if it needs a wash but maybe not too bad that another day will do. Taking his lighter out for a cigarette, he remembers the empty carton he chucked on the kitchen table last night. Pulling on his trainers, he checks what the weather is doing then heads out the door to buy some more.

The two women who live along the road are standing on the pavement talking. The short one lives in the bottom-left flat with the net curtains in the next block, number 15, and the fat woman stays in the bungalow round the corner. She has two cats that hiss when they see him. Still talking, their attempts to ignore his presence and continue their conversation don't quite work, as the gaps between their words lengthen and he becomes an uncomfortable focal point for them. One of them tugs the others arm, as if to bring her attention back to what they're talking about and somehow ignore his neglected appearance. He hasn't established a method of dealing with the locals, preferring to dip his head forward and look down at his feet and the pavement. This morning, it's hard going because any strain on his neck means the pain of his sore head worsens. The sick feeling from the tablets on an empty stomach returns, churning into the acid build-up, with small belches bringing up the hellish bile. He pulls out a flattened packet of chewing gum from his jeans pocket and launches one in his mouth, causing the two nosey women to visibly turn away and, he's sure, start talking about him. He hates this town, fucking hates what it has done to him. If he could, he would sell the flat he bought with money from the school trust fund. He'll speak to his grandparents, see what they think. They are due to pop in and visit him. It's Friday, after all, and maybe by then, this sore head will have cleared.

'You know we can't help you if you won't help yourself. I mean, look at the state of the flat.' His grandad has arrived just as he gets back from getting his cigarettes. He hasn't had the chance to do a quick tidy. Maybe now isn't the time to discuss selling the place.

'Just me that lives here, not as if anyone else is gonna see my dirty plates.' And his attempt at smiling falls flat as his grandad just shakes his head. He can smell the disappointment puffing out into the air.

'What are you doing with yourself these days? You started your job hunting yet?'

'And who's going to want to give me a job? I asked around, but there's nothing going.'

'You been in touch with your friends then? That's good.' He isn't about to start telling his grandad that he hasn't actually seen his friends, or rather, they haven't been to see him. It's best to let them come over and make the first move then he can tell them about the new dens he's made, and they will be able to use them again. 'Put a wash on then at least. I best get going now. Your gran isn't feeling well today, so I'm just picking up a few bits and pieces for us. See you now.' And at that, his grandad heads out, pulling the door hard shut behind him. It needs a good pull because the hinges are loose again. Kicking off his trainers, he lies back on the sofa and lights the cigarette, see if that will cure this bloody sore head. He'll tidy up after that.

He isn't sure how long he sleeps for, but his head seems to have cleared when he wakes up with the bright sun shining in through the window on his face. Hot and agitated, he goes into the kitchen and opens a can of cola and takes a long drink. His stomach makes a funny noise as the cola goes down, so he thinks it's better to eat something now and puts bread in the toaster for a snack. He glances at the time on his mobile phone and realises he needs to be out before it gets too late. He quickly eats the toast, picks up matches and his cigarettes and heads up the road towards the school. He's chosen his spot carefully at the back of the large playing field. Flanked by houses, there are a few spots that afford him privacy in his den. Where the fence ends and the tall stone wall starts, there are the big houses you pass on the main road. Their gardens are big, and he'd climbed the wall a few times to get wood for his den. The council never come to this corner to cut the grass, so it's overgrown and has a few trees and bushes in it. The kids never come this far either, always was out of bounds; it was the same when he was at school, but he did like the den he'd chosen. School is over for the day, so the field is quiet, which is handy since he has put a few things in a carrier bag to keep in his den and he needs peace to sort through it. There's a loose stone in the wall behind him which makes a good place to store spare cigarettes if he's caught short. Wrapped in foil with a few matches, only he will know they're there.

His viewpoint is pretty good and again he feels relaxed watching folk come and go with them having no clue he's there. Two kids walk along the back road, kicking a ball and chatting away, must only be about ten or eleven. One taller than the other. Any other time, he'd have stopped and talked to them and shown them his den. They'd be pretty impressed, and they could even have some of his booze. They'd look up to him, he's sure of it, and there would never be a shortage of them wanting to hang out in his den. A while ago, a couple of kids trashed one of his dens and that pissed him off when he went there the day after and saw what they had done. Waited for them to see if they came back like they usually do to gloat and call him a freak. Grabbing a kitchen knife that day, he was going to make them sorry. When they did come back, calling him names, he jumped out and chased them up the back of the park where there were paths in the hills and bushes. Told them he'd cut them because he had a knife. They ran home screaming and told the police, who let him off with a warning. Told them he didn't have a knife and wasn't waving it at them, and they believed him. Today though, these kids are just heading out to play football and head over to the faraway corner of the field where it's flatter and they can put out pretend goalposts and not disturb him.

Standing up, he peers over the wall into the garden of one of the big houses. A woman is in the kitchen at the rear of the house, busy at the kitchen sink. He's seen her before in the early days when he was building his den. She was putting rubbish out in the bins parked at the side of the house. Nearly caught him that day. Luckily the overgrown bushes and crab apple tree, with its bushy broken branch he was about to step over, camouflaged him. Wearing only her dressing gown to keep out the cold, the wind had picked up and blew it open, the floral nightie sticking to her round legs and tight pants that dug deep around her belly. It had been earlier that day when he went to his den. She looked like she had just got up out of her bed, with her pasty face visible below bushy, unwashed hair and she had grey rings below her eyes. Walking down the side of the house to where the bins were, she had left the door open, and anyone could have got in. She wasn't moving that fast because of the heavy bag of rubbish and old slippers she had on, with the heel support folded down, the backs of them scuffing and slapping down on the path to the bins. After she threw the bag in the bin, she headed back into the house and shut the door. Walking past the big window, she pulled her dressing gown around her and picked up what looked like a nice warm cup of tea. She just stood there with the tea heating her up from the cold morning air. Moving about the kitchen, he imagined her being warmed up now.

Today the woman isn't in the kitchen. He sits down in the back of his den where the grass slopes down into a shallow egg-shaped dip, pulling his jacket around him. The padded lining and corduroy collar soon generate a bit of heat and he lies down. Bringing up his knees to his chest and into a ball, he is still, the ground and his clothing falsifying his longing. It's hard to find the comfort, seeking it on his worst days. With the desperate pain that clawed into him, it was all he could do, lie still until the weight moved and smell of mint gum was far enough away to let him know it was over. He can still hear the stifled, rasping words of pretty boy, thinking over and over again how the raw, heady grip became the familiar consolation.

He really should head back to his flat now. He'll go via the chip shop; he quite fancies a bag of chips.

## 37

The late evening sky over the island is peaceful and beautiful, like the previous night but different. With my feet up and leaning into the back of the sofa, I scan the panorama outside. My eyes follow the low-level hills on the Isle of Rum on the left, their smooth grey tops rising and falling into the sea, in contrast to the 'join the dots' rock edges and pinnacles of the Cuillins on my right. Low-level crocodile clouds snapping as they form a visual loop in my dreaming, hanging over small fishing boats further out at sea, searching for the silverback herring. I can't see the boats tonight, only imagine them beyond the line of the sky as they head out, manipulating the herring's nocturnal weakness. Watching the ghostly mist freckle the horizon, I want to follow them, to witness their hunting as a means of safeguarding their return. Walking along the cliffs the other day, I sensed the danger below, hypnotic deep pools with breached surfaces from the cutting rocks beneath the water line. Tonight feels different; I'm not succumbing to the lure of another low mood. Instead, I'm lifted then slide into a powerful sleep, the tartan blanket draping me with a warmth. This island is good for me; I'm coping.

My sleep is good too, lasting a few hours despite my default bed in the living room. At 4am I wake up and my mind resumes the fishing tale, as I turn to witness any further seaward activity. Breaching the horizon, I can see a small boat head towards land, the Kelvin wake with its feathery infills following it downstream. I'm pleased to see the boat at this early hour. Its successful return reaffirms the notion I have that things are changing. I can sleep without the panic. I can wake up without my usual instant dread. I wonder what time Jenny finally settled in her bed.

# – 38 –

Archie Connell had seen Grace a few times passing Darren's flat. That way when you see someone briefly in a car, their face pointing blankly ahead, ignoring the people who are out walking. The windscreen dulls a clear image, and at night time especially, it gives the impression of something sinister. Only there was nothing sinister about Grace that night. Concentrating on the road ahead, you couldn't glean anything really from her expression, other than a numb horror or pain but not a hint of badness.

He's done his best to *alert* Grace with the notes he has written since he needed to buy time, to think things through. And here she is, subconsciously doing all she can to scupper any plans he might have. But none of this is fair and what enrages him is that it was all preventable. He never understood how Darren had avoided being dealt with before all this, other than the local police doing their usual softly softly approach. Bloody hindsight though; if they knew what they know now, it would have been different. Caring for his father is a daily prescription for him, a reminder of what did actually happen. This was no simple housebreaking, far from it. I mean, his father is a wreck. He can never accept they could not possibly have known what a dangerous predator he was, repeatedly clocking up habits that beggared belief, and when combined, it was fucking obvious what it might all add up to. Did no one do the profiling or maths then? Christ, the police truly were shit at the maths.

And like a grating punishment, unrelated news stories appear in the news when horrific stuff happens to poor folk. He follows the spoon-feeding of all the gory details about the depravity and evil in folk like it's something they've just eaten that leads to some murderous gastroenteritis. And then when they announce guilty verdicts, it all comes out how they've done this and that previously, but some person high up still thinks it will be okay to let them roam the streets. Hoping that one day, there is never some poor bugger in the wrong place, creating the combination of circumstances that will light the fuse and boom.

It upsets him too seeing Grace, someone he doesn't know, getting paler and thinner and visibly decline more and more. She has a daughter too, that much he knows, and he can only imagine what she makes of all of this. Unfair, so bloody unfair this disease that's eating away at her and, at the same time, filling his veins with this painful hatred.

* * *

I flick the kettle on, following what has been a long and stupid phone call with my brother John. It isn't my fault he's changed his statutory 'ring and see if my sister is still alive' phone day only to find I'm not at home with Jenny. But for some reason, he has and seems pissed off I have just 'buggered off up north', leaving Jenny to somehow fend for herself, even though she has her friends with her and, more importantly, is more than capable of looking after herself. Now isn't the time to remind him of her age. But the phone call has left me anxious, and I play back the conversation over and over again, partly because I'm annoyed and partly because there's something else I can't put my finger on.

'Do you know, Grace, how selfish you are just swanning off like that?' John was clearly on a roll, and despite a weakening phone signal, I can hear him loud and clear.

'Selfish? What do you mean selfish? Jenny knew I was heading away, tell a lie, she actually encouraged me to *swan off* as you put it.' I don't have to defend myself, but I'm preparing to hold my ground on this unjustified tirade.

'Well, perhaps you could have considered the fact you might be needed here, close to home?'

'What? *Now* you suddenly discover you have abandonment issues? *And* that's meant to be my fault?' I have no idea what's behind this nastiness, other than since this all happened, I think the entire family had descended into this shared madness. Oh yes, we've all freaked out on more than one occasion.

'Yes, actually, families stick together, and right now, I would have preferred you here closer to home and not in some, oh, wherever the hell it is you are in the back of beyond.'

'Well, I'm sorry you feel like that.' And I think why the fuck am I apologising as usual. I've been there for them throughout this whole episode and now, *now*, he picks on this one time I decide I need a break. Unbelievable. And I end the call.

The phone call has unsettled me enough though to ring Jenny to see how things are at home. Damn it, how my brother's pathetic arguments always land on my failure step. 'Did I ever mention your uncle is a dick, Jenny?' I laugh and I can hear her giggle too at the end of the line.

'Mum, it's fine really. I told him I'm doing great, and he has no need to worry, but you know he just gets on his high horse about things. Yeah... he is a dick, you're right.'

'He probably can't quite recall what age you are, Jenny. After all, it has been a while since we had our last family get-together.'

'Yip, at the funeral; it was at Nanny's funeral. Jeez, that makes us sound like a brilliant family, eh, waiting for the next stiff to gather the family together.'

I burst out laughing, delighted to see Jenny hasn't lost her dry sense of humour through all of this. And more importantly, she's on side, on my side. 'Well, I'll be home in a day or so anyway, darling, so you get some rest, or rather, make sure you tidy up all your crap before I get back.'

'Crap? That's a bit harsh. Yeah, it stinks a bit. Best get the rubbish out soon. They're just sitting in black bags in the kitchen just now.'

'*Jenny*, I told you...'

'*Kidding*. Mum, you are so easy to wind up, I tell you. See you soon, luvs ya.'

'Luvs ya too.' I switch my mobile off and toss it onto a corner of the sofa, angry as if my brother is inside it.

I can't settle after my cup of tea, twice flicking on the kettle to re-boil the water for a cup of tea that's never getting made. I consider walking down to the jetty for some fresh air but decide against it since it's getting a bit dark. The steep hill back up from the jetty is also persuading me to give it a miss tonight. Whether it's the fact John has temporarily trip-wired my buoyancy, I'm not sure, but my mood is dropping, and I can feel it like someone is draining the blood from my body. It looks like I am in for a treat tonight, with another bright moon. If I could, I would rub it out and ask the day to place a wedge in its circadian clock and stay for a short while longer, to wait for my mood to catch up. And then the immense agitation settles, the way I used to feel Mum's sun downing, the pressure building up when every part of her body started to shake, her eyes darting about the room, looking at me like I was a stranger. It was so strong at times it carried itself over the air and inside me, and as hard as I tried to comfort her through it, by that stage, I was fighting my own collapse.

Then the tiredness hits me, starting in my head, and I pull my arms into my sides sharp and press the way you would an airbed, to rid it of all the air before packing it away. And then my habit, my thumb gently circling the palm of my opposite hand, switching one hand to the other like Mum did when I was a baby and sleep was escaping me, no matter what exhaustion I felt. My fists are now big tight balls of protruding knuckles, my veiny skin pulled taut, creamy and shiny. If I squeeze any more, the skin will rip apart and the bones poke through. Madness, it's like a madness that follows by my side, waiting for the kill when I am at my lowest.

Eventually I head up to bed and I fall asleep; it's all my body is capable of. I dream of cadavers on the floor, painful, wretched creatures with torn souls, stepping over them, the mess, the blood, that awful smell. Faces screaming with the volume turned to mute, hands clutching at clothes, tugging, suffocating and still not a sound. I hide amidst it all, unable to run and make my escape because Darren Rodden is there, with his pulled sideways smile, opening wide as he kicks the bodies, over and over again, their arms flying up and down with a thump. Dignity, sucking the dignity from them, large bundles of bed clothes, sheets and pants, dirty, soiled, strewn all over, covering up a pair of broken spectacles. I'll die if I don't wake up, and suddenly, I sit bolt upright in my bed. Swinging my legs out, they catch on the sheets that drape off the side of the mattress, where I have been kicking them in my nightmare. Stumbling, I have nothing familiar to catch on to to break my fall and I tumble over, hitting my head on the side of a large oak chest of drawers. I'm out cold.

Around 2am, I come round, utterly terrified, terrified that I find myself so far away on my own and, it would seem, incapable of looking after myself. I pick up the corner of the bed sheet and wipe the tears from my face. I need to blow my nose too but decide using the sheet would be too ignorant. I head to the bathroom and tear off a yard or so of toilet roll, sending it flying across the tiled floor. I'm disgusted and disappointed at what Jenny would make of all of this, how she would despair at her mum in this state. And I burst into tears, knowing once again, I failed to find my foothold in time. More upset comes in waves. I've pierced the reservoir and it lines them up one by one, reminding me there's so much missing here. I pull my hair back off my face and flinch at the enormous lump I've left myself with where I bumped my forehead. And now I only have a couple of days to let it heal or I shall be returning home resembling the Elephant Man.

In desperation, I pick up my mobile and switch it on, noting there are two bars worth of signal. I've found the lucky spot in this black hole. I scroll down the contacts and pause at Julian's number. Christ, I can't ring him at this hour, what if he is at home? I look at the time, half past two. I press the green ring button and tentatively put the phone to my ear, preparing myself to hang up. That's of course assuming I'm blessed with a continued signal. It rings only twice before he picks up.

'Grace! Where the hell are you?' Julian sounds scared but, at the same time, ready to give me a row.

'I'm not at home. Why?' I'm not sure what the fuss or urgency is about. But admittedly, I thought I owned the fuss and urgency but clearly not anymore, judging by the tone of Julian's voice.

'I know you're not bloody at home. When I couldn't get hold of you on your mobile, I tried to find you, but you were not at the gallery and your car wasn't outside the cottage. And well, well, I could hardly knock at your door and suddenly introduce myself to Jenny.'

'I'm up in the Isle of Skye. I've done something terrible and now I keep getting these nightmares. I have a huge bump on my head, and I don't want to be alone, Julian.'

'I'm coming up. Jesus, Grace, what the hell have you done?'

'It's the rabbits. I just don't know what came over me.'

'Rabbits? What about your head? The bump? Grace, are you okay? You won't do anything more stupid, will you? For Christ sake, stay safe.'

'What's more stupid than the rabbits?'

'Grace, I haven't a clue what you are on about. You *have* heard the news, eh?' It's all I can do to break down and drop the phone by my side.

'*Grace! Grace! Pick up the ruddy phone.*'

And it glues to the side of my face, against tears and sticky stuff from my nose.

'He's *dead*, Grace. Darren Rodden's *dead.*'

And I wait. Wait for the morning, when Julian will be here.

# – 39 –

To somehow justify it as a moment of provocation or diminished functioning would be helpful, but that would be kidding himself. The seed was firmly sown that day in the courtroom, hearing about Grace's mum. Archie Connell's rage formed like a human incendiary device, and it had taken all his strength to contain the pressure from over-spilling and causing a drama in front of everyone. He'd never experienced such emotion, anger forming into tears as he was drawn into all the doubt and ambiguity of what might have happened that night to his dad.

When Darren Rodden took to the witness stand, he had to grip the sides of the bench to stop himself jumping over towards him and, using his bare hands, damage him, damage him till he bled and suffered. As if mocking the gravity of events, Darren told his story, his story of disillusionment of being a superhero out to save someone. The resultant hell for those involved was cast aside, as if he was making a mockery of it all. That day, looking across the rows of the jury, he felt sorry for each one sitting on the bench, sensing they'd been deprived of a proper accused's account of events. But that was the thing; there was no hilarity or tempered amusement in his account.

Darren Rodden really did believe those words he was spouting out. Clever or naive or dangerous or even insane, it was hard to tell, and that's what got to him. There was no settlement, no words that could somehow make anyone hearing his testament sit up and say, 'Well, now we know what happened that day.' Nothing, absolutely nothing. Darren Rodden's face was round and pallid and with an absence of honest living for someone as young as he was. Monstrously nondescript and hiding heinous secrets in his mind behind this boyish schoolboy façade. Casting his story out to everyone in the courtroom, hooking them into the unfortunate, innocent timing of stumbling across the old lady's flat with the door ajar. There was no way he was responsible for what really happened that night, well, in his mind anyway. An innocent passer-by, he'd have us all believe. Demonstrating his panic by spinning round in the witness box as he sort of stumbled past the old lady, concerned she'd be scared to see him. She hadn't fallen that hard, in fact if at all, more of a few backward steps, losing her balance, but by that time, he thought it best to leave. Oh, and coupled with this 'other person' he spotted coming down the road, not simply a passer-by; maybe he or she was the real culprit.

The old lady was never able to identify him in the photos they took to her in hospital. Could have been anybody.

He'd been on a first aid course, he stated proudly, his expression changing in anticipation of the sighs of relief from the jury. This would be the saving grace. He was more than capable of assisting this frail old lady, for which she'd be full of praise over the coming days. The relief that there was someone close at hand to assist her, if indeed she had fallen, but of course, he wasn't to know that, because he'd scarpered by then. Running out the back door before someone heard her screaming, and with him being there, finding him at fault, somehow responsible for those terrible injuries she appeared to have suffered at some point in those early hours. Always distancing himself from the reality. His defence team, by this point, were bursting with nervousness, desperate for his time on the witness stand to be over before he uttered more incriminating information. In all honesty, their hearts had already sunk into their socks and shoes after those opening 'superhero' lines.

The previous week in court, Archie sat in the courtroom listening to the catalogue of savagery the old lady had endured. The punches, the kicking, dragging her fat, heavy body. The slapping and bloodied hands pressed brutally over her mouth to muffle her screams. Trying to bite her attacker, and then being punched into silence. His account was simply further insult. His attempt to remove the jury's thoughts further away from their horror at what the old lady had endured, and to feel their understanding seep towards him, the innocent party. How difficult it would be for him to portray his full intention that morning to somehow save her, but he'd give it his best shot.

Sitting there in the public gallery, Archie's mind was racing. Grace's mum, his dad; Archie couldn't assemble the connections and similarities. The lack of physical injuries made it impossible to hear first-hand what had happened in his dad's bed that night, nine months before the attack on the old lady. In court, Darren Rodden never spoke of the evil attempt to rape the old lady because, according to him, it never happened. Archie was left to imagine from the inference given by the prosecution. Naked, the old lady was naked, stripped of her nightclothes and underwear, thrown around the room like an overgrown rag doll, a room where order and tidiness were taken over by the perpetrator's sick endeavours. What inhumane appetite had Darren satisfied, what twisted facial relief was there when the act was over? Imagining the tears and crying he left behind as she lay terrified, his dad too, alone and in their darkness.

Weeks passed after it was over, Archie's attempts to come to terms with it all dashed amidst the worsening situation at home with his dad. Things still utterly misunderstood without the verbal acknowledgement, just silence and an emptiness from the old man. He was left to only imagine, with days when not knowing gave rise to bouts of anger. Unable to push his dad when he was chatting to him, to find the truth, accepting he'd never know. Archie could still recall the day of the brutal assault of Grace's mum, and so soon after the business with his dad and the break-in. When they announced Darren Rodden had been arrested, it was like some wiring circuit suddenly being connected, a pulsating loop of strained energy. And then clarity, in his mind, of what actually happened at the farmhouse that night. History had repeated itself and there was no saying what he might do next. He just had to warn Grace.

Archie lived with what was a daily reminder, looking after his dad, clumsily finding ways to ease his nightmares. His dad never went upstairs anymore, after Archie had turned the disused dining room downstairs into his new bedroom, terrified that the stairway led to some hell. Truth of the matter was, he'd never get over it.

Archie witnessed Darren's return to the flat to restart his temporarily halted life. He imagined it would go away, this hatred and sense of ruined, wasted months. Maybe he'd felt the odd moment when there was hope for a new outlook, but the angry stain had become engrained and without prospect of redeeming itself.

His mind had been made up on that morning when he'd gone to the old shed at the bottom of the farthest away field. Next to the old orchard, it had been used by his dad years ago to store the apples that he carefully twisted and pulled from the heavily laden branches on the apple trees. That was until apple canker had savaged most of the trees. The sunken rotting holes appeared on the odd branch but quickly took hold, the gnarled and disfigured limbs appearing steadily as if in sympathy with his dad's arthritic hands and joints. His dad joked, saying the trees spoke to him, and when Archie couldn't convince him to give up the copious harvests of apples, the trees had started to visually convince him. Archie hadn't been down to the shed for a long time. The disintegrated roofing felt hinted at an imminent roof collapse and it had been on his to do list to fix it before this year's winter storms finally pulled it to the ground.

Parking up his pickup, Archie grabbed some tools he had thrown in the back. As he slowly made his way through the orchard, ducking below the sickened cankerous branches, he stopped and looked at the flattened path that led to the faraway side, the side hidden from the roadway. Placing his tools down on a dry mound of soil, he weaved his way through, pushing aside the branches in his way as they pinged back, sending their rainwater droplets flying back onto his jacket. Sure as hell, there it was; someone had been here and he knew instantly, knew within a stomach-churning split second, it was Darren Rodden. Making his way back to the main path through the orchard, he quickened his pace towards the front of the shed, not really knowing what he was expecting to find there. With the full force of his shoulder and side of his body, Archie pushed the old wooden door open and stumbled forward, his breathing heavy and sweat building up on his forehead. There had definitely been someone in here. Bundles of wood had been neatly laid out, to dry perhaps, and the floor was littered with empty juice bottles and chocolate wrappers. The wooden frame, thick and damp where the weather had caused its damage, gave off a stale aroma, masked only by a hint of cigarette smoke, probably from Darren Rodden smoking as he stored up useful bits and pieces ready to strengthen his den. He felt panic, his mind racing, thinking about the close proximity to the farmhouse, to where his dad lived, lived alone for a lot of the time in between his short visits.

Archie needed to know, needed to know for sure, and that's when it all began, his plan, following Darren, seeing where he was going. The first few weeks had been futile, but he had rotated his route and changed into the various old jackets, coats and parkas he had up at the farm in order for him to spy on him without anyone noticing. And he'd got away with it. But building dens again, that was bloody serious, and whenever he could, he just couldn't stop himself venturing out and watching him, seeing what he was getting up to. Those days that he had followed him never provided him with the solid proof he had returned to his old habits of building dens. He told himself he had to be careful and spun out the days in between, but like a cancer, he could not stop himself and rid himself of the need to know, to watch his every move. Even his dad wondered why there had been more and more visits to the farm, but he'd been too confused to ask. The carers never seemed to come at the same time, so he was sure he would be able to blend in to his dad's confused daily schedule.

Since that day in the orchard, seeing Darren's den, Archie knew something in him had switched and somehow taken over his thinking. On visits to his dad, he'd park his pickup out of sight of the front lounge window, hoping by the time his dad had got up out of his big chair and over to the window to watch him drive off, he would see his pickup missing and assume he'd just missed him heading down the farm track. He was always in a hurry anyway and his dad knew this, forever apologising for taking him out of his way and inconveniencing him when he had tonnes to do without him adding to his burden. But Archie didn't rush off. Quite often, he would head up behind the farmhouse and towards the large barn where they stored the equipment. Climbing up to the roof space, he headed over towards the apex window, the wooden frame rotting due to the perpetual damp weather but providing the ideal view down the fields towards the old orchard and path leading up to it. And he'd watch, day after day, his breath misting over the dirty window panes but patiently waiting for his reward, a sighting, seeing Darren Rodden return to the den. It was only a matter of time, and he had all the time to sit and wait.

He crouched down on a makeshift hay seat in front of the barn window, going over in his mind what he'd done in the weeks before, when he had dabbled with watching the evil bastard head out of his flat. Mentally recording his movements for no purpose other than to stimulate his increasing appetite to settle this score.

Like the night he'd ventured out, and on the road up to Darren's flat, he thought he spotted Grace driving up the same road. With his hood pulled around his face, he slowed down, looking around him for a place he could bunker down to see what was happening. When her car didn't return, he walked slowly, nearing the flat, and spotted her, spotted her walking to his front door. At first, he thought it was a bag of shopping she

was carrying and that confused him, since he couldn't understand why she was there. Did she know one of his neighbours?
Obsessed now with what was slowly unfolding, he watched her
further, watched as she took something out of the bag before
hooking it onto the handle of his front door. Just as he was
about to turn and creep back down the road before Grace
spotted him, he was bolted to the spot as Grace stepped onto
the narrow flower border and pushed something onto the front
window of Darren's flat. Archie turned and then, with some
speed in his step, headed in the direction away from the flat,
before decelerating back to a normal walking pace as Grace
drove past him, calmly, as if nothing had happened. He waited
until she turned onto the main road further down and then he
turned back up towards the flat to see if the bag was still on the
handle or if Darren had opened the door and collected it. He
could see its shadow though as he approached, still hanging
there. There were no visible signs of movement from within the
flat. Curious, he had to know what was in it, so he walked up to
Darren's front door, his heart pounding with his focus darting
from the hanging bag to the front window, half expecting a
light to switch on at any moment. There he was, right outside
the front door, confused by what he saw, not so much in the
bag but the blood smeared on the front window. Opening the
bag and peering inside, Archie took a sharp intake of breath
as he saw the rabbit corpses, and with a stench that had him
almost bellow out loud, he flung the back of his hand up
towards his mouth to muffle any noise that was about to come
out. Panicking, he yanked his old scarf from around his neck,
tugging it a few times to loosen the grip it seemed to have on
him. And then with one hand, using the scarf, he vigorously
wiped the bloody mess off Darren's front window and dumped

the scarf into the bag as he ran as quietly as he could down the road with the carrier bag and away to safety. Taking the back road towards the farmhouse, he passed the river and tossed his scarf in, keeping hold of the bag of rabbits. He walked faster to the part of the river where the rapids began, and checking behind him for any sight of anyone who might see him, he threw the bag in the river, staring as it splashed right in the middle of the rapids, the white of the bag slowly disappearing as it bobbed just below the water line, being dragged further and further downstream.

It was close, too close for comfort, but Archie was relieved he'd cleared the delivered bag away. He wasn't prepared to just leave it in case Darren called the police the next day. It was the sort of pathetic thing he would do, bleating about what someone had hung on his door and splattered on his window. As it turned out, there was nothing, nothing in the local papers, no local gossip about events that night. He'd got away with it, or rather, Grace had got away with it. It meant his plans were still on track.

Sitting up in the loft of the hay shed that morning, Archie stretches out his left leg since his muscles are seizing up from the awkward way he has been crouching for the last hour. Rubbing just above his knees, to get the feeling back in his leg, he glances back up and out of the window, only to see someone in a dark red hoodie heading up the path and towards the den. Ignoring his stiffening limbs, he gets up and heads down and out of the barn, grabbing an axe in the process. Opening the gate to the large field, he makes his way down towards the old orchard, not once looking down at his steps, his eye firmly on the path leading to the den. Pulling his jacket tight around him, he feels the hard wooden handle of the axe press into his ribs. Slowing down just before the start of the path, he stops and moves over towards the old apple trees, their branches covering up his arrival. Still, he needs to see Darren Rodden close up to be sure before making his move. *Noises*, there are noises coming from the old shed. Someone is inside; it must be Darren. *Smoke,* he can smell the smoke in the air, seeping out of the frail walls of the shed. Archie takes two steps out from behind the branches of the trees, and suddenly there is movement; the shed door slowly begins to open. Luckily, Archie hasn't fully positioned himself out in the open, and instinctively he crouches down again, quietly, his heart racing by now and the sweat building up. He checks access to the axe and it's there, in the wide inside pocket.

The shed door scrapes fully open and Archie is poised, ready to pounce. This is his one and only chance. Pulling the axe out from his pocket, he grips the wooden handle. Appearing at the door, he can see an arm, but whoever it is isn't wearing the same dark red hoodie. Has Darren taken it off? Archie feels like his heart is about to launch out of his mouth, terrified he's been spotted. His hand with the axe rapidly rises upwards, nearly making contact with his forehead. Christ, he almost clocked himself with the darn axe. It isn't Darren Rodden exiting the shed. It's bloody Grace's brother! Throwing something on the ground, John bolts out of sight, towards the south field, *thankfully* in the opposite direction to where Archie is crouching. He stands up, the confusion still upon him, and slowly but stealthily, he makes his way towards the open door of the shed. Still clutching the handle of the axe, Archie spots the blood-stained pointed rock on the ground. Holding the axe mid-height, he creeps into the shed.

Darren Rodden lies, fallen on the ground; no movement

from his awkward limbs, static, resting in a dark pool of blood, growing rounder and spreading below what he assumes is a broken skull. Taking no risks, Archie kneels down beside the body and checks for a pulse. Nothing. Welling up inside him, he feels the panic and disbelief at Darren lying there in front of him, dead. He stands up and looks out of the still-open door and once again sees the bloodied rock, the rock that's been used to kill him. Turning, Archie quickly heads outside, the fresh air hitting him with a gut-wrenching nauseous pain. Steadying himself with one hand on the shed, he straightens up and heads back to the den. As if possessed, he gathers up the remnants of wood scattered around Darren's homemade den, throwing in the bloodied rock and finally pulling the shed door shut behind him. He needs to think about what to do next. What to do with the body. And Christ, he can't ring the police. He's hardly been a saint in all of this. And he still can't believe what Grace's brother has done. Jesus.

# – 40 –

I'd fallen asleep quite quickly after Julian's phone call, but waking up to this tiredness can only mean it was a disturbed night for me. I'm not sure what to make of the news from last night. *Darren's dead?* It reaffirms how remote the last few days have been at the pointed end of this island. The simplicity of living and eating clearly spreading, and I'm lacking my usual indulgence of reading the national and local news online. Glancing over at my laptop, it's still in its leather case, having not been switched on since my arrival. I wonder what else I have missed, but there's nothing I can put my finger on. I think and worry about Jenny every day and I've spoken to her since my arrival at the holiday cottage. Picking up my cup of tea, I blow on it to cool the temperature and loudly sip through the darkened water of what the packet claims to be organic Earl Grey Green Tea. I try to add to my meagre list of close acquaintances. There isn't anyone else I can mentally annotate onto it and therefore claim as being someone I miss. It's the way things are of late, a withdrawal that hasn't jarred into monumental proportions, but festering over it now, I realise how far I have removed myself from reality.

The more I think about my involvement in delivering the

rabbits to Darren Rodden's flat, the more anxious I become. Looking out the window at the closed farm gate, there is still only my car on the driveway. I keep glancing out to see if Julian has arrived, but I know it's too early to expect him to have covered the five-hour drive up here. And then I wonder, how the hell do I explain this to him?

Outside, the night has lifted and rather than sit and look at my morning view, I'm pacing up and down the full length of the large expanse of windows like a zoological human being trying to smell the outside beyond these four walls. The hills and sea are giving no clues in their colouring, no hint at the day's impending weather. In fact, it's all a bit grey, and I stop for a moment to take on board the disappointment that, unlike the last few days, the landscape hasn't succeeded in endearing me to it. Even the sheep are a bland grey, having lost their invigorating purple demeanour from the other night. Surely to God, something is accessible to me that will lift me out of the gloom this morning. My only hope is Julian's arrival will dust me with security and nurturing.

In the shower, I dig my fingers into the rich lather from the shampoo in my hair. I can see my faint reflection in the glass screen as I lift and mould my hair to form an amusing pointed peak. I resemble a garden gnome now as I bob my head to the side, causing the pointy bit to topple over, adding to my internal comedy. There's a glaze of desperation now to find new muses that just might manage to break the spell. It's an unknown spell now.

And what about Darren Rodden's death? Yes, his death, and how he died? That's one I would rather wait and share with Julian when he gets here, since I'm confident he will be able to break the news to me in a format that moves it beyond the angst

I'm carrying around with me. I think it would be safer that way. Pulling on comfortable jeans and a black top, I give myself a final scoosh of perfume, with the warmth of my skin mellowing the amber and lavender scent and filling the area around me. A light spread of makeup lifts my pale skin and I start to feel a renewing glow now as I head downstairs to wait for Julian.

His car slows on the gravel at the start of the driveway up to the cottage. I can see his face clearly as I slide open the large, glazed door and wander down to unbolt the heavy cattle gate for him. Briefly he glances up at me before concentrating on parking up. We walk in together, his arm over my shoulders, pulling me towards him. Nothing has been said beyond hello. He puts down his aged leather bag and I look at its volume to gauge how brief or otherwise his visit is likely to be. Things look promising.

'Let's see you then.' And he positions me to face him, his steely grey eyes giving the first hint of a smile. 'Headbutting random strangers, I see.' He pulls my hair to the side to check on the swelling on my forehead.

'You see it all, Julian.' Keeping his attention, I want him to talk, to tell me what's happened but not until I have fully savoured his smile, a mixture of caring and amorous. Coffee is needed after his long drive, and as I organise this in the kitchen area, he walks through to the lounge, looking upwards and sideways like a potential home buyer. Finally he settles on a spot in front of the large, glazed area and takes in the views of the islands and the Cuillins. I know his mind thinks exactly the same as mine did a few days earlier. It pleases me, knowing that finally I get to share the breath-taking scenery with him, share it beyond flicking through photos on my camera, which don't come anywhere near being able to absorb the character and beauty of the place. I also know there will be more joy to share since neither of us will be capable of restraint, with the recent events I'm about to hear about only adding to the need for mutual comfort.

'So, you best tell me what's happened.' I know one of us has to start the inevitable conversation.

'I only know the basics, Grace, and to be honest, that was about as close as I wanted to get. But they found his body, mashed up on the railway line, not far from where he lived. In fact, just down the road from you.'

'So he killed himself?' And immediately I'm relieved, relieved he's done the decent thing, but then I feel instantly bad for equating this with his death.

'That's the thing, it's not conclusive that he killed himself.'

'Eh, well, I'm no expert, but given where he turned up, it would seem obvious that's what he did?' And for the first time, I am made to feel guilty by the expression on Julian's face, an expression that's firmly conjured up for my benefit. I try and work out how I can redeem myself, but I'm struggling.

Julian's medical background kicks into play now as he explains the theory of head wounds caused by hitting the tracks and head wounds caused by blunt trauma after a heavy blow. It's like a scene from *CSI*, but even that doesn't lighten the intense horror of my involvement. And although it's clearly unconnected to my misdemeanours that night when I deposited the rabbits, I'm terrified that when they find out I did it, I could still be linked to this potential foul play.

'Well, it wasn't me, Julian, if that's what you are thinking.'

'Oh, Grace, you don't think I'm remotely suggesting you did it, do you? Crikey, you've lost the plot a few times, but this would be taking things too far.'

'That's a relief then.' My tone is ungracious, appalled, because I'm convinced the thought did cross his mind and that he's just trying to make me feel better by quashing the idea. He's looking for my reaction now, I can bloody well sense it.

'What's this with the rabbits, Grace? You said something about rabbits on the phone.'

There's a sudden disparity over events that waves over me, and I feel faint. I can still recall how determined I was that night, scooping up the rabbits then this overwhelming courage as I walked to Darren Rodden's front door and did the deed. It comes nowhere near to what I'm feeling just now, panicky and guilty and almost removed from any sense that I am capable of such an act. I don't know what to say to Julian because it's just hellish what I've done, and I don't want him to think even worse thoughts than he probably already has about me. After all, he's here now, in front of me, and I just want him to stay.

But it comes out, the whole sorry saga that I try and sculpt into normality, but I know I'm failing abysmally. I've got him to the disbelief stage in even getting the rabbits that night, and Christ, I've still to tell him what I then did with the rabbits. Losing the ability to hold his gaze, I stop directing my account to his face; instead, it's being delivered to the entire lounge area, hoping the furniture will dilute the effect. Finally, I conclude without reason or justification. I just sit forward and place my hands on my knees and position my feet parallel to each other, another of my nervous afflictions.

'I have no idea what to say, Grace. I take it no one knows or saw you?'

'No, doesn't seem to have even been reported.' He nods, pursing his mouth in a dignified heartening way and I think, yes, I'll settle for that. I'll settle for just forgetting about it, a confessional cleanse minus the two Our Fathers and three Hail Marys. 'How long are you here for, Julian?' I look towards his full overnight bag sitting on the floor.

'As long as you'll have me here. I've nothing to hurry back to. You might as well know I've moved to the flat in Edinburgh. Permanently.'

'So, still problems with life at home?' And this time, I want to know more. I want him to tell me in more detail what is happening and not leave me in a state of perpetual guessing.

'Yes, she's leaving. Moving back down to the Borders to her folks. The house will go on the market soon. I suppose you can say we are through, finally.'

I say nothing, just look at him as he turns and looks out the large windows over towards the hills. I'm resisting my insatiable urge to know what the final blow was that ended it, whether it was him or his wife who first spoke of their intention to move out. But it's final, I can tell. He's not following his usual dismissive pattern of moving in for the pounce, cutting off the awkward conversation that he knew would never set things out conclusively. Changing channels on this television of life. He's still staring out at the sea, not expecting anything more from me, it would appear. I struggle to conjure up a question seeking more details on their separation since anything that I come up with in my head tells me it really is none of my business. But I want to know eventually. 'Penny for your thoughts?' I move behind him and wrap my arms around his waist, my head resting somewhere between his shoulder blades.

'One day I'll tell you, Grace, I will, one day.'

And I accept this; it seems the only thing I can do, short of spotlighting him for a full interrogation. The subject is closed for the rest of the day as we head out for a short walk close by the cottage. I want him to see the places and views I have found over the last few days that I have been here. Sounding more like a local rather than this new interloper, I share everything with him. I ask him to stand and take in the views where I had halted previously. Each and every one of them secures one of his special smiles until I feel he has finally caught up with me in this quiet lazy corner of the island. He tells me how perfect the colours are, describing them in colours sometimes different to how I had witnessed them previously. But that's the thing, the light moves and changes all the time, and it never repeats the shades and textures of the previous days. The sheep are no longer purple.

It's what we do to forget events of the last few days. Pretending, that's what this is, living the last couple of days on Skye as if we are in a different, less turbulent timeframe. But removing the clutter is easy when Julian is here, and we are so utterly absorbed in each other that nothing matters anymore. I count the hours until I have to begin the last tidy-up of the holiday cottage in readiness for handing back the keys in time for the next guests to share this lovely home. Stretching out what's left of the days, we walk and laugh, and I suppose succumb to the idea that we just might be able to keep this up after our holiday is over. And I don't want this to end up like our usual goodbyes, with him driving off, not knowing when or if we will meet up again.

'I need to know, Julian, what happens after this?'

'Things are different now. You could say I'm a free agent.'

What he's said is not what I want to hear, since it says so very little about his true intentions. I don't want to be promoted from an option for him to a fully declared partner on the grounds that suddenly this position has now become vacant. Playing the highs and lows of this pinball relationship, I move rapidly from one flipping paddle to the next, never resting comfortably, instead waiting for the gaping pit to swallow me up. And there I'll lurk until he puts another 50-pence piece in the machine to play me again. But it's hard to ignore how all his attention during these few days, and especially in the dark hours of the night, have cultivated new roots, new growths that are helping me see things in a more content light. He's somehow lifted me towards a newfound happiness. Still the nagging doubt; her move to her parents, is it permanent? He's not mentioning how it will all end. Selling the house implies a certain end of the road. I just want him to say it, to use language that puts it beyond all reasonable doubt, but at the same time, I don't want to be the one squeezing it out of him. He should have the ability to declare his intentions without me badgering him for it.

'What is it you want, Julian?'

'You have to ask? Is it not obvious?' And there he goes again, infuriating words that have me picturing him with one of his scuffed, brogued feet firmly placed close to the exit. It takes all my restraint to stop me just wanting to fucking punch it out of him.

'Julian, why now? Why not last year? Why suddenly now you decide? Have I moved from second place up to the winning podium because she's out of the equation?'

'Grace, you know how much I care for you. I'm here, after all, and what a bloody five-hour drive that was!'

I'm occupied for the next few hours, or rather, I find something to occupy me. Preparing the cottage for leaving the next day means avoiding Julian for a short period of time. It gives me time to think, and I hope gives him time for the penny to drop and for him to begin the conversation I truly want to have with him. Instead, we reach an impasse, with neither of us budging and with the prospect of a continuation of this fraying relationship that once again has avoided some robust hemming.

Standing in the driveway, we glance at our independent cars and prepare for the awkward drive back home. I know he'll make better time than me down narrow roads, so at least I don't have to tailgate him for a punishing five hours.

'So this is it, Grace. When will I see you again?' I avoid the strains of The Three Degrees filtering through the air and instead just shrug. I don't want him to go. It's like the same old feeling I had when he left time and time again, window down on his car and a wave that said nothing, no hint of an impending preoccupation that would smother him for the remainder of the day as he drove out of sight.

'Nothing's really changed, has it, Julian?' And I can see the hurt in his eyes, as if I have just told him I don't love him, when it's quite obvious he won over my heart a long time ago. But I can't tell him. I just can't tell him.

'I will explain one day, Grace. One day, when you just let me, I will explain it all.'

One day? I wasn't stopping him *now*.

# – 41 –

Archie feels the heat on his face as the flames lick up the side of the wooden shed panels. There has been no further rain for the last two days, so the wood is engulfed and crackles and sparks loudly. Stepping back, he watches the air lift the glowing floating embers, eradicating the building's history, now tainted with what has taken place. There's nothing worth keeping inside. Old apple crates once stacked neatly on the wooden benches are thrown into the burning mix, their robust nailed encasing now contorted, the panels made skinny as they quickly disintegrate and slip into the molten pile of ashes. It's hard not to think back to his younger days growing up on the farm, passing each nail to his dad as the four walls took shape, the shed rising up from the foundations. It had taken days to build, longer than just now, when in a short space of time, each hour of careful building is diminishing, burning out the memories in a bittersweet halcyon way.

Of course, there is a purpose to burning the shed. Returning to the corpse that night, Archie parked up the pickup truck and removed the body. Wrapping it up in the plastic hay bale sheeting, he'd taken it to a remote location, next to the metal railway bridge over the north line. He timed it some 15 minutes before the midnight Aberdeen express train was due to pass under it. With careful positioning on top of the metal bridge, he rolled Darren's body out of the sheeting and watched it land perfectly across the railway line below. And there he lay, exposed, weak and broken, resting at an awkward angle in an almost surreal way. He headed off before the Aberdeen express train reached the body; it felt too unnatural to witness the actual moment the train would then shudder across the body. In the distance though, he heard the click of the signal going up, paving the way for the train to pass. He could hear the train but then dispelled his thoughts as far away as he could from what was inevitably about to happen.

On the day of the body moving, Archie couldn't wait for the daylight to fade, and for once, it was him and not his dad watching the clock constantly. And always with a sideways glance down the farm road, watching and listening for any signs of someone going near the shed and finding Darren lying there in what must now be a larger pool of blood. If someone had asked him before all this happened, what he would do if he found a dead body, there would be no hesitation; go to the police. But *this, this* was different. His notes to Grace now felt like he'd been brandished with somehow being responsible for all of this. Documentary evidence of his escalating obsession towards the ultimate killing. And give or take a few minutes, he quite clearly would have murdered the bastard. Darren's den being so close to the farmhouse too would have the police sniffing about him, especially now he realised they'd been hiding the awful reality of what might have happened to his dad during the break-in. *They knew, okay, they bloody well knew the score.* They just kept their mouths shut and decided not to open the sick can of worms. If he'd rung the police, it wouldn't have taken Sherlock to offer Archie up as a prime suspect.

It was a risk though. There was Grace's brother too. Unless he suffers memory loss, he surely isn't going to *not* wonder how Darren's body found its way from the shed to being minced further in the wheels of the Aberdeen express. He's also bound to notice the untimely burning of the shed, like a local Up Helly Aa but without the crowds. But now wasn't the time to make panicky light of it; he simply had to hope that whatever was going on in Grace's brother's mind, it wouldn't involve incriminating himself even further by trying to join the dots and seeking out the truth.

He had been a bit concerned by the early reports of the body on the line. Worrying about being spotted, worrying that Grace's brother would start snooping around. But a silence shifted across the whole affair, draping a darkness that settled over the town, a town afraid to disturb another shocking truth.

Today the plastic sheeting burns along with traces of Darren Rodden as he lay bleeding on the ground. Watching the last bits of identifiable wood disappear, Archie sits down on the grass bank and tries to gauge how he now feels. Numb, he feels numb but in a cowardly way, hiding from the hellish truth. Would he have actually killed him if he had arrived a few minutes earlier? He was convinced the hatred and anger within him truly was strong enough to carry out the heinous act. But there was no point thinking this way; he didn't kill Darren, but his cold, methodical way of disposing of his dead body hardly provided a buffer to the fact he had blood on his hands. He could kill; he was about to kill. Archie considers the change that might take place when the reality descends on him, that same darkness shifting its weight above him and luring out a fresh madness inside him.

'Son, that was some bonfire, eh? See, still life in the old shed. Made it good, I did; it could have stood for another 50 years.' Archie's dad had been watching the burning from the front lounge window.

'Dad, I doubt that. It had already practically plummeted to the ground. It was dangerous leaving it as it was in that state.' And he flinches at the awful truth behind what he said.

'Aye, rotten it was, I bet. Still, that's it done.'

'Safer now so it is, Dad, safe and no one can get hurt anymore.'

'Many of my auld apple trees left?'

'Not really. They died off a long time ago.' Archie can still picture the three old trees that remain, trees that must have witnessed the awful deed. There's no point, though, telling his dad they were still standing since he'll only want to head down to see how they are, convincing himself they can still summon a crop of fruit next summer. He can't handle that prospect, can't handle seeing his dad stand so close to where it all happened. It would be too much to bear.

## – 42 –

B ack home, I head into Edinburgh and to the gallery, keen to restore more regular opening times and somehow repair the neglect of late. Aiming for Thursday through to Sunday lunchtime, I'll start work on the new pieces I've sketched out, ready to begin choosing fabrics for sewing onto the heavy linen. The gallery space has also started to transform, working late into the nights with Jenny as I put up a new exhibition, including a handful of lace works inspired by Mum's wedding album.

The new works look delicate and thought-provoking, and as I lean over a newly started work and stitch away, I take in each slow pull of the thread, nurturing my sense of loss and grief. The bold and exposed slate-coloured background being smoothed and softened as small cuts of pale grey madras fall over the expanse and start to bury the dark nothingness and create a round bird-like eclipse, sitting below two wings of transparent lace. I allow myself to think and drift towards unravelling recent events. It feels like my life has had a spring clean, but not that it's so intense as to block new shoots, un-curling deep down, waiting for an ambivalent cloud to make up its mind and yield a transformative elixir. And like the immediate aftermath of the assault on Mum, the town has once again rallied subconsciously and draped a silence over the death of Darren Rodden, deciding the least being said about it, the better.

There has been no word from Julian, as I had expected after our parting in Skye. We both need time, I think, to get ourselves back on track. For once, the singularity of focussing on my artworks doesn't make me feel I'm lacking or not filling my day. Numbness sets in to my fingers and yet I dare not halt this sewing activity, since I'm convinced my work is taking me on my path that will have space and peace at the end of it. The time has come to embrace those steps and move on.

I accept it's going to take time to pick up on the footfall at the gallery. I begin picturing new works to hang in the window, a display with a bit of difference to tickle and entice people inside and view the new exhibition. After a final sweep out of the floor of the gallery window, I bring a few of my works through from the back-office area and prop them up against the wall. Taking off my shoes, I step into the window and double check the strong wire hanging rail, measuring carefully the three different hanging levels for the three works I have finally settled on, one large and two smaller works.

Yards of vintage lace, loosely braided, dropped theatrically to the floor in large wave-like swathes. With ease, the three works fit securely on the railing and position themselves perfectly amidst the lace, creating a romantic cobweb effect almost. I prepare a card with details of the works and place it amongst the lace on the window floor. Despite a moderately high price for the hand-sewn works, the positioning of the card and pricing amidst the softening effect of the lace patterns was my subtle way of introducing the window shoppers to what they might expect inside. Slipping my shoes back on, I venture outside to hopefully see the full glory of my window display.

Like some sort of rejuvenation, I have worked steadily making new pieces and of course finishing off pieces I had already made progress on. The half-complete works return memories of when I first started them and ultimately what had happened to halt their completion. The assault, long chats with Dad at the nursing home, Mum's funeral, dinner at the water tower with Julian, standing staring into his office and the midnight visits to my gallery. The unfinished state and lack of shape in my works index the repeated chapters of loss and failure in my life. Yet in between, I've salvaged moments of reparatory vigour, when needles and threads and fabric seem to harness and control the emptiness of the spaces and gaps that move like uncontrollable apparitions. As if paying homage to this, filling the new window display, the centrepiece is my latest work, just back from the framers, a large hand-sewn coin on a heavy linen background, a one-penny piece titled *Penny for your Thoughts*.

Fifteen works hang inside the gallery, and I enjoy the feedback visitors to the gallery have offered up. Jenny has even taken a week off college to, as she put it, share the joy of my new exhibition. Clearly those early years dragging her around galleries and exhibitions have paid off and she is quite at home amidst my work and dealing with customers. She regularly heads out to the small deli down the road and brings us in lunch. After devouring the tasty salads and frittatas, we sit with our cups of regular tea and pop bubble wrap in the back office. Finally, my friend, who had triggered my last exhibition with the other two artists, buys one of my works whose influences she says are that of Hindu feminism. With spirals of fabric that radiate outwards like multiple arms, I can see where she is coming from, but for fear of showing my ignorance on Hinduism, I steer the conversation on to how the exhibition is going generally. Later, in my own time, I'll no doubt stop and ponder over the work, if only to try and link, in some futile way, my failing subconscious mind to the intellectual teachings of this religion. I don't hold out much hope.

In total, I've placed the little red dots on six of the works, including, to my delight, my lovely penny in the window display, secured by a cash deposit Jenny had taken from a lady who came into the gallery a couple of days ago. With the end of the exhibition nearing, I am feeling happier that my at times troubled efforts which created the works have finally resonated with buyers.

My walking has resumed too, finding favour with both the familiar and new places. The miles I covered on foot seemed to transmute with time. It's as if I knew the sounds, smells and visual offerings would eventually strengthen and embolden me to the point where I'd see myself in a new way. With each walk, I'd be mesmerised with this newfound unflinching trickery surrounding me. Gone are the bouts of dread, a stalwart affliction that used to visit at the end of one of my good days. I feel able to relax, sensing the wafts of positivity, and signalling a change for the good. And so the walking days would end, returning home tired and being rewarded with a decent night's sleep. Of course, I can't resist the odd wake up and make myself a cup of tea, sitting and talking to my moon. She's content now, I think, less likely to begin the self-doubt arguments that were so rife. In recent nights, I yearn for nothing more than a visual appreciation of the swirling clouds and surface on my moon. And she accepts this, doesn't offer up anything else

that might divert my strengthening spirit. With the exhibition ending, Jenny and I have been busy in the gallery, redesigning the layout on the walls. We take down the sold works and replace them with other works to avoid the gallery looking like thieves have been pilfering from it. Jenny has admittedly got to the stage where anything will do to fill the gaps, whereas the perfectionist in me is keen to ensure the works still flow for people browsing. This evening, I finish packaging up one of my older works, which had been spotted by a customer who immediately bought it. Unhung and propped up outside my office, I'd moved it only to gain some space. I felt bad as she paced up and down alongside it as it sat inappropriately at floor level. Offering several times to hold it up, she declined, and I could see Jenny in the background, rolling her eyes as if she was yelling at me to stop fussing and let her be. With the sale complete, she was keen to take it home there and then. Jenny, on the other hand, was itching to head off, but I'd asked her to stay to allow me the peace to bubble wrap it tidily and securely for the customer.

'Can I head off now, Mum?' With the customer on her way, Jenny locks the storm doors and dulls the inside lighting. 'Said I'd meet friends for a bite to eat and I'm already going to have to rush to get there.'

'Yes, yes, of course, you head off. Before you go, who is it that's coming in for the Penny work tonight?'

'Her name's in the book, Mum. Still to pay the balance, but she rang earlier and said she'd be here around 6.30pm. Is that okay? Look, I really need to go, Mum.'

'Of course, yes, you head off. It's all bubble wrapped and everything, eh?'

'Yes, paperwork in the envelope in the diary there.'

'You are a star, Jenny. Right, off you go, have a great time.
I'll tidy up a bit here then lock up after she's been to collect
the Penny.' And with that, I kiss her and off she goes into the
night. I can still smell the perfume she'd hurriedly scooshed on
herself. She's been a great help the last few weeks in the gallery.
I loved spending the time with her but sense she's reached the
end of playing gallery assistant for me. Pity, she is rather good
at it, and I wonder if in all the busy chaos, I've actually told
her this. Unexpectedly, and with such brevity, failure's scythe is
never far away.

Sitting at the desk in the front of the gallery, I have been
daydreaming for a while, or rather scanning the walls, still
unconvinced at my choice of works that fill the gaps. I have
been trying to work out what it will take to persuade Jenny to
help in another late-night shifting which she'll clearly argue
is unnecessary. I think I miss the first knocks on the storm
doors, either that or the lady has a robust set of knuckles on
her. Standing up and brushing off any thread remnants stuck
to my suit, I head over to let her in. As I pull open one side of
the storm doors, I bend down to unbolt the other side, keen
to avoid damaging the work when she takes it away with her.
Looking up and with a cheery hello, I'm suddenly faced with an
enormous bunch of sunflower heads, tightly bunched up into a
big yellow and brown ball that, to be honest, will need the full
two doors open if they're to ever to fit through.

'Hi, Grace.'

'*Julian!* What on earth...' Handing me the heavy sunflowers,
he steps back outside briefly and lifts in an equally giant card-
board box.

'The girl in the florist shop said she hoped I had a big
enough vase for them. I wasn't sure, so I bought the vase too.'